They Write Among Us

New Stories and Essays from the Best of Oxford Writers

Edited by Jim Dees

Foreword by Willie Morris

Jefferson Press
Oxford, Mississippi

A Jefferson Press Book

Published in the United States of America by
Jefferson Press LLC
1533 Jefferson Avenue
Oxford, Mississippi 38655
www.jeffersonpress.com

Jefferson Press books are distributed by Independent Publishers Group of Chicago, Illinois. Books may be ordered by calling 1-800-888-4741 or writing to Independent Publishers Group, 814 North Franklin Street, Chicago, IL 60610.

Cover design by Kelly Tidwell Kornegay
Cover photograph by Maude Clay Schuyler

They Write Among Us: New Stories and Essays from the Best of Oxford Writers

ISBN # 0971897417
First printing

CIP Data

For Willie Morris

CONTENTS

Why Oxford? They Right Among Us

"Oxford is the United Nations with catfish on its breath."
–Barry Hannah

When asked repeatedly over the years why his home state had produced so many writers, the late Mississippi author Willie Morris had his answer honed with an editor's economy: "Sour mash and memory."

While one of the attributes Morris cited often cancels out the other, his answer had the ring of truth. Southerners, and Mississippians in particular, have a way with a tale, and convivial drink often prompts the telling.

I'm proud to say I've shared both drink and stories with every writer in this collection. Indeed, this book exists because of simple friendships with extraordinarily talented people. Half of them happen to have the same zip code, a quarter of them live within walking distance of each other.

So the question remains and probably always will: Why are there so many—at this count 30—published authors living in a single, small northern Mississippi town of 10,000?

There may be several combinations of reasons; perhaps it is the whiskey, or the slow pace or the lack of distractions. Certainly William Faulkner made Oxford, Mississippi, a credible literary address. For twenty years after his death in 1962, the Nobel Prize winner was the most notable writer associated with the town and always will be. In 1984, however, Willie Morris arrived to teach writing at the University of Mississippi (known as Ole Miss) in Oxford. Morris was known in literary circles for a memoir, *North Toward Home*, that had prompted the *London Times* to compare him to Mark Twain. Two other non-fiction books on Mississippi followed. Morris' writing career began after a successful—if not volatile—tenure as the youngest editor ever at *Harper's* magazine.

Morris was relieved of his command by the magazine's stodgy owners after he published a 50,000 word anti-Vietnam War essay by Norman Mailer that included earthy expletives never before printed in a mainstream American publication. Morris' arrival in Oxford caused a stir among bookish folk. Here was a living, breathing author who counted among his close friends, William Styron, James Jones, Irwin Shaw, Peter Matthiessen and even the famous New York restraunteur, Elaine.

That was the pleasant paradox of Willie Morris, for all his big time associations, he was surprisingly approachable; a Rhodes Scholar with the heart of a Yazoo City good ole boy, late night phone pranks being just one specialty. His students became accustomed to his holding class in local taverns. After his lectures he would often invite the class—bartenders included—back to his faculty bungalow for further discussions. These usually turned into a Willie monologue lasting into the wee hours and centered on everything from the Civil War to Faulkner to the exact tenets of the infield fly rule.

Morris, master of memoir and literary journalism, was soon joined in town by author Barry Hannah who struck literary fame in 1978 with a brilliant short-story collection, *Airships.* Hannah arrived with a colorful affinity for drink, handguns and motorcycles, but he never stopped honing his talent. Thus, his fiction remains; all of his 12 books are still in print, still translated into several languages and he continues to write the most interesting sentences of any major writer.

His literary voice—a kind of prose jazz—is very much informed by music. At its best, his work is the literary equivalent of his heroes, Miles Davis and Jimi Hendrix. Hannah's sentences dance all over the page, reveling in new, unrehearsed steps. Even his everyday conversation sparkles with uproarious riffs. And yet, for all his accolades and worldwide literary stature, (not to mention more lucrative teaching offers elsewhere) Hannah has remained in Oxford. Bumping in to Barry Hannah on the street and exchanging pleasantries is reason enough to live here.

Hannah and Morris became the foundation of Oxford's growing literary house; a bookstore and research center provided the walls and roof.

The Center for the Study of Southern Culture opened at Ole Miss in 1977 and immediately provided serious cultural study of all things southern: from Faulkner to kudzu, from Richard Wright to okra.

Square Books, now one of the nation's premier bookstores, opened in 1979 and immediately provided sustenance for Oxford's growing literary appetite. The store specialized in southern writing and author readings and became an oasis that proved that the citizens of Oxford not only read books but also would stand in line to pay for them.

With these crucial elements in place—and the broad shoulders of Faulkner's legacy to stand on—Oxford began to thrive as an unlikely cultural mecca. This is a town that Pat Conroy has called the "Vatican of Southern letters" and a community Willie Morris affectionately referred to as a "boondocks avant-garde."

Over the last twenty years, Oxford and the University have seen their community flourish in all of the arts, including a successful art gallery, Southside Gallery. When mega-selling author John Grisham signs books at Square Books, the line snakes past the art gallery all the way down to the video store, As Seen on TV. Grisham has been an integral part of Oxford's literary emergence.

Grisham moved to Oxford in the early 1980s after a successful career as a lawyer and state legislator. With encouragement from Morris, Grisham wrote two novels in the early morning hours before work and eventually scored unbelievable literary—and financial—success in 1991 with the publication of *The Firm*. His subsequent thrillers, published one per year since then, have catapulted Grisham into a stratosphere of worldwide sales unmatched perhaps by any American author.

To his credit, Grisham has donated generously to Mississippi schools including the endowment of a visiting writer's chair at Ole Miss. The John and Renee Grisham Visiting Writer's Series, named for the author and his wife, brings a different author to Ole Miss each year to teach writing for two semesters. Some of the writers in this book have held the Grisham chair including, Tom Franklin, Mark Richard, Shay Youngblood and the poet Claude Wilkinson.

Richard was one of the first Grisham writers and one of the most popular. His novel *Fishboy* still stands as one of the finest achievements in southern literature, a true blend of storytelling and high art. As if his literary talent wasn't enough, of all the writers in this anthology, Mark Richard looks the best in a tuxedo.

Shay Youngblood was the 2002-03 Grisham writer. Her stories are at once lyrical and compelling storytelling. While personally friendly and outgoing, Youngblood's work is layered and often dreamlike but always soulful. Another Grisham writer included here is Claude Wilkinson (2000-01), one of the first poets to be so honored. Claude takes poetry to the great outdoors for blackberry picking, quail hunting, or just plain daydreaming. During his stay in Oxford Wilkinson was also very much admired for his snazzy red 1972 Dodge Challenger.

Tom Franklin and Beth Ann Fennelly decided to move to Oxford permanently after Tom's stint (2001-02) as Grisham author. Tom's story collection, *Poachers*, and Beth Ann's debut poetry volume, *Open House*, are considered classics. On a personal level, the two are universally loved in Oxford. When the couple announced they were moving here, school was dismissed for the day . . . okay, but it should have been.

Carly Grace's "Southwest Georgia Haiku" rounds out the verse section of this book. Grace is a recent graduate of Ole Miss from Georgia who has chosen Oxford as her home to pursue her nascent writing career.

One writer who didn't have to move here is Larry Brown. Brown is one of two Oxford natives in this book, Dean Faulkner Wells being the other. Brown splits his time between two rural communities ten miles outside of town, Yocona, where he lives, and Tula where he is building a writing shack overlooking his pond.

Brown may be the closest Oxford has to a Faulkner-type writer, one who tends his home fires by day and then at night writes novels for a living. Like Faulkner, Brown's books all take place in a fictionalized world of his making, but are based not so loosely on real-life characters in and around Oxford. Brown was a fireman and jack-of-trades for years before his literary career became successful enough to allow him to stay home and write. He still remains very much a down-to-earth craftsman and prolific author. Brown also hosts an annual squirrel dumpling party that is a major event locally.

Dean Faulkner Wells and her husband, Larry, both featured in this book, live in the home William Faulkner's mother built. They have seen Oxford grow from sleepy hamlet, into its current status as a "hot" real estate market. Besides being fine writers, the Wells' were in the forefront of efforts to slow the over-development of our town. Simply put, I can't imagine Oxford without them.

With such literary folk and "infrastructure" in place, writers from all sorts of backgrounds and with various literary interests have moved to Oxford.

For example, author John T. Edge has helped turn southern cuisine into a serious area of study at Ole Miss. Edge himself has prowled the streets of Paris (France, not the real one) in search of the best fried catfish. A University of Mississippi food symposium, founded by Edge, is now as anticipated an event as the University's annual literary conference.

Noted blues photographer Dick Waterman arrived in Oxford to work with the southern culture center after a successful career photographing and reviving the careers of forgotten blues masters such as Son House and Skip James. Waterman was later the longtime manager and confidant of Bonnie Raitt. His forty years of photographic work includes everyone from John F. Kennedy to the Rolling Stones and Bob Dylan, as well as every major blues star you'd care to name from Muddy to Precious Bryant.

William Gay has made his mark in southern letters with two novels and his most recent story collection, the best-selling, *I Hate to See that Evening Sun Go Down.* Gay, a former carpenter, lives in Tennessee where he says he still occasionally "hangs a little sheet-rock just to keep my hand in." He is such a frequent—and welcome—visitor to Oxford that he feels like family and is included in this volume as an "honorary" Oxford writer, a beloved "ringer."

Another beloved ringer, screenwriter Anne Rapp (*Cookie's Fortune* and *Dr T. and the Women*) is also a frequent visitor to Oxford after having lived here for three years in the early 1990s studying under Barry Hannah. Her story, "Snakebit," came to her in a fever dream after a night out drinking in Santa Monica with Mark Richard and Larry Brown.

Also representing the "ringer" category is South Carolina native, George Singleton. With two hilarious short story collections to his credit, and a third on the way, Singleton may be the Lewis Nordan of his generation. If George Singleton is giving a reading within driving distance of your town be sure to go and you can thank me later.

Right down the road from Oxford is Paris, Mississippi, where Ace Atkins cranks out his best-selling series of "blues mysteries" featuring his fictional sleuth, Nick Travers. After publishing his first three novels, Atkins bought an old farm house near Paris, some ten miles south of Oxford, where he writes, rides a tractor and tends orphaned dogs.

Jonathan Miles has moved from Oxford to New York City to write for various magazines and serve as a contributing editor to *Men's Journal.* He began his career here at the local paper, the *Oxford Eagle.* Miles is remembered fondly: he spent so many post-reporting hours on a barstool at City Grocery, a local pub, the owner put a plaque at his spot on the bar.

Curtis Wilkie moved to Oxford (and sometimes New Orleans) after years as the national correspondent for the

Boston Globe. He can be easily spotted around town with his Gen. Robert E. Lee-like white beard and hair. He was a student at Ole Miss in 1962 when federal troops occupied the town to oversee the bloody integration of Ole Miss. Wilkie fled the state back then but has moved back and now lives the quiet life of the country-gentleman writer.

Jane Mullen is a longtime resident of Oxford who has published a powerful book of short stories. Mullen continues to quietly ply her trade as a writer with no fuss, no fanfare, just a steadily nurtured talent. Mullen represents the best of Oxford's literary community through her quiet appreciation of the written word and her strong commitment to her craft.

Masaru Inoune is from Japan, but takes periodic sabbaticals from his teaching at Ferris University in Yokohama to live in Oxford for a year at a time. Inoune is an American Literature professor with an emphasis on Faulkner. While in Oxford he often becomes mesmerized by things we Southerners take for granted: the first appearance of honeysuckle, the sweet sting of Jack Daniels, or, as he recounts here, the bewitching inaccuracy of southern courthouse clocks.

Lisa Howorth has edited two books on the south and is also the co-owner, along with her husband, Richard, of Square Books. The Howorths are as responsible as anyone for Oxford's emergence as one of the south's leading cultural communities. Lisa is well-known in Oxford for her wicked humor and her story, "Importance"—her first published fiction—is proof of that.

Jamie Kornegay is a bookseller at Square Books and is perhaps the town's most promising young writer—quite a distinction in a town full of youthful scribes. His apprenticeship is drawing to a close and you will no doubt have the opportunity to read novels bearing his name in the very near future.

David Magee is a lifelong Oxford resident who was once news editor of the local paper and later became the City's first non-fiction business writer. His book, *Turnaround: How Carlos Goshn Rescued Nissan*, is published in seven languages, and he is currently working on another, *Ford Tough*, slated for a Christmas 2004 release.

All of these writers are celebrated individually as they should be, but I'm also proud to have them assembled "under one roof" for the first time. In fact, perhaps this book should be read as if the reader were making a visit to Oxford. If you come in spring the honeysuckle will be out, you know the Jack Daniels will be in season and there will be an unfathomable courthouse clock.

Like any small town, there is gossip here, tragedy, drama and plenty of human comedy. On your visit we'll drive around town and visit some of these friends, they all live nearby. I think you'll find them very entertaining people with some very cool stories to tell.

So hop in and pop a cold one. I'll drive.

Jim Dees
Taylor, Mississippi
Full Moon Lunar Eclipse May 15, 2003

Foreword

My Two Oxfords

By Willie Morris

Editor's Note: Willie Morris passed away in 1999. He wrote this essay while living in Oxford in 1984.

I am a singular creature, among the handful who has dwelled for any length of time in two of the world's disparate places—the Oxford in England and the Oxford in Mississippi. On the one hundred fiftieth anniversary of the founding of the Mississippi one, I address myself to the subject. May I suggest there are similarities, but not all that many?

Still, it has always struck me as poignant that the white settlers who first came to this spot in the red hills of northeast Mississippi in the 1820s and 1830s, cleared the piney woods and made churches and roads and schools and jails and had a courthouse square for themselves by the time of the Civil War (everything being in readiness for Federal General A.J. "Whiskey" Smith to burn it all down in 1864), named their town Oxford. They wanted to acquire the new state university to dignify their raw terrain, and they were happy they got it, by a one-vote margin of the legislature.

The name-sake is rather more venerable. Its first mention was in the Anglo-Saxon chronicle of 912 AD, and of the university in the twelfth century, although legend ascribes the origins to Alfred the Great. My own Oxford college, New College, was new in 1379, and God knows what might have been transpiring in the forest and swamp bottoms of Lafayette County, Mississippi, in that auspicious year.

Has any single place on earth of comparable size produced such an august and eclectic array of human beings as the English Oxford? Indulge me this casual list, in random order: Thomas Browne, Samuel Johnson, A.E. Housman, William Penn, John Wesley, John Carroll, Phillip Sidney, Edward VII, Cardinal Wolsey, Randolph Churchill, Max Beerbohm, Bishop Wilberforce, Matthew Arnold, Robert Peel, T.S. Eliot, Walter Raleigh, Cecil Rhodes, Cecil Day-Lewis, Lord Bryce, Christopher Wren, William Blackstone, Lord Salisbury, Percy Bysshe Shelley, Clement Attlee, Joseph Addison, Richard Steele, Oscar Wilde, Edward Gibbon, John Galsworthy, Charles James Fox, Siegfried Sassoon, Thomas Hobbes, Admiral Blake, Evelyn Waugh, Walter Pater, General Haig, Lawrence of Arabia, Charles Lyell, Lord Baltimore, Cardinal Newman, Arnold Toynbee, Adam Smith, Robert Southey, Algernon Charles Swinburne, Quiller-Couch, Thomas De Quincey, Lord Asquith, Lord Grey of Fallodon, King Olav of Norway, Prince Felix von Singer, who commanded the German forces at Monte Cassino. This is a mere sampling, but imagine the oppressiveness of their footfalls as their spirits stalked a callow young American there a generation ago.

I lived almost four years in the classic Oxford in the late 1950s. I came down from New York to the Mississippi Oxford in 1980 to be Writer-in-Residence at the University of Mississippi and I have been here ever since. Was it the call of the name? Was there something in the blood compelling one to risk assimilating these most dissimilar landscapes? As with other of the curious and divergent experiences of a lifetime, can the two Oxfords be assimilated at all? Or are they both to me a dream?

Certainly that other Oxford is dreamlike to me now in its unfolding, a Lewis Carroll fantasy for a golden summer's afternoon. From the summit of the years I find it difficult to conceive I was actually there. Does this seem strange? Surely it was the first and last time I would ever live in a museum. Its spires and cupolas and quadrangles, its towers and gables and oriels and hieroglyphs, its ancient walls with the shards of glass embedded on top, its chimes and bells resounding in the swirling mists, made home seem distant and unreal. I lived in frigid rooms overlooking a spacious Victorian quadrangle, a stone's throw across the greensward from a massive twelfth century wall with turrets and apertures for arrows. A boy's choir sang madrigals every afternoon from the somber chapel across the way. I dined in a gloomy medieval hall with its portraits of parliamentarians and ecclesiastics, warriors and kings. The dons at first were as terrifying to me as nuns in my childhood.

The sacrosanct privacy of the place, the perpetual fogs and rains, elicited a loneliness, an angst, and melancholia such as I had never before known. The mementos of death were everywhere, in the ubiquitous graveyards, in the interminable rolls of the war dead in the chapels. The spirit of Kipling and Rupert Brooke resided amidst these scrolls to the fallen young. It was "the City of Dreaming Spires," and "the Home of Lost Causes." The burden of the past was ominous and incontrovertible. The college gates were padlocked at midnight, and within our forbidding fortress we were at the mercy of the ghosts of the centuries, and a squinty-eyed mystic from New Delhi peregrinated in the doomed hours conjuring all of them. After four years at a huge American state university—the final one as editor of the largest student daily in the United States—the change was horrendous. I began spending considerable time in the pubs with the Australians. Emerging from the Turf Tavern one foggy late afternoon into a secret medieval walkway which led to the college, we happened upon a curious assemblage: elves and fairies and Elizabethan princes and princesses and a girl in white robes playing a flute. "I had too bloody much this time," the Aussie from Brewarrina, New South Wales, said, unaware that the college drama club had just finished a Shakespearean rehearsal.

Lectures were optional. One of the English students explained to me that they had gone out of vogue with the invention of the printing press in the fifteenth century. Examinations were comprehensive and came at the end of three years. The tutorial system was the core of the Oxford education. Students wrote weekly or twice-weekly essays and discussed them in private sessions with the dons.

I remember my first essay. The tutor, Herbert Nicholas, had assigned me the Reform Act of 1832. I read seven or eight books and perused a half-dozen others. I stayed up all night polishing my effort to a thundering conclusion. Before a gentle fire in the don's rooms above the college gardens I read the next-to-last sentence. "Just how close the people of England came to revolution in 1832 is a question we shall leave to the historians," and was about to move on to the closing statement. "But Morris," interrupted the tutor, "we are the historians."

With essays the only formal requirement, one might do as he pleased; read novels, write poetry, walk along the river, sleep till noon, go to London, bicycle through the Cotswolds, or spend sixteen hours a day reading for the next tutorial. A West Point man claimed he went to the bulletin board near the tower-gateway twice a day looking for an order telling him what to do. The community did not judge, nor interfere with, one's personal habitudes. In fads and eccentricities, as in the paths the mind took, the Oxford student was protected by a subtle yet pervasive tolerance. There was an abiding homage there to independence and self-sufficiency, to intellectual candor, to one's own intensely private inclinations.

The paradox and variety of the place were vivid in its social life. There were social functions right out of Edwardian Oxford—from sherry in a don's room on Sunday morning to the raucous society dinners with their several courses and four or five wines. On one such evening W.H. Auden, brandishing a large carafe of red wine, wagered me a one-pound note that he could consume the contents in less than a minute. He did so, then collapsed on the floor. There were the fabulous commemoration balls on the college lawns with the all-night champagne, the tables laden with turkey and goose and pheasant and beef and fish and caviar, and the London society orchestras playing through the dusk-like lingering midsummer nights. At twilight one evening in the college cloisters, the guests, ranging from recent graduates to lords and ladies of the realm, sipped champagne and heard madrigals sung by the boy's choir. There was a time, also, for pork pie and inexpensive sherry at someone's lodgings—the Saturday night parties given by the working-class students where, in one or two close and smoky rooms, dozens of undergraduates were crowded inescapably together. Here invariably was a white wine concoction, American jazz from the gramophone, the shy and awkward English talk between boy and girl.

All this has been hard for me to fit into the whole of my American life, and I am no exception. A number of other American writers, from Robert Penn Warren to Reynolds Price, have studied over the years in Oxford, England, but by and large they have not written very much about it. It was an exotic interlude, and I remember it with affection and love and fulfillment and no little bemusement.

Oxford, England, is likewise a commercial and industrial center of well over 100,000 people. Oxford, Mississippi, minus the university students, is an unhurried courthouse-square hamlet of about 11,000, surrounded by a rough and authentic rural countryside. In physical aspect my latter Oxford is closer to the more pastoral Cambridge, without its aura of age or its majestic colleges. Of all the towns and cities in America which are home to the historic, capstone universities, this Oxford is the third smallest, just behind Orone, Maine, and Vermillion, South Dakota.

Ole Miss is small, too, by measure with other state universities, with slightly more than 9,000 students who are suffused with the flamboyant 'elan of their American state university contemporaries everywhere. Indeed, unlike the historic Oxford of my past, I find too little loneliness here. The emphasis is on gregariousness. The Greek system is strong and entrenched and dominates the social and political life. The rich sorority girls drive baby-blue Buicks with Reagan-Bush bumper stickers. They are noted for their beauty and their gossipy style. Many of them major in "Fashion Merchandising," an intellectual pursuit absent from the curricula of Oxford, England. Their social life is elaborate, organized, and not especially introspective. A New York writer described the rituals of the sorority rush week, "What screams, what cries, what an amplitude of passion. The proceedings are more exotic than the Romsiwarmnavian rites of the primitive Shirenes of Brazil's rain forest." Yet the legendary beauty of the Ole Miss coed is not a myth. The girls of Oxford, England, so stringently screened by some of the world's most demanding academic requirements, were often dour; yet the occasional warm-spirited beauty among them was always worth the waiting, and these were the girls, I am pleased to say, that the Yanks got. By the same token, the intellectual Ole Miss sorority girl of good and gentle disposition is a joyous song in the heart, and will endure.

Surely, it would be frivolous and indeed self-defeating to compare the students of one of Western civilization's greatest and most ancient institutions with those of a small, isolated Deep Southern American university. Yet in moments there is a palpable, affecting sophistication to this stunningly beautiful campus in the midst of the rolling rural woodlands of the American South. In the juxtaposition of town and school many have been reminded of the Chapel Hill of a generation or so ago, which bustles so now within the perimeters of the Research Triangle. It has so lost its touch with the Carolina land. One often recalls at Ole Miss Thomas Wolfe's description of his only slightly fictional Pulpit Hill years ago in *Look Homeward, Angel*, "There was still a good flavor of the wilderness about the place—one felt its remoteness, its isolated charm. It seemed to Eugene like a provincial outpost of great Rome: the wilderness crept up to it like a beast."

Ole Miss ranks high on the list of American Rhodes Scholars, and as with all state universities there will always be its cadre of bright, imaginative, and hard-working young. Gerald Turner, the resourceful new chancellor who is the youngest in the history of the Mississippi Oxford, wishes to build on the sturdier traditions. Turner has succeeded in a $40 million fundraising campaign to improve faculty salaries and the library at the university of the poorest state in the Union, and to strike a more wholesome balance between the Greek and independent students, and to stand fast with the First Amendment.

Nowhere is the contrast between the undergraduate life of the two Oxfords more striking than in two enduring institutions of these locales: the Junior Common Rooms and the Hoka. The "J.C.R's" of the colleges of Oxford, England, were the traditional student retreats for relaxation and conversation. These were sedate and proper places with frayed carpets and overstuffed Victorian furniture where one retired for tea and crumpets or to read *The Times* or *The Guardian* or the *TLS*. Women were not allowed (in the English Oxford of my era the colleges were rigorously segregated between the sexes) and the repartee was—shall one suggest—restrained. In the quiet and civilized gloom one could gaze out the windows at the darkening mists or the incessant rain. I was the only person who read there the *Paris Herald-Trib* for the baseball scores. If time weighed too heavily on my contemporaries and me in this setting, we might retire at pub-time to a little oasis of tranquility called the Turf Tavern—an ancient inn accessible only by a narrow medieval passage and presided over by two old maid sisters and their soporific cats—for warm ale around its stone and timbered bars. Here Thomas Hardy's Jude the Obscure courted Arabella the barmaid, but that was before our day.

The Hoka of the Mississippi Oxford, named after the tenacious Chickasaw princess, is situated across an alleyway from a bar reconverted from an old cotton gin. One is witness in this boondocks avant-garde coffeehouse to the true variety of Ole Miss and Oxford life, as opposed to the enclaves of Sorority and Fraternity Rows. It is presided over by Ron Shapiro, a much beloved St. Louis transplant, a kind of white Jewish Rastaman, and one Jim Dees, a Deltan who writes essays under the nom-de-plume "Dr. Bubba." The auditorium in back will have classic European and American movies. Up front B.B. King will be on the stereo, or the Grateful Dead, or Hank Williams, or Elvis. The Memphis and Jackson papers are there on the counter, just as the London papers were in the New College J.C.R. So, however, are vintage issues of *Playboy*, and *Field and Stream* and the *Yazoo City Herald*, and a wicked journal called *Southeastern Conference Football*. The patrons will include black athletes, willowy sorority beauties, nocturnal professors, a few carpenters or truck drivers or hairdressers from town, tousled student intellectuals in from a lecture by William Styron or Alex Haley or Eudora Welty or C. Vann Woodward, a black and white softball team, attractive female pharmacy students dining on Hoka chef's salads sprinkled with Dixie herbs and seeds, young editors who have just put the student paper to bed, a defrocked fraternity man or two sitting in a corner writing poems, a group of Ole Miss men recently returning from frog-gigging in the Tallahatchie River bottoms who smell of frogs, legal secretaries of both races from the courthouse square, a table of black sorority girls talking football, law students discussing torts and civil liberties, graduate history students arguing the Wilmot Proviso, the writer Barry Hannah between books, and an invariable blend of foreign students trying to make something of the perfervid and eclectic dialogue. One recent evening I joined two black and two white South Africans engaged in heartfelt, almost brotherly talk of their tragic nation.

Two or three of the village dogs will wander in expecting a sampling of the cheese nachos or a nibble from the most popular sandwich of the place, called mysteriously "The Love at First Bite." Instead of tea and crumpets, here and there are cinnamon coffee, bagels, and New Orleans-style beignets. The mood is mischievous but well-behaved, and some of the soliloquies are lyrical. On the walls are posters and circulars announcing rock concerts in the Delta, or blues festivals in the darkest canebrakes, indigenous sculptures, and photographs of Mississippi writers. There are portraits, too, of Vietnam veterans by a talented young photographer. In the girls' restrooms, I am told, there is graffiti too graphic for the toilets of St. Hilda's College, Oxford, England. Yet, as with the English J.C.R.'s, in its own mode this, too, is an honorable place, where words matter yet.

A casual stroll through the English Oxford of my youth would lead one, of course, to some of the impressive landmarks and monuments of the western world. Many was the afternoon I toured the town and countryside alone, or with a favorite English girl, or with visitors from home, absorbing its fleeting grey auras. The winding High Street or St. Aldate's or the Broad was always crowded with the red double-decked buses, bicycles, and trams, and the sidewalks with the townspeople and the undergraduates in their odd truncated academic gowns.

There were the sudden cul-de-sacs and alleyways, the Broad Walk with its avenue of towering elms, the fragrance and intense greenery of spring along the Isis or Cherwell. The afternoon offered limitless possibilities: the lavish interiors of the college chapels and the serene college gardens, the eerie facade of Mob Quad of Merton dating to the early fourteenth century, the grandeur and sweep of Tom Quad in Christ Church, the Crown Tavern near Carfax frequented by Shakespeare, the Georgian houses along Beaumont Street, the grotesque sixteenth century gargoyles in the Magdalen Cloisters, the Martyr's Memorial in front of Balliol with the statues of the doomed Cranmer, Ridley and Latimer, the regency elegance of St. John's Street, the opulence and isolation of Trinity, the self-proclaimed splendor of Rhodes House, the wonderful private retreat of Blackwell's book store where clerks left you alone as you browsed through Gibbon or Macaulay. One might pause in the Bodleian to look at the first editions of Chaucer or Shakespeare or Milton, or in the Ashmolean for its timeless collections. Or one might tarry in a favorite pub and eavesdrop on discourses about Toynbean cycles, French existentialism, the foreign policy of the United States, or the latest debate in the House of Commons. How I grew to love these walks of my youth in the noble, heroic old town! And touching everything on this day would be the omniscient, indwelling past.

A similar afternoon's tour of Mississippi's Oxford will be another study in catastrophic contrasts. Foremost are the Faulknerian landmarks. Beginning at the courthouse square with its Confederate soldier facing southward and the benches on the lawn crowded with sunburnt men chewing tobacco, one will follow the shady, settled streets with the antebellum houses hidden in magnolias or crepe myrtles. Their names are Shadow Lawn, Rowan Oak, Memory House. One may stroll by the oldest domicile in town, which was built in 1830. In front of the jail aged white and black men wearing Ole Miss baseball caps sit in haphazard conversation. The Ole Miss students speed by in their cars, their shouts and laughter trailing behind them, and there will be dusty pickups with farmers in khakis from Beat Four. The sorority girls have been in their rooms on campus painting their toenails, when one of them shouts, "Anybody want to go buy some shoes?" Everything is a blend of the town and the enveloping, untouched country.

The campus will be only a few blocks down University Avenue. Here the town and the university come together. In the bowers and groves lush with dogwood and forsythia in the spring, white and black students sit together under the trees, or drift languidly toward their classrooms. The old Lyceum is at the crest of the hill, and the library with its inscription: "I believe that man will not merely endure . . . he will prevail." Not far from here is the football stadium, where 40,000 people—four times more than the population of the town—will unquietly congregate on the autumnal afternoons.

The differences between my two Oxfords are even more emphatic in their countrysides. The miniature Oxfordshire country beyond the factories and modest brick homes of the industrial workers is one of manicured landscapes, tiny rivers, stone walls, and cottages and comforting greens, ancient parish churches and crumbling graveyards and manor houses at the horizon, perfect vegetable and flower gardens, and pristine village streets with antique shops and tea houses. In any direction from the campus or the courthouse square of the Mississippi Oxford, a two-mile drive or less, is the rough red earth, hard and unrelenting. Black and white farmers amble along the roads. The dark, snake-infested kudzu vines are everywhere, the landscape dotted with creeks and swamps and abandoned wooden houses, and country dogs bay in the distance. In the fields are scraggly cotton and soybeans, and on the horizon are the violent rains and windstorms of the Deep South. The rural hamlets of Lafayette County consist of a few derelict stores, a catfish restaurant, a church or two, a minuscule U.S. Post Office with firewood more often than not stacked on the front porch, and an untidy graveyard—"the short and simple annals of the poor." In such terrain at the proper seasons, one might sight more than a few of the male students of Ole Miss, hunting in the swamp bottoms with their dogs. This is the closest equivalent in the Mississippi Oxford to following the hounds and will not invite an especially intimate comparison.

On returning from their countrysides to each of the two Oxfords, the vistas from afar will also be dissimilar. The sight of the English Oxford from a distance is one of the most imposing and unforgettable in Europe. The sun breaks through and catches its silhouettes, its spires and walls and cupolas all in filigree, its gaunt and self-contained fortress aspect, and this exists for me in memory now as an apparition. The vista of the Mississippi Oxford from a high, wooded hill is of the campus half-shrouded in its dense vegetation, and of the twin water towers, and always the courthouse.

Finally, each Oxford, indeed, has been a "home of lost causes." In the English Oxford there were the successive changes of religion, the Civil War in which the University declared for the Stuarts and the town for Parliament, the bloody and immemorial political disputes, the executions and public burnings.

Of Mississippi Oxford, Gerald Turner speaks of the "extraordinary resilience" Ole Miss has shown in its 140-year history. It too is a place of ghosts. Almost no other American campus envelops death and suffering and blood, and the fire and sword, as Ole Miss does. In the American Civil War it was closed down and became a hospital for both sides. The bloodbath of Shiloh was only eighty miles away. Hundreds of boys of both sides died on the campus, their corpses stacked like cordwood, buried now in unmarked graves in a nearby glade. There is a Confederate statue on the campus also, given to the

University by the Faulkners as the one on the courthouse square was. The University Greys, all Ole Miss boys, suffered bitter casualties in that war. One hundred and three of their numbers were in the first wave of the charge at Gettysburg. Through later poverty and political interference and racial crises the institution somehow survived.

In 1962, John Kennedy dispatched almost 30,000 federalized troops during the riots over the admission of the first black student, James Meredith. As we know all too well, two people were killed and scores injured; it could have been worse. As recently as five years ago, several hundred white students marched on a black fraternity house protesting the abolition of the Confederate flag as a university symbol. In 1982, the University observed the twentieth anniversary of the Meredith confrontation. Interracial audiences gathered for an awards ceremony for distinguished black graduates of Ole Miss and for speeches by blacks and whites. The keynote address was given by Meredith.

Black enrollment at Ole Miss today is just under eight percent, in the American state with the largest black population, thirty-six percent. The black students have sometimes complained that they are left out of the social life of the campus. The Greek system remains completely segregated. The varsity athletic teams are, of course, totally integrated, and the outstanding black athletes are genuine campus heroes. The Ole Miss Rebels football team has the highest ratio of black players in the Southeastern Conference and perhaps in the nation—fifty-four percent—and the white-and-black band plays a rendition of "the Battle Hymn of the Republic" and "Dixie" called "From Dixie with Love" at sporting events which would bring tears to the eyes of a Massachusetts abolitionist. The chancellor has pledged to recruit more black students in substantial numbers and to increase black faculty members. One cannot help but note here a new spirit of interracial good will. As Professor David Sansing has written, who would have imagined in those precarious days of 1962 that Ole Miss's most recent Rhodes Scholar would be black, or that the grandson of Mohandis Gandhi would come in 1987 to study race relations in America?

Ultimately, one supposes now, I was only an interloper in the English Oxford. When the moment came, I collected my paraphernalia, mostly books, and returned home again to America. It had been the freest time of my life, and I learned there something of myself—my abilities, faults, convictions, prejudices.

As for the Mississippi Oxford, it lurks forever now in my heart. For it is the heart which shapes my affection for my two Oxfords, and across the years brings them ineluctably together for me.

FICTION

BARRY HANNAH

All the Old Harkening Faces at the Rail

A few of the old liars were cranking it up around the pier when Oliver brought his one-man boat out. He was holding the boat in one hand and the motor in the other. Oliver probably went about fifty-seven or eight. He had stringy hair that used to be romantic-looking in the old days. But he still had his muscles, for a short guy.

"What you got there," said Smokey.

"Are you blind, you muttering old dog? It's a one-man boat," said Oliver.

Oliver didn't want to be troubled.

"I seen one of them in the Sears book, didn't I? How much that put you back?"

"I don't recall ever studying your checkbook," said Oliver.

"This man's feisty this afternoon, ain't he?" said a relative newcomer named Ulrich. He was sitting on the rail next to the steps where Oliver wanted to get his boat down them and to the water. For a moment this Ulrich didn't move out of Oliver's way.

"You buy it on credit?"

Oliver never answered. He stared at Ulrich until the old man moved, then went down the steps with his little boat to the water and eased the thing in. It was fiberglass of a factory hue that is no real color. Then Oliver went back up the steps where he'd left the motor. Then he pulled the back of the boat up and screwed on the boat clamps of the motor. It was nifty. You had something ready to go in five minutes.

All the old liars were peering over the edge at his operation.

"Don't you need fuel and a battery?" said Smokey, lifting up his sunglasses. One of his eyes was taped over from cataract surgery.

"A man that buys on credit is whipped from the start," said Ulrich.

When Oliver looked up the pier on all the old harkening faces at the rail, he felt young in an ancient way. He had talked with this crew many an evening into the night. There was a month there when he thought he was one of them, with his hernia and his sciatica, his lies, and his workman's compensation, out here with his cheap roachy lake house on the reservoir that formed out of the big Yazoo. Here Oliver was with his hopeful poverty, his low-rent resort, his wife who never had a bad habit in her life having died of an unfair kidney condition. All it's unfair, he'd often thought. But he never took it to heart until Warneeta passed over to the other side.

There was a gallery of pecking old faces scrutinizing him from the rail. Some of them were widowers too, and some were elaking away toward the great surrender very fast. Their common denominator was none of them was honest.

They perhaps had become liars by way of joining the evening pier crowd. One old man spoke of the last manly war, America against Spain. Another gummed away about his thirty pints and fifteen women one night in Mexico. Oliver had lied too. He told them that he loved his wife and that he had a number of prosperous children.

Well, he had respected his wife, and when the respect wore off, he had twenty years of habit with her. One thing was he was never unfaithful.

And he had one son who was a drum major of the band at Lamar Tech in Beaumont, and who had graduated last year utterly astonished that his beautiful hair and outgoing teeth wouldn't get him employment.

But now I'm in love, thought Oliver. God help me, it's unfair to Warneeta in the cold ground, but I'm in love. I'm so warm in love I don't even care what these old birds got to say.

"Have you ever drove one of them power boats before, son?"

This was asked by Sergeant Fish, who had some education and was a caring sort of fellow with emphysema.

Oliver walked through them and back across the planks of the pier to his car that was packed in the lot at the end. He opened the trunk of his car and lifted out the battery and the gas can. He managed to hold the marine oil under his armpit. He said something into the car, and then all the men at the end of the pier saw the woman get out of Oliver's Dodge and walk to him and pull the marine oil can from under his arm to relieve the load. She was about thirty-five, lean, and looked like one of those kinds of women over at the Rolling Fork Country Club who might play tennis, drink Cokes and sit around spraddle-legged wit their nooks humped out aimless.

Jaws were dropped on the end of the pier.

Smokey couldn't see that far and was agitated by the groans around him.

Sergeant Fish said, "My Gawd. It's Pearl Harbor, summer of forty-one."

When she and Oliver got near the liars, they saw her face and it was cute—pinkish big mouth, a jot pinched, but cute, though maybe a little scarred by acne.

Oliver rigged up the gas line and mixed the oil into the tank. He attached the battery cables. The woman sat two steps above him while he did this alone in the back of the boat. There was one seat in the boat, about a yard wide.

Oliver floated off a good bit while he was readying the boat. The woman had a scarf on her hair. She sat there and watched him float off thirty feet away as he was getting everything set. Then he pulled the crank on the motor. It took right up and Oliver was thrown back because the motor was in gear. The boat went out very fast about two hundred yards in the water. Then he got control and circled around and puttered back in.

The woman got in the boat. She sat in Oliver's lap. He turned the handle, and they scooted away so fast they were almost out of sight by the time one of the liars got his tongue going.

"It was Pearl Harbor, summer of forty-one, until you saw her complexion," said Sergeant Fish.

"I'll bet they was some women in Hawawyer back then," said the tall proud man with freckles. He waved his cane.

"Rainbow days," lied Fish. "The women were so pretty they slept right in the bed with me and my wife. She forgave me everything. It was just like stroking puppies, all of them the color of goldfish."

"Can that boat hold the two of 'em?" said Smokey.

"As long as it keeps going it can," said Ulrich, who featured himself a scientist.

"Oliver got him a babe," said another liar.

"I guess we're all old enough to see fools run their course," said old Dan. Dan was a liar who bored even the pier crowd. He lied about having met great men and what they said. He claimed he had met Winston Churchill. He claimed he was on friendly terms with George Wallace.

"You'd give your right one to have a chance with Oliver's woman, indifferent of face as she is," said Sergeant Fish.

"When the motor ever gives out, the whole thing will sink," said Ulrich.

They watched awhile. Then they all went home and slept.

WILLIAM GAY

The Iceman

Birds called him awake where he slept on the riverbank, a veritable madhouse of caws and chirps and twittering that began with the advent of day and increased with the encroaching light. He struggled against waking as if the day held more than he could handle and he wanted no part of it but he'd fallen asleep in some curious aviary walled only by the trees and when the cries grew more strident and persistent he discarded his strange dreams and sat looking out across the river. There was no commerce on it as yet and the surface was calm, warped and wonkylooking as distressed sheet metal. Far across in distant haze the other shore looked new and unspoiled. There was no trace of man or his works and the countryside looked like the shore of some vague and lovely world only rumored, not yet tainted by civilization.

He arose and made ready to go, glancing about once like a man checking out of a hotel room checking to see has he forgotten anything. He had not. There was nothing to take into the day save Yates and the clothes on his back. He struck out up the riverbank. Curious little town built on hills. Winding precipitous sidestreets, you seemed always to be climbing or descending stairsteps. He came upon the main drag where folk were beginning to mill purposefully about then veered south through a warren of shacks clinging to hillsides with parchedlooking nighvertical gardens attendant where nothing he recognized grew and through backyards strung with clotheslines where hung ragged graylooking clothes and through front yards past silent watchdogs on tangled chains. No one seemed up save some old grandmother warming in the sun and did not acknowledge his existence, he seemed to move through here in furtive invisibility. Begarbed shacks halfpainted as if their tenants had given up and thrown the brushes away, blownout automobiles deceased and stripped of their viable organs, some already buried in honeysuckle and kudzu. He moved through a land locked in silence, a place that seemed to be reeling in the aftershock of some cataclysm that had come in the night and whose impact had not yet been assessed. He quickened his steps.

He came out near the railroad tracks four or five blocks up from the depot. He went past a sprawling clapboard building that had been remodeled and added onto endlessly as if constructed by carpenters who could come to no sort of agreement as to what they were building. It moved backward in a series of diminishing rooflines and the last addition seemed designed for littlefolk or leprechauns so near the ground it was. There was a red Diamond-T truck backed to the front porch and a heavyset man was loading blocks of ice onto it with a set of tongs. Another man sat leaning against a porch stanchion with his face in his hands. He seemed to be grieving. Yates had seen this truck before or one like it and he went closer to inspect it. When he turned his attention back to the seated man he saw that he was holding crushed ice in his cupped palms and he was rubbing his face with it.

The man with the tongs slammed a fifty-pound block of ice onto the bed of the truck and stepped back to the porch.

"You better get to coverin this shit up," he told the seated man. "I get paid to sell it and that's all and here I am loading it. But I'll be damned if I'm covering it and everything else."

The man lowered his palms and looked at the melting ice and rubbed it into his sparse gray hair. Chunks of ice lay there and began to melt and the cold water ran down his forehead. His eyes were fey looking and drunken, one with a rightward cast as if it would have a wider vision of the world or at the very least a different perspective on it.

"I was tryin to remember where I stayed last night," the man said. "It's right on the edge of my mind but I just can't get hold of it. I wish I could. Seems like I done somethin awful or somebody done somethin awful to me but I'll be damned if I can remember what. I wish I could just remember where I stayed."

"Where was you when you woke up?" Yates asked, becoming interested in this mystery in spite of himself. "That always seems to help me. Generally where I wake up is about where I fell asleep at."

The man looked at him and then he looked away. He shook his head and didn't say anything.

"Where was your truck at when you woke up?

The man studied Yates without expression, with a face that bore him no animosity that perhaps welcomed the rationalizations of a logical mind.

"Ahh," he said. "My truck. My truck was here, where I left it yesterday when the ice plant was closed. I can keep up with my truck. It's me I keep losin."

"None of this is gettin ice loaded and covered up," the man with the tongs said.

"Ain't I seen you on Allens Creek? Who are you?"

"I'm the iceman," the man said. "You liable to see me most anywhere. I'm the iceman, he sang in a tuneless crooning: I'm the iceman, the iceman, better get out of my way."

Yates turned to go.

"Hey," the man said. Yates stopped.

"I'll give you two dollars if you'll get that scoop and sawdust that ice down. Cover it over and put the tarps over it."

Yates looked at the size of the truck. The ice stacked in its bed. The mounded pile of sawdust.

"I already got two dollars," he said.

"All right, I'll give you four. Hellfire, ain't you got no ambition? Here I am offerin you double, I say double your worldly goods for a few minutes work and you don't even want to hear it. What's the matter with these young folks today."

"Where you takin this ice?"

The iceman studied. Monday, he told himself. He looked at Yates. "I'm goin out Riverside and up Allens Creek. Back through Oak Grove."

"I'll do it if you throw in a ride to Allens Creek."

The man stuck out a hand and Yates shook it. The hand was wet and cold as ice, just the way an iceman's hand should feel, Yates thought.

He took up the scoop and the man with the tongs showed him what to do. The blocks of ice were spaced two or three inches apart and Yates carefully filled in between them with sawdust and between the ice and the sideboards. When that was done, a layer thrown loosely over all, the man with the tongs began to stack more ice. A layer of ice, a layer of sawdust. At last the man signaled he was through and Yates covered the last layer and drew the tarp over it and lashed it down.

The iceman was up and about and with enormous effort he opened the truck door and climbed in. Yates got in the other side.

"You have to hold onto that handle," the iceman said. "Door'll fly open on a curve and sail your skinny ass down a hillside."

Yates sat clutching the door handle both handed. The iceman was staring out the windshield.

"Well now," he said. He was looking at the world with intense concentration, as if it were coming at him at a hundred miles an hour and he was charged with negotiating its curves and byways. He reached out and turned the ignition and the truck coughed into life and set idling. He nodded. "All right, all you unrefrigerated sons of bitches," he said. "Here comes the iceman."

Four or five miles out of town they went through a flatlands where the road paralleled the river and Yates could see not the river itself but the upper half a barge that seemed to be cruising by some miraculous locomotion through willows and a stand of sassafras. Then the road curved upward into the hills and he could smell hot piney woods baking in the sun, astringent and somehow nostalgic.

The iceman at first drove with the exaggerated care of a drunk who doesn't quite trust himself. As his confidence grew and the pitch to the motor wound higher he began to croon mindlessly to himself, "the iceman, here comes the iceman, better get out of my way."

He walled his off eye up at Yates. "You ever been so drunk you couldn't remember where you was or what you done?"

"Lord no," Yates said, clinging religiously to the door handle. "I can barely find my way through a day cold sober. I'd not even attempt one drunk."

"I never could make much sense of it drunk or sober," the iceman said. "Seems like it just went easier drunk though."

Yates didn't reply. The road had climbed into terrain near mountainous that he was wary of and the road was snaking around narrow switchback curves. The off eye kept glancing at Yates and Yates wished it would watch the road. The truck kept rounding curves and the blind side and Yates was watching them apprehensively. Red rock climbed sheer on the left and looking down from his window he could see the earth dropping away in a manner that took his breath away and he tightened his grip on the door handle as if in some talismanic way it was holding the truck on the road.

"It's in like a dark place," the iceman said. "I can almost see in there but whatever's in there slips back out of sight. Sometimes I nearly think of it and then it's gone."

"Godalmighty," Yates said.

They'd rounded a leftleaning curve on the wrong side and two enormous black mules were just suddenly upon them, the left mule rearing with wild rolling eyes and its hoofs slamming onto the hood then its head turning against the actual glass with white walled eyes frantic then gone and the wagon with the old man's face a rictus of absolute horror and him trying to whip the mules onto an impossible course, sawing the lines and cutting them into the sheer wall with the wagon tilting and the iron rims sparking against the granite bluff. The truck struck the left rear wheel of the wagon and carried it away with the wagon turning and sliding crosswise behind them, Yates whirling watching through the back glass the overalled man spilled from the wagonbed then whirling back to see coming at him across the hood a frieze of rock and greenery clockwise in such elongation the landscape seemed stretched to transparency as the brakelocked truck swapped ends in the gravel and the horizon itself fleeing vertically downward as the truck tilted backward off the shoulder of the road and the truck cab filled with intense blue sky.

The iceman was humming crazily to himself. He'd locked the brakes and now when he released them the truck accelerated backward down the hill with him watching out the windshield trees that seemed to come from nowhere fleeing backward, brush that sprang erect from beneath them like imaged brush in a pop-up book, him giving the steering wheel little meaningless cuts right or left. He seemed not to know where he was.

"Hit the Goddamned brakes," Yates screamed. Yates was peering out the back glass, at once trying to see where they were going and fearful of it.

When the iceman slammed the brakes the motor stalled and died and the load of ice shot backward down the slope, disappearing off the bed like a frozen waterfall then the truck lurching and jouncing across it and the ice reappearing magically before them, great chunks strewn like gleaming hailstones from a storm of unreckonable magnitude.

"Cut it into a tree," Yates yelled, but before he'd even finished saying it the truck slammed into a treetrunk so hard the force of it whipped his head into the back glass then forward into the windshield. They sat in a ringing appalled silence, Yates clutching his head, the iceman staring up the hillside the way they'd come. Outraged crumpled saplings, crushed cedars, ice everywhere.

"All them folks," the iceman said.

"Do what?" Yates asked. He thought the iceman was talking about the collision with the wagon and he'd only seen one man.

"All them folks waitin on me. With their hot jugs of tea. Their ice cream freezers. 'Where's the iceman,' they'll say. He ain't never been this late before."

Yates was shaking and he couldn't stop. "You are absolutely the craziest shitass in the whole history of the world," he said.

The iceman was trying to get his door open. It seemed to be stuck, jammed where it struck the wagon wheel. At length he turned in the seat and kicked it hard bothfooted and it sprang open.

"Help me," he said. "We got to get that ice gathered up."

"I wish I had sense like other folks," Yates said. "I'd be better off in hell with my back broke than ever crawlin in a truck with you."

"I got money tied up in this ice. Help me reload and we'll scotch this truck somehow and I'll try to drive us out."

Yates looked. He was shaking his head.

"You couldn't drive up that bluff in a Goddamned Army tank," he said. "She ever comes out of here she'll have a block and tackle tied to her."

"Nevertheless it's got to be done," the iceman said. He staggered up the slope clutching to saplings. Yates clambered out of the canted truck cab. It was hard even to stand here, so precipitous and undependable was the earth. He looked down on a fairyland of treetops, tiny pink road winding somewhere, so far. He sat down and began to inspect himself for wounds.

The iceman had selected a fifty-pound block of ice. He was stumbling toward the truck with it clutched before him like some offering he was making. Suddenly he halted stock-still as if the ice had frozen him in his tracks. He had a peculiar look on his face.

"Son of a bitch," he said.

"What?"

"A dance," the iceman said. He sat the ice down carefully then seated himself upon it. Elbows on knees, hands clasped before him. He seemed to be in deep thought.

"What?"

"I killed somebody," the iceman said.

"Who?" Yates was thinking about the wagon, the man sliding roadward.

"Some girl," the iceman said. "Some woman. We was at a dance. One of them beerjoints down by the river. I don't even remember what we got into it about. I took to beatin her with somethin . . . seems like it was a singletree but I don't know where in the shit I'd get a singletree."

"A stick maybe. A big stick. I remember she kept tryin to crawl off into the bushes. I kept hitting her and hitting her."

Yates was watching him apprehensively. He could feel ice water tracking down his rib cage. He glanced upward to the rim of the earth where the road ran, figuring perhaps angles of inclination, speed when fleeing madmen.

"Maybe you just slapped her around a little," he said hopefully.

The iceman thought about it a while. He took a package of Camel cigarettes from a shirt pocket and tipped one out and just sat holding it. His hands were wet from the ice and after a time it shredded in his fingers.

"No," he finally said. He shook his head. "No. I killed her all right. She was all busted up and limber. I remember rakin wet black leaves over her face."

Yates arose. He dusted off the seat of his jeans.

"I got to get on," he said. "It's a long way to Allens Creek."

The iceman appeared not to hear. Yates climbed a few feet up the slope and then he turned. "I need to get that money," he said.

"What money?"

"That four dollars for loading the truck."

The iceman fumbled out a wallet, sat studying its contents.

"I'd double it again if you'd help me reload."

"I got to get on."

The iceman carefully counted off four one dollar bills, rubbing each one carefully between thumb and forefinger. Yates took the proffered money and pocketed it.

"Appreciate it," he said.

"Anytime," the iceman said. "You want to help me as a regular thing the job's open."

Yates didn't reply. When he was halfway up the hillside he looked down. The iceman had risen and he had begun to gather the blocks of ice and restack the truck. Yates went on. The next time he looked back the iceman raised a hand in a curiously formal gesture, farewell, and Yates raised an arm, farewell, and clambered onto the road.

He stood breathing hard. Far down the winding road toward Clifton the farmer appeared riding a mule. The wagon and the other mule were nowhere in sight.

He turned. Beyond the rim the world lay in a crazyquilt patchwork of soft pastel fields, tracts of somber woods. Folded horizons so far they trembled and veered in the heat and ultimately vanished. Somewhere in that dreammist lay Allens Creek. He'd have traded a year of his life for a handful of its dust. He spat and wiped the sweat out of his eyes and struck out toward it.

Lisa Neumann Howorth

Importance

On the second-to-last day of his life Jack Ernest came to with the sickening but sexy sensation of something foul and warm and wet in his face. Aunt Nana's nasty little Yorkie was, in fact, standing on his chest, feet foursquare, lapping away. With one hand Ernest chunked the dog across the room where it landed with a wheezing squeak like a child's rubber squeeze toy. He reached for a Marlboro. Since his return from Bosnia he'd switched to filtered, not entirely unconcerned about his health before he was ready to consider being awake. Eventually he would rise, shower and descend to the kitchen where he would have breakfast with his aunt and grandmother. Then he would go back to his room and write about the war. He did this eighteen days out of the month. Every other weekend he went up to Oxford, where the University was, to party. This was what he planned to do tonight.

"You know, if you're going up there tonight for your fun, it's a winter storm warning all across the TV," said Aunt Nana. She was actually Ernest's grandmother.

"It's true—DeLoris called and she had just spoke with her daughter in Memphis who said it was already snow up there," said Abelia, who was an aunt.

"You might could use those tire chains," said Aunt Nana. "The ones we had to get in the Rockies that time." She rocked the skillet back and forth to distribute the grease.

"I've got plans for those chains, my good grandmother," Ernest said. "And they don't include putting them on the car." He winked salaciously at his grandmother, and then looked at Abelia and winked again.

"Honestly, Jack. What a white-trash thing to say," said Aunt Nana. She sniffed to signify indignation. Abelia chuckled.

Ernest sat down at the table and surveyed the women. Sisters, but they could not have been more different. Aunt Nana, conservative and provincial in all her notions but first with the latest fads at the mall, wore a wind suit—a plastic abomination of turquoise and fuchsia geometric designs. (Ernest thought that after jogging suits, which people now actually wore out in public as if they were real clothes, wind suits were one of the most hideous affronts to civilization ever. As a child he could just barely remember leisure suits, but then his fashion sensibilities had not been highly developed. He had never, however, forgotten the shocking sight of white shoes and white belts on his grandfather and uncles and the cheesy feel of their polyester Sans-a-belt slacks. Even at eight, running around shirtless and shoeless, he wanted to look like the guys at Ole Miss: khakied, tweedy, club-tied). Abelia, on the other hand looked like Florence Bavier; hen-breasted, brooched, tiny of foot and voice but she held advanced ideas and had a sharp sense of humor. She had had two husbands, six children, and was never without an escort for a movie or church event. She enjoyed David Letterman. Nana had had only the one husband, Toy, who had simply sat down under a bodock tree on the fifth hole of the Attala County Club golf course one day and never got up. Nana was as prim and prissy as Abelia was loose and generous of disposition.

"Lord, what a time that Rockies trip was," said Abelia. "I'll never forget that. A blizzard in June." The sisters weren't given to travel, especially west of the Mississippi, or actually, even west of the Yokanakany, which ran close by Wallis, but they had won a trip to Branson in a church raffle and Abelia decided that they ought to go on and at least see the Rockies before kicking the bucket.

"Well, I kind of thought the blizzard was an improvement on things, myself. Nothing but rocks, rocks, and pine. I thought the Rockies were just plain *tacky*," said Nana.

"How in the hell can a mountain range be tacky, Nana?" Ernest asked.

"Oh, you know what she means," said Abelia. "Too new. Too brown. Too full of *strangers*." She laughed.

"Exactly. They just *are.*" Nana sniffed. "Now the Smokies—there's some pretty mountains for you."

The insectoid dog crept nervously into the room. "And why is this dog acting like it's been beaten?" asked Nana. The wind suite gave off a lot of irritating noise as she moved toward the coffeepot. "Come here, Ashley," she said, making little air smooches, "Mwa."

"That dog is a loser," said Ernest, pushing back his plate.

"Ashley, oh Ashley," Nana said. She scooped up the little dog. "Don't listen to him. You're such a gentleman. And so handsome."

"He might look handsome at the end of a fishing line, or on the lazy susan at the Ruby Chinese," Ernest rose from the table. "But there's no other way he would."

Upstairs, Ernest took a pair of Duck Heads from a clean, ironed stack of a dozen, and a crisp white shirt from a sizable row in his closet. He added a blazer and shades and the look was complete—the relentless and correct uniform of the Mississippi boulevardier. To get the testosterone percolating for the day's and evening's events, he decided to take the AK-47 out and shoot some things. He took the gun from its case next to the bed and petted it.

It was an older gun; the wooden stock had been painted red at one time, for identification, he supposed. The gun had been handled so much that the paint had worn away, leaving the wood with a rich cherry patina. It was lovely to look at and even better to feel. Ernest traced a whorl in the grain with his finger. He had bought the gun for almost nothing—fifteen American dollars and a couple packs of Marlboros—from a wounded teenager returning from the Bosnian front.

The kid, broken in every way, had no wish for anything other than slivovice and cigarettes. He had laughed in spite of a neck wound when Ernest said that he himself was headed to the front to write about it. A Red Cross medic, a Georgia girl of Ernest's acquaintance, had translated the soldier's exhausted remarks. "He's more or less telling you to *go on,*" she said. "*Get you some.*" He had smuggled in the AK-47 by sending it home Fed-Ex—you could send anything Fed-Ex, bless them. The Mercury of the twentieth century. In Bosnia Ernest had known guys who had sent amazing things stateside. He met a GI whose great-great-great grandfather was the Cherokee chief, Ridge. The solider had scalped a Serbian prisoner's unit, taking away pud, pelt and balls, and sent it Fed-Ex to his girlfriend. Another GI had sent exotic mushrooms and rare plants to his boyfriend in San Francisco.

Ernest passed through the kitchen to the back porch, casually aiming the gun at Ashley.

"This dog is worth hundreds of dollars at stud," Nana called after him. "So please point that thing somewhere else."

Ernest let the screen door slam. "You're crazy, Aunt Nana," he said. "You know that dog has failed at love."

"I know no such thing," Nana called. "A random Rottweiler twice his size is no test of his abilities."

To Ernest, if you couldn't get it up for exotic, strange pussy, what was the point? Instead of uttering this he said, "Well, I wish he'd quit testing his abilities on my hunting boots."

He began firing off rounds into a dirt bank behind the house. It was wonderful the way the orange clay exploded. In the overcast winter daylight, the gun glowed, a thing of high beauty and precision. A joy forever. It was Ernest's intention to sell the gun for a big pile of cash now that they had been outlawed. Even though every ghetto gangster in America owned an AK-47 he figured he could sell it for enough to live on for a year or so, somewhere cheap, Cracow or Spain. He had always wanted to run with the bulls.

Ernest shot off a few more rounds. He felt pumped up, but it was getting chilly and the day was turning bitter and threatening. He thought of Kalashnikov, living in Siberia and working at the munitions plant, not giving a fuck about the cold and communism and lack of attractive gash as long as he could jink with his guns. Ernest pictured him in his tiny, immaculate dacha, cheesecloth spread out on a table where dozens of oily steel pieces lay scattered like watch parts, or jewelry. Kalashnikov would work at the guns into the night with the wind and the wolves trying to out-howl each other outside his door in the vast taiga. In the morning he would gather up a few parts, tying them up in an old babushka and take them to the factory where he'd fool with them some more. He would mess with them until he got it right, honing and tooling until the gun became a perfect little piece of clockwork, an artifact of impeccable craftsmanship and satisfying—thrilling—to hold and behold. This was just the way Ernest intended to write his novel; refining each little thing until the whole worked flawlessly. It would be the AK-47 of novels. He would get to work on it seriously after the weekend.

He'd expended himself. His hands were freezing and if he was going to make that party in Oxford he'd better hit the road before the weather turned. How bad could it get? He'd seen unbelievable snow in the Dinari Planina south of Sarajevo—snow that fell in clumps for days, covering tanks, cows, and tires. Snow in Mississippi was puny and accidental and didn't last much past sunrise. Things never got covered-over. You could always still see the ugly kudzu tangles underneath, like piles of chicken bones. But now the sky had turned that ominous steely gray like he remembered in Bosnia—low and solid and not like there was going to be any breaking up to it.

Ernest gathered up the things he would need for the night. It was a birthday party at Janky Jane's, black tie, but would they be lame enough to cancel it for a little weather? Surely not. A band was lined up, and even though all they did was R&B covers the Velvatones were not cheap. It had to be happening. At any rate, he was out of here. He had had no fun, *zero*, in weeks, unless you counted the night at the boats in Greenville, where he'd lost a wad and seen his real father.

"I'm gone!" he shouted to Nana and Abelia. "Y'all'll see me when you see me!"

"Be careful! Drive safe! Everything safe!" they shouted back.

Ernest threw his party clothes and a batwing of Tanqueray into his MG. Backing down the long, rutted dirt drive he stopped to throw back a couple of little white pills. "Godshpeed," he said, chewing. He was off.

He went by way of French Camp to collect a poker debt from Tork Hazelrig. Tork (the nickname came, as they often do in high school, from something to do with his private parts. Other classmates had been Weege, Bull, Bone, and Rat Cods. In fact, when Tork had played ball with Ernest at Attala—Wallis Christian Academy, better known as Tally—Wally, even the team was called the Tallywhackers.) Tork now worked at the Hep-R-Sef and had done some time in Chicago. From behind the pickled eggs. Mini-Thins and condoms he said to Ernest, "You goin up to Oxford, it's bad up there. Memphis is all froze up, too, I heard."

"A little ice on the road is nothing to fear, old friend," said Ernest.

"One time Lake Michigan froze up so hard we drove a Buick Roadster out onto it. Me and my wife and kids. We parked out there and the kids slid around and we ate that kaboosa sausage on buns and listened to Willie."

Ernest was always amazed at how white Tork was—the whitest person he'd ever seen, almost blue. He never went out in the daylight.

"I don't believe I would have taken a chance with a car like that, Tork," Ernest said. "There aren't many Roadsters left around."

Back on the road, he decided to head up through Sweatman and Kilmichael, escaping the charmless interstate as far as Tie Plant where he had to cut over to avoid all the log truck traffic. A Mississippi log truck was the most dangerous thing on earth: long, skinny pines drooping down practically to the road and overloaded onto ancient trucks that pooted oily blue smoke and had no signal lights. People had been skewered. From Tie Plant he could sail on up I55. If he hurried there would be time to call up a few women, gauge the poontang availability, and shoot some pool at Purvis's.

By the time he hit the interstate Ernest could feel but not see that there was a little ice. The MG was so low to the ground that he could sense the road slipping away beneath him, tire treads unengaged. At one point he fishtailed, sending him into a cheek-stinging adrenaline rush and a lower gear. The little car righted itself and Ernest patted the dashboard. "Good dog," he said, and plugged in a Stones tape. The Stones—you could always count on them to supply intestinal fortitude and a surge of confidence. God bless Mick and Keith, although sometimes Ernest had a nagging fear that they had gone soft on him. He didn't mind all the models—that was good—but all those kids, the health food and tennis and tans, the repaired teeth—what was going on with those guys? Ernest had missed out on the early days; Brian Jones, the incredible drugs and parties—he was just about being born when Marianne Faithful had done the candy bar thing. He had read about it. Now *that* would have been a party.

The light, Ernest noticed, had gotten really strange, like tornado weather, but that was a good month or two off. The clouds seemed so low—like they were barely clearing the trees. Sleet was coming down in hard little lines, and few cars were on the road. Almost none were coming from the opposite direction. Here and there a car had run off into a ditch, or had pulled over. Still, it was just a little glaze—nothing so unusual. Southerners just did not know how to drive on ice. They would try to brake, and they would turn against a skid. It was probably the only thing that Yankees could do better, Ernest thought, taking another pull of Tanqueray. Sorry bastards.

By the time he reached Coffeeville, the dex was kicking in good, which made it even harder to deal with the fact that he was creeping along, doing maybe thirty, thirty-five. What was this shit? The trees sparkled even in the low light, their branches drooping slightly. The surface of the interstate had a high and alarming sheen to it now, as if it were coated with Vaseline. Ernest lit a cigarette and fast-forwarded to "Memo from Turner."

Didn't I see you down in San Antone on a hot and dusty night?

You were eatin eggs in Sammy's when a black man there drew his knife.

Inspired, he sucked on the Tanqueray again. Yes. Mother's milk. He would probably not arrive in time for an exhaustive poon check but he and Sto could still shoot a few. Maybe.

Ernest took the almost circular Oxford exit at a crawl. For the last half-hour he hadn't seen a soul on the road. The freezing rain was falling thickly and noisily now. The trees were burdened with ice and hung low; in some places branches were welded to the ground with ice. Wires sagged heavily. Although it was only about three in the afternoon it was already getting dark. What the fuck? thought Ernest.

He decided that first he would go to Boudleaux's where he could change and leave the MG. From there he could walk to the party. Clearly there would be no driving anywhere tonight. He could probably crash with Boudleaux in the unlikely event that he did not get lucky.

Upstairs, in Boudleaux's little apartment overlooking the town square Ernest flopped down on a crusty plaid burlap sofa. He brushed away some waxy sonic Foot-Long wrappers and a puckered nub of hotdog bounced out and rolled along the floor. The Tanqueray was about a third gone, so Ernest, wanting to conserve gin for the evening, switched to the beers in Boudleaux's fridge.

"Ah, PBR," he said. "Piss, But Refreshing. My favorite." He shook his head.

Boudleaux came in with a sack. "Hey, man," he said. "Why don't you have a beer?" He began unloading batteries, candles and more beer.

"All they had left at Family Dollar were these faggy pink candles. But like the saying goes, in the dark, they're all pink, right? Haw Haw." He carried two beers to the window. On the outside window ledge was a narrow painter's trough for spinning beers. Boudleaux could spin one to icy perfection in ninety-six seconds.

"What in the fuck is happening out there?" Ernest asked. "What's going on?"

"I don't *know*, man." Boudleaux was excited. "It's the *weirdest*. I walked back through the cemetery and some kids were in there sledding, and all of a sudden, the trees were, like *exploding*. The kids were freaked—they were screaming."

There was a huge crash. Ernest jumped up to look out the back window. "Jesus God," he yelled. A big old oak, weakened by target practice, had split in half. Two enormous limbs, each as large as a tree trunk, fell from another tree in the lot beyond. Ernest pushed the window up all the way and he and Boudleaux stuck their heads out. All they could hear around them was the din of branches and trees shattering and crashing under the weight of the ice. The sound was like gunfire, the shots amplified by the low sky. Two or three cars moved along slowly. They stopped and skidded every few yards, trying to avoid the limbs that fell in the road. Within a few minutes there was nothing, not a living soul, out on the streets. Or at least that Ernest and Boudleaux could see. They had never seen the town so deserted. The trees continued crashing steadily.

"The power's bound to go," said Boudleaux. "I'd better cook something."

Bryant Boudleaux was a sort of faux Cajun. While still in his tender adolescence he had left his unbearably white middle-class Ohio home to work on the rigs off the Louisiana Coast. Taking advantage of his French last name he had managed to pass as a local and to pick up some useful skills. He had learned to play a wicked blues harp from a small criminal named LeNigre and learned to cook from a three-hundred pound woman whom he only occasionally had to service in exchange for meat and groceries. She had been a wonder with seafood, from catching it to having her way with it in the kitchen. Boudleaux had felt like just another crustacean in her hands, soft and peeled and defenseless, waiting to be plunged alive into a boiling pot of pungent Zatarain's. It actually wasn't too bad a deal except sometimes on red bean Mondays.

"I guess this means the bars will be closed," Ernest said glumly.

"It doesn't seem unreasonable that the bars *might* close for the end of the world," said Boudleaux. He was busy taking paper packages from the freezer.

"It's supposed to end in fire and brimstone, not in ice," said Ernest, opening a seventh beer. "Ignorant heathen. You know—the two hundred thousand horsemen: 'And thus I saw the horses in the vision, and them that sat on them, having breastplates of fire, and of jacinth, and brimstone. By these three was the third part of men killed, by the fire, and by the smoke, and by the brimstone, which issued out of their mouths.' "

"Yeah, well, whatever. Apocalypse is apocalypse is apocalypse," said Boudleaux. "You get that from Star Wars?"

At that moment the lights went off and the old Frigidaire quit its friendly hum. Ernest and Boudleaux looked at each other in the silent gloom.

"I wonder how long this will last," said Boudleaux. "If it's doing this all over town, trees and shit falling on lines, then it's not going to be coming on anytime soon."

Stovall Bott III came in with more beer, which was good since Ernest and Boudleaux were working on the last two. Ernest was glad to see it was an up-grade—good old skunky Rolling Rock. They lit all the candles Boudleaux had bought. They were all red and pink.

"Where'd you get these pussy-ass candles," said Sto. "Jeez. Reminds me of my sister back in high school, smoking dope in her room listening to the Carpenters."

"This was all they had. You know—Valentine's." said Boudleaux. "I hope we don't have to fire up the tarbaby and the Jesus candles." The tarbaby was a huge brown voodoo candle in the shape of a man. You could light him upright from the wick on top of his head or lay him down and light his dick. Next to his Hohner chromatic the tarbaby was Boudleaux's favorite thing.

"Sto, do you think this party will still be on?" said Ernest.

"Definitely, man. It will *definitely* be a party," said Sto. "It may not be the *same* party, but it will *be* one. Who needs electricity?"

Boudleaux, who was scheduled to play the gig, said, "Well, we've got to plug into something to be able to play. Think about it: the Velvatones unplugged? A little acoustic 'Higher and Higher?' Mr. Excitement would be spinning in his grave."

"Gentlemen," said Ernest. "It's the pluggin-in-thing that concerns me. Are there any women in town?"

"Who knows?" said Sto. "Let's get the news and see where this situation is going."

They tried to pick up the local stations on the jambox but there was nothing but static. Finally, they picked up WLVS from Tupelo, which was talking about slippery streets over there, a little danger and inconvenience.

"But we understand that over in Oxford they're having a major *thing*, a major ice storm," said the deejay, "We've been told that the power is out everywhere over there and a lot of trees are falling on power lines—that kind of thing—it's an emergency situation—Oxford folks—don't go out of your houses unless absolutely necessary. We'll be giving you more information on that ice storm in Oxford as soon as we get it."

"Cool," said Stovall.

"Damn," said Ernest. "That means local talent, no imports."

"I'm just gonna cook up *all* this shit," said Boudleaux, bending over to light a smoke on the gas eye. "This freezer could get funky. And we'll need gumbo to keep up our strength."

"Don't forget the oysters," said Ernest.

All the rest of the afternoon, the icing continued. Branches and trees kept falling. The power stayed off. The phone went dead; luckily not before Ernest and Sto had had a chance to determine that some women were still around; hadn't wussed out and run home to diddy. Then, for some reason, the water cut off. This did not perturb the men because they were not huge consumers of water. Flushing might be a problem, but for the moment the beer was gone. Humpy and Teeth had straggled in, excited about conditions outside. They sat down and began a game of boureé and finished off the last beers. They would have to make a run to James Food Center for more.

"You think it's even open?" said Boudleaux.

"Are you kidding? Mr. Paul knows that business will be better than the day before Thanksgiving," said Sto.

Ernest was getting bored with the card game even though he'd been winning. When Sto accused him of cheating Ernest said, "Fuck y'all, bastards," and volunteered to go for the beer. He was curious about outside, and restless. The standing half of the target-practice oak was now only a jagged spike, all but one of its branches gone. The remaining limb was bigger than the trunk. It had to go any minute. In fact, Ernest thought he could hear it groaning, but maybe it was just all the Rolling Rock beating against his eardrums.

"That son of a bitch is coming *down*," he said to the other men. They looked out the window. In the last of what little light there was, they watched as the branch tore away from the tree, exposing a gaping hole. Out popped a confused looking raccoon that looked around and tried to scrabble away on the ice.

"Damn. Look at that," said Sto.

"Cute little fucker, ain't he?" said Boudleaux.

"Where's my gun?" said Ernest.

Ernest ventured out. He had gone ahead and dressed for the party in his tails, but realized the folly of it as soon as he hit the ice. There was no way. He had had way too much beer chased with slugs of Tanqueray to negotiate the ice. Not to even mention the dex and a couple of ludes provided by Boudleaux who said, "Lagniappe, boys" as he had passed around the packets of physician's samples.

If he put on his Orvis boots he might be able to make it. At the bottom of the apartment stairs, he grabbed the back of one of Boudleaux's mule-ear porch chairs. He shuffled behind it like an old man with a walker. When he reached the MG, he opened the trunk and exchanged his Cole-Haans for the hunting boots. The boots smelled vaguely of dog effluvia. Damn dog.

Still, he needed more traction, but he could probably make it to the Food Center which was only a block away. The AK-47 lay in the trunk. It was tempting. If he wore his heavy overcoat he could conceal the gun and take it along. He might need it. One never knew. What if those fraternity bastards picked a fight again? Although he really felt that the coat, a thick wool British officer's coat, detracted from the formal appearance he wished to present, it had an important feature. Inside was sewn a sturdy holster large enough to accommodate the AK-47, simply and ingeniously designed by Peggy at Peggy's Sew Nice Alterations. Peggy, happy to have something to do other than reconstruct prom and beauty review dresses for Tally-Wally girls with disproportionate boob jobs, installed the holster in exchange for a deer tenderloin from deep in Aunt Nana's carport freezer chest. Ernest slipped the pet weapon inside the coat. Even if he didn't need the gun to defend himself he could shoot up a lot of shit. No one would notice the sound of it in the din of all the trees exploding. He could wait on that, though. The night was young.

There was some kind of light on at the Food Center. Lots of people scurried in and out, some forgetting to slow down when they hit the ice and busting their butts. A group stood talking excitedly in front of the sign painted on the building that said, "DO NOT STAND HERE AT ANY TIME FOR ANY REASON." There was a major buzz in the air; Ernest could hear bits of conversation. "P and L says we won't get it back for two weeks," "Sap was up already from that warm spell at Christmas—they were top heavy."

Inside it was like the fun house at the Mississippi-Alabama State Fair, or a seedy used car lot at night. Mr. Paul had gotten hold of a small generator somewhere and it was making enough electricity to dimly light a few orange bulbs that were strung across the checkouts. Back in the dark aisles people skulked slowly around with flashlights. A face would suddenly loom out of the darkness, smiling crookedly with panic and excitement, causing Ernest to think for a minute that he was tripping but then he remembered he hadn't done any mind stuff. He maneuvered to the beer aisle and picked up the last two suitcases. Keystone. Fuck. With no heat in the store it at least would be cold.

At the check-out he noticed the things that normal people thought they needed to tough out the storm: charcoal, diapers, toilet paper, paper plates and cups, Styrofoam coolers, matches. A big damn picnic.

The suitcases of beer seemed to center his weight more and negotiating the ice was a little easier. He'd pick up Boudleaux's chair later, and anyway a breathless old lady was sitting in it. She looked to be in some kind of distress but Ernest didn't have time for it. What could he do, anyway? Deliver the beer, have a few more, and he'd be off. He wasn't going to hang around Boudleaux's all night. Women were out there: frightened, cold, in a tizzy about the storm and they needed the special kind of consolation and comforting that only Ernest could offer. It had been what? Three weeks? Since New Year's Eve. That made it *last year*! Totally unacceptable.

At Boudleaux's the men were impressed that Ernest had returned at all, let alone with beer. The game had become unruly and mildly entertaining. Ernest sat down to watch, popping two Keystones. For every pat hand, knock and boureé in the game there was a somehow appropriate line from *Deliverance*:

"Now let's you jes drop'em pants."

"You don't know nothing."

"Aintry? This river don't go to Aintry."

"Give the boy some money, Drew."

"Get on back up thar in them woods."

"Don't say anything—just do it."

"L-l-l-louder."

"Don't you boys try nothin like that again."

"I could play with that guy all day."

"This corn's special."

The men did Jagermeister shots out of Boudleaux's collection of NASCAR jelly glasses. The cheap red candles stuck into Rolling Rock bottles formed bloody puddles on the floor. Boudleaux's gumbo simmered forgotten on the stove; a dismal swamp of fishy sludge that Ernest found unsettling. A quick trip to refresh himself in the john and he was ready to go.

"Enough of this cozy little homosexual scene," he announced. "Don't any of y'all want to check out this party?"

"Ernest, why in hell are you in that monkey suit?" said Sto, lurching toward the bathroom. "This is an emergency situation, man. It calls for emergency attire: flannel shirts, camouflage, Carhartt, day-glo, big boots."

"Got my boots, asshole," he said, "And besides, 'Clothes make the man, right?'"

"Who said that anyway?" asked Humpy.

"Gandhi, I think," said Teeth.

"No, Gandhi said, '*No* clothes make the man,'" said Humpy.

"Yeah, Teeth, when ya ever gonna *loin*?" said Boudleaux. They laughed.

"Speaking of which, mine are girded up for the evening," said Ernest. "See y'all."

"Hey, who did this in the tub?" Sto's voice came muffled from the john.

"It's not my vomit, bastards," said Ernest, slamming the door.

Outside again, Ernest realized that even with his boots on, the ice was more treacherous now that the sun had gone down. By Boudleaux's dumpster lay some pieces of chicken wire. He mashed these around his feet and clumped around. Only a little more traction, but as one of his favorite mottoes went, *some is always better than none*. It would have to do. He needed to be *getting* some ass tonight, not busting it.

The air didn't actually seem too cold out although everything was frozen. Must be the Jagermeister antifreeze effect. The thick glaze of ice gave things an arctic appearance, like the ice palace scene in Aunt Nana's favorite old movie, *Dr. Zhivago*. Against that romantic image, or any other warm, fuzzy thoughts, Ernest threw back a couple more dexes. Ludes were nice but they really had a way of taking the edge off. Ernest liked an edge. He patted his left pocket to be sure that he still had the batwing of Tanqueray.

Things were looking extremely spooky. Even though there was no electricity, the sky was weirdly illuminated with a pinkish glow. Branches were still falling. Ernest had to climb over a few downed trees and dodge a falling limb which came down slowly and surreally and shattered like glass. The broken trees were silhouetted, their fractured stumps raw and jagged against the icy glitter and the strange sky. It reminded Ernest of those peopleless German landscape paintings he had seen in the museum in Prague, but without the ruins. "This is what the war will look like," his Croatian girlfriend had whispered. "Except that there will be people scurrying like rats, and the bodies of children." Ernest shuddered at both memories—the burned-out Bosnian towns, and his lovely woman with her pale, celadon skin. When she stood in front of the old brass lamp in his shabby room he could see through her beautiful breasts. He lit a smoke and pulled on the nearly empty gin bottle, tucking the flask into his cummerbund for easier access. He hoped he wouldn't fall on it and disembowel himself. Or worse.

Dead Larry's was not far and Ernest decided to check that out and refuel. Normally, Dead Larry's was noisy with college kids shouting at each other above their loud, retread music. The bar had actually hosted some epic live performances. Mose Allison, Junior Brown, David Lindley, but the fratboys just forked over the stiff covers to spin their lips the whole show complaining about the bands that *just did not know how to jam*, man. Tonight the place might as well have been the Attala County public library, it was so quiet. Ernest peered through the window. The gin bottle clanked against the glass. There was the dim glow of a candle far back in the cave-like bar and he could make out some of the bartenders playing cards. Each one had long hair, a beard and a toboggan. To Ernest they looked like the seven dwarfs. He went in anyway.

"This is quite the Disney moment," he said. "Where's Snow White?"

The bartenders turned. Their glazed eyes were half-concealed by drooping lids. "Hey now," said one. "Why are you so duded up, man?" asked another. "What's with your fucking *feet*?"

"It's the latest," said Ernest. "Y'all might think of getting some. Chicken wire goes pretty well with hippie couture."

"Yeah, yeah, it would," said one of the dwarfs, seriously interested and leaning over the table see Ernest's feet better. "It's definitely a look."

"So can I get a drink or what?" Ernest said.

Another dwarf, whose red lips, moustache and sparse soul patch made his face look like somebody's private parts said, "Help yourself. Here's the flashlight. We'll take the tails in exchange for what you drink." They all cracked up. Last year, when he'd returned from Bosnia, he had gone on a week-long bender and to pay his bar tab had had to auction his cashmere Harris Tweed jacket, the one he'd worn all through the war, right there in the bar. "Doesn't matter, bastards," he'd said to a protesting Boudleaux. "War is hell on a blazer."

Ernest scanned the rows of bottles looking for the Kahlua and vodka. He decided that a few White Russians were the way to go. At least they had some nourishment and the syrupy liquor would give him a little sugar buzz. Good—there was milk in the cooler with a yellow wedge of hoop cheese and a bowl of peeled hard boiled eggs. He popped one of the eggs into his mouth and not seeing a knife bit off a few hits of cheese from the wedge. Something else floating in the ice water caught his eye—a baggy. Hoping for contraband he pulled it up and held it to the flashlight. A snout, claws and dull little eyes looked back at him.

"God damn, y'all. What is *this* shit?" Ernest said.

"It bit Jamie this morning," said a dwarf. "On his thigh—very close to his good stuff. We can't take it to the health department to see if it has rabies 'cause it's closed down. We're saving it till whenever."

"Yeah, can't you see how I'm foaming at the mouth?" said the dwarf named Jamie. "And I've become *so aggressive*," he added with a fey inflection, punching another dwarf.

"Jesus." Ernest spat out the cheese and threw the baggy back. Thinking to sterilize his mouth, he quickly slugged back the rest of the Tanqueray, gargling far back in his throat. He built his White Russian and sat down with his back to the poker game. He was starting to feel really lit. With the flashlight, he examined the stuff behind the bar. It was the usual college bar décor—a Porky Pig cookie jar Ernest knew to be full of multi-colored condoms, football gew gaws, cute happies the sorority girls had given the bartenders, a row of old lunch-boxes, a Shriner's hat. What the fuck was Al Chymia? What was the deal with the middle-eastern thing, anyway? In Bosnia the bars were all austere and strictly business. In a real bar nothing should distract you from your drink or your thoughts. Unless it was a woman. At his favorite bar in Bratislava there had been an incredible, medieval barmaid. For an extra five bucks she would lift one long, beautiful breast from the top of her dress and, giving a tug not unlike the pumping action on a gun would aim a thin stream of bluish milk into your slivavice, turning it a cloudy lavender. Plums and cream. For another five bucks she'd dip the breast in the drink and allow you to suck it off.

Ernest smoked a couple of Marlboros and polished off another drink. Awash in the sad, milky sweetness of memory and White Russians, he jotted down a quick Byronic ode on a napkin: "Ode on a Dirtyleg." He loved odes.

He felt fortified, but instead of the sugar rush he'd expected he felt a sinking spell coming on. Rummaging around in his breast pocket he found some blue pills. He couldn't remember what they were, but it didn't matter; they would alter the mood one way or another. Ernest shook them in his hand like dice, then popped them into his mouth. What the hell. He chewed them—time suddenly seemed of the essence—and washed them down with a swig of vodka.

Just at that moment a guy entered Dead Larry's with a large, greasy-looking black lab. The dog went immediately to Ernest, attracted by the Ashley-violated boots. Suddenly, out of the dark corners rushed more dogs, who charged the lab. Instantly Ernest was in the midst of a roiling dog fight. They barked and snapped furiously, whirling in a vicious pack. It was too dark to see how many dogs there were, as of course, they were all black labs, but Ernest could hear the muffled snarls as teeth met fur. "Denali!" "Dark Star!" The bartenders tried to separate the dogs but couldn't. Ernest lunged for a bottle and threw it into the black ruckus but it didn't stop. He pulled the Kalashnikov out of his coat and fired down into the fray, hoping not to hit anything and mess up his tux pants. The dogs yelped and scrambled, knocking against him and sending some shots upward. Someone screamed like a girl, then there was silence. The candle flickered. The dogs had disappeared.

"Jesus, man, you hit the fucking dough machine!" said one of the bartenders, shining a flashlight into the kitchen. Large, fleshy globs extruded through a ragged hole in the stainless pizza crust machine.

"Sorry, gentlemen," Ernest said, gathering in his gun and napkins. "Just trying to help."

"It is definitely *so not cool* to have that thing around here, man," shouted the nose-ring dwarf. "I mean, that thing is not even *legal*, is it?"

"You need to pay for this shit, man," said another. "I'm calling popo. You could a taken out one of us. Or one of the *dogs.*"

"That's the thing about y'all, and those designer dogs," said Ernest. "You can just call 1-800-H-I-P-P-I-E and order up some more." Sensing a decidedly hostile atmosphere, Ernest retreated as quickly as he could on his chicken wire snowshoes, deftly swiping the Kahlua bottle as he did.

Back on the dark street he worried that the bartenders might really call the police, but surely they realized that they'd get busted if they did. Anyway their phone probably wasn't working. Cops ought to have their hands full tonight with better things to do than harass decent party goers who, after all, had the right to bear arms, especially on an unpredictable night like this. At the very least they'd confiscate the AK-47. At the worst—Christ, a night in the county jail. With no electricity. One could only imagine. He needed to stay off the streets—but how? If anyone saw him creeping through their yard they'd think he was a burglar. A *looter*. He'd just have to keep low, stay on the trail, but not in the middle, off to the side, dodging into the brush at the approach of enemy vehicles. OK. It could be done. He'd done it before.

The sky was weirder still—that bizarre orangeish glow from an unknown source. Transformers were blowing close by and in the distance and exploding like rockets. Fewer branches were falling now so that the crashes were more separate and distinct and, to Ernest, more nerve-wracking. More like a war zone.

Ernest slunk along, cradling his gun and thinking about Bosnia. Evasion—that had been the difference there, the difference between him and the real soldiers. He remembered a night like this. He had been trying to reach his room one night after drinking with soldiers in a café. Fighting had been going on intermittently all day, but it had stayed a few streets away, near the river. Suddenly, it was in his street, all around him, and the few people who were out ran for cover.

He had continued walking stealthily, ducking into doorways at every burst of gunfire. At one point, a man toppled out of a darkened stoop, slumping to the street. Looking in the direction the shots had come from, Ernest recognized one of the soldiers from the café. He'd been covering his ass. The solider looked Ernest in the eye but gave no sign of recognition and moved off into the night. Ernest had crossed the street to the wounded man. A crummy Chinese knock-off Kalashnikov lay next to him. His chest was open and his heart pumped out his life across the icy, glittering cobbles.

Ernest froze. There, just ahead, were the shapes of several people standing around a yard. There seemed to be too many sizes and shapes for it to be the police—a family with children? They weren't talking but each held something—what? Guns? Baseball bats? They seemed to be turned toward him expectantly, hearing his approach. No fucking wonder—his chicken wire kept getting hung up in branches. Ernest tried to quietly step backwards in retreat but instead fell over a downed branch. The AK-47 let off a burst. The figures jumped out and bellowed and clutched each other but did not run away. In fact, they turned on flashlights and aimed them as they advanced. With huge relief Ernest recognized a familiar group of retards from the local half-way house. What were they doing loose on a night like this? Ernest, who had a way of knowing all sorts of people on the fringe of things, recognized most of these guys, each of whom had a distinct public persona. There was a municipal worker guy, a suburban leisure guy in a powder blue jumpsuit, a large set of cowboy twins, and a small, colored pinheaded guy, who Ernest knew to actually be the brains of the group. Two more guys he didn't know; they had no act and might have been caretakers; sometimes it was hard to tell. Encountered individually the men were meek and amusing, but in a pack like this? The two strangers stood over him with their hands on their hips in an authoritative and threatening way.

"Geh up," one said. Where *were* the handlers, then?

"I sure will," said Ernest pleasantly, although he was not at all sure he could pick himself up without assistance and still maintain control of his gun. His head spun a little. The worker guy approached looking pretty excited. He had on full gear: an electric department hard hat, massive ring of important keys, a hammer hanging from his belt. Probably he had just enough smarts to realize that the storm was going to mean a lot of city service people with chainsaws, trucks, cherry pickers and walkie talkies come morning. His deal—Ernest had seen this several times—was to stand around a work site with all his stuff on and look involved. The city workers very sweetly tolerated this and sometimes he would be sitting in a Bobcat or a truck. It had occurred to Ernest that it was entirely possible that these guys were put on the earth for the sole purpose of making the rest of us seem smart and attractive.

"Evening, gentlemen," said Ernest, rising unsteadily. "Nice night for a stroll, wouldn't you say?" the men stared at him. "No, I guess you wouldn't," Ernest said. He drew the Kahlua from his left pocket. "Care for a drink?" he said, swallowing three big gulps before passing the bottle. "Seen any good TV lately? What about Beavis and Butthead? Y'all boys watch that?"

One of the no-act guys spoke up. “We not allowed to on account of it makes fun of the mentwee chowinged.” The worker shuffled in an agitated way, hand on his hammer.

“I see your point,” Ernest said. He knew it would be extremely bad form to mess with retards but the substances and adrenaline in his blood had taken over, doing away with any notion of *form.* He knew he needed a way to bond with these guys, soothe their savage breasts, so to speak. What could he have in common with all of them?

“Y’all had any lately?” Ernest inquired in a concerned tone.

“Ha what?” said the spokesman guy.

“You know, pussy,” said Ernest.

“Jonas had him a little cat,” the small colored guy said, “But Wiley back over it with the van. When it dried we had us a sailcat.”

“A sailcat?” said Ernest.

“You know!” he said, flipping his wrist frisbie-style.

The worker guy couldn’t stand it any longer and stepped up closer. He was huge. With the exception of the pinhead they were *all* pretty huge. “What about that gun,” he said. “Theter G.I. Joe?” The other men moved up behind him. Ernest smelled mildewed clothes and Kahlua. Before he could answer, the leisure suit guy said, in a tone that was both admiring and menacing, “I like to have that suit.” He stroked Ernest’s satin lapel.

“Tell you what, how about these fine shoes?” said Ernest. “They’re not Dorothy’s, or Carl Perkins’s but they’ll take you far tonight.”

Using the Kalashnikov as a cane, Ernest teetered on one leg and then the other, prying off the chicken wire booties. The leisure guy did not look impressed, nor did he extend a hand to accept the shoes.

“We taken the van over to the Progressive just on Monday, for shoes,” said one of the cowboys. “Henry Earl thowed up on his new size 14s. Cotton candy’s what did it. Cotton candy and I don’t know what all. Had him a sack to do it in causen he always thows up when we ride, but there he went. Mr. Ivory said he don't have the sense God gave a gar."

"Couldn't be hepped," said the worker guy, apparently Henry Earl. He rhythmically clenched and extended the hands hanging at his side. "What about that gun," he said again.

Sensing that the conversation was not going well and that the situation, these men riled by the storm and the gunfire like angry bears startled out of hibernation by an earthquake, had taken an ugly turn, Ernest said simply, "Night, boys. Enjoyed visiting with you. Excuse me, now." Amazingly, they parted and allowed him to move off into the night.

He needed to keep moving—the gunfire or the bellowing might have attracted other attention. Without the chicken wire but with the energy and strength of the pills and the grace of the White Russians he found he was able to glide down the icy street. Incredibly, South 11th Street was straight and flat and smooth with only a few branches down, over which Ernest elegantly leapt. Every few yards smudge pots burned, as if the street were a driveway illuminated for a party. Ernest gathered speed and confidence—an Olympic distance skater with the AK-47 held behind his bent back, his right arm swinging in time to his strong, measured glides. Then he relaxed a little and held the gun before him and across his ribs, like it was a fur muff. The wooden stock of the gun was oddly warm in his hands and the icy air and adrenaline burned his cheeks. The night had finally become black and the stars twinkled gorgeously against it.

"It's darker than Egypt," he said to himself. It was one of Abelia's lines. All the broken pine and cedar made the air smell like Christmas. Lovely! He sailed down the long street. Hans Brinker on the canal, on his way to put a finger in, well, he hoped not a dike, ready to save the town. He flew and flew.

The party seemed to have been going for some time, maybe all day, or it was way later than Ernest thought. Janky Jane's living room was illuminated by a few stubs of candle. The air was thick and smoky and smelled of pot, bourbon, burnt sugar and a gas space heater. A wood fire was petering out. From the ceiling hung an oil lamp that swayed and smoked like the censers in Sarajevo cathedrals. Billie Holliday moaned from an old jambox, complaining about men. The song dragged a little as if both Billie and the jambox batteries lacked the will to go on. Catching a glimpse of himself in a mirror over the mantel he noticed that his mousse-stiffened coif glowed regally in the candle light. He imagined himself, for a second, as the Emperor Jones. Or Kurtz. A few people were dancing, wrapped together tightly. Others had just tumped over like the trees outside and lay on the floor. Everyone wore coats and boots. Ernest scanned the room looking for friends and opportunity. He was in dreadful need of a woman. He saw a French graduate student lying on some pillows in a corner and he allowed himself to remember a night with her last summer. She was good-natured and had let him wear her yellow panties as an ascot afterward, but she bored him to death with her graduate student babble about Derrida, deconstruction, postmodernism, blah, blah, blah. What the fuck was postmodernism anyway? Besides, the French? Losers. Fuck'em. He had sprung an equine tuffy and thumped it down with his thumb.

He made his way to the dark kitchen where he recognized a number of late-night people: a line chef from Town Market danced sensuously with an older woman, a bored housewife of known moral turpitude, a shaggy, smelly blues enthusiast, a handful of pale, scrawny boys in dresses. Ernest thought them not to be gay, or even sexual at all, but he shied away from them anyway. Sorry bastards. Someone had lit a small fire in the sink, and the two backup singers for the Velvatones were toasting tiny marshmallows with roach dips. Healthy, pretty girls, they worked hard at maintaining their sickly, fluorescent pallor. Their hair was mayonnaise-colored; one nearly bald and the other's hair hung lankly on one side as if it had been pressed; the other side oddly frizzed up. Grayish straps always hung out of the few clothes they wore although tonight they were wearing what appeared to be dog fur coats. Ernest admired their skanky pulchritude.

"Ernest!" the short one said in a cheerful voice. "Want some marshmallows? We're on a bourbon and marshmallow diet." Her eyes glittered with reflected candlelight and God knew what else. "That's all we've eaten for two days."

"Girls, I'll just skip the sweets if you don't mind," he said, reaching behind the girl for a jug of black Jack. "I'm on kind of a liquid regime, myself."

"It's not, you know, totally unlike, you know, a mint julep," the other one said, raising a glass in which some blackened marshmallows floated. "But without mint. Maybe we could just throw in an Altoid."

Ernest poured a big plastic cup half-full of sour mash. "What the hell happened to your hair?" he asked.

"Caught fire in a marshmallow-related incident," the girl said. The Velvatones laughed.

"Scorch becomes you," said Ernest. "Skol."

He could just make out Jane in the pantry with Boudleaux and one of the boys in dresses, a waiter with a shaved head named Porter. They were smoking a number and offered it to Ernest, who declined. "I've got some X, if you'd rather," said Jane. "Or a Delaudid?"

"I don't do mind drugs, but I think I'm in some pain," Ernest said, chewing the proffered Delaudids.

Porter, who had what looked to be either a busted lip or a small disease, was leaning slightly on Boudleaux. Boudleaux, although not in the least effeminate, had been known to occasionally lapse into unnatural relationships. He had also learned to believe in, ever alert to the nether world of late-night possibility—their old credo that something was always better than nothing—although Ernest believed Boudleaux took things too far.

"Jane," said Ernest. "You look lovely this evening." He took in Jane's long, skinny form and scant but downy, freckled cleavage. A hot glow came over him. "Happy Birthday."

"Some thing, this ice storm, eh?" said Jane, smiling at him, checking him over. "You clean up pretty good, Ernest. Want to see something cool?"

"Uh, yeah," said Ernest, thickly. He was suddenly finding it difficult to speak.

"Watch." Jane stood a flashlight on end and held her fingers close over the lens. Her long, witchy fingernails were punched through with tiny stars. Shining through the stars, the flashlight beam projected a little Fourth of July galaxy across the ceiling. Ernest was transfixed. Jane moved her fingers as if casting a spell. The stars danced sensuously. Ernest thought he'd never seen anything so wonderful.

"Porter and I were just saying, in an emergency like this, nothing is true, everything is permitted," said Jane. "None of the rules apply." She smiled; not young, but beautiful.

"Ernest don't go by rules anyway," said Boudleaux. "*Pimp* law, maybe."

Ernest tried to say, "Son, I take exception to that," but his face had gone numb. He could only manage to mumble between teeth that were beginning to clench, "I live by many rules, bastards."

"Rules rule," said Porter. "Ernest, you OK? You want to go lie down?"

"Just a little prayer," he said, as his legs gave out and he sank to his knees in front of Janky Jane. He buried his face in her long coat. "A little prayer." The AK-47 clanked heavily against the floor.

When Ernest came to he was on a bed with Jane and Porter, sandwiched between them. His shirt was open and his pants were undone. He was freezing, his coat was gone. He vaulted sideways over Jane's comatose form, pulling his clothes together. Ernest's coat lay on the floor, and miraculously still had the gun swaddled inside. Jane and Porter were wearing their coats but both of their dresses had hiked up. No underwear. Ernest shuddered. He sniffed the air for clues and tried to focus on his various orifices to see if anything seemed amiss. Everything seemed to hurt, but nothing hurt inordinately, except his head. Ernest left the house in a hurry.

Once on the interstate he relaxed a little. The interstate was a longer haul but the backroads were a mess. It had been hairy. The pines bowed to the ground and had been chainsawed back to the shoulder of the road. Beyond them, scattered around the edges of the cotton and bean fields the hardwoods stood, stripped and raggedy. By Water Valley things were considerably improved—the trees, all but the tall, skinny loblollies, looked okay. The landscape was frosty, but not crystalline. By Coffeeville, it was completely clear. He stopped at the Stuckey's in Vaiden for beer, smokes and a BC, and mentioned the ice storm to the woman taking his money. "What ice storm?" she said. The beer eased his headache a little—his head felt cleaved. Ernest felt around to see if he might have sustained any wounds. Nothing, other than a small scabby knot on his head. It would take a little extra mousse to make his hair lay back and cover it, was all.

By the time he crossed the Attala County line, which was only an hour or so away, it wasn't even cold. The sun shone warmly and there was no ice on the ponds. Things weren't too bad. He wouldn't think too much about last night. Or he'd think about it tomorrow. No, tomorrow he was hunkering down on the novel, if Nana and Abelia would leave him alone. It was really a gorgeous day. The red MG buzzed along on the wide, dry road, perfectly ten miles over the speed limit. The sky was blue.

About to turn off at the Wallis exit, Ernest lit a cigarette and reached to put in the Stones tape. He wanted to hear *No Expectations* but couldn't seem to punch it up. As he turned off onto the long, ascending exit, he was fiddle-fucking with the buttons,

finally finding the song. When he looked back to the road, an old, beat-up pick-up truck slowly came at him. Maybe it wasn't moving at all. He had time to say to himself, "You're going the wrong way, bastard," and then Jack Ernest was sailing again, remembering last night's awesome skate down the icy street, the sparkling winter wonderland of frozen trees, the stars in the deep, infinite night sky, twinkling and winking at him like so many beautiful, beckoning women.

TOM FRA

The Ten-Thousand-Sixty-Eighth Hour

After his second affair, when his second wife left him, Gary dated around. Unlike the other members of his Victims of Abusive Spouses group, he felt ready to dive right back into the Singles Scene. The other members, all women, sobbed and choked in the church basement where they met each week. They said they needed time to heal, to be alone. Gary hit on them all.

He had a table-side lamp that cut on and off when you clapped your hands. Gary and a paralegal were underneath an afghan, struggling. When she slapped him, the light came on.

He got a breedless dog at one of those Adopt-A-Pet side-walk fairs. It wanted to be walked all the time and he hated to do that. When he did, it ate the shit of other dogs—which Gary took as low self-esteem—and barked exclusively at Asian-Americans. He left the dog tied to a light pole at the animal shelter and sat in his car down the street, pretending to read a newspaper, until somebody came out, looked around, and took the dog inside.

Now things were very bad. There was even an incident at work, where he was the safety man at a large chemical plant. It made pesticides. Gary was in charge of seeing that no one got killed or hurt. He drove a yellow pickup with a clip-on siren and could often be seen updating the large poster in the plant cafeteria that said how many Safe Man Hours there had been. At present the figure was very high, 10,067.

The incident was this: He showed up for work, hung-over and unshaven. One of his chief responsibilities was to make sure everyone's gas mask fit tightly—imperfect seals were a pet peeve of Gary's, as everyone knew, including the big black rent-a-cop named El Roy, who refused to let Gary on-site with his three-day-thick growth of beard.

A shoving match ensued and El Roy had Gary in a headlock when a golf cart arrived and the plant manager, dressed in a tie and hard hat, tried to get to the bottom of things. First he sent the uniformed onlookers to their stations. Pesticides could not make themselves. Then he made El Roy let Gary up and ordered somebody to radio for the medics to check out Gary's head injury.

It might be a concussion, someone said.

"I feel fine," Gary said. A line of blood ran down his nose and he let it drip onto his white shirt.

"Should we warm up the helicopter?" asked the helicopter pilot.

"No," the plant manager said. "Take him in the Chrysler."

At the emergency room they bandaged his head and gave him sample packets of orange pills that he took with alcohol, though the tiny writing on the label advised against it. When he called the plant manager's office, the plant manager's secretary told him he was to stay home for a week, without pay. He'd been officially reprimanded.

A letter on its way to his file.

In his rental house, his cable had been turned off because he'd forgotten to pay the bill, so he drank beer and watched the television snow until he noticed the time on the VCR clock. At Abusive Spouses the women confronted him despite his bandaged head. They'd voted him out of the group. You're the abuser, they said, not the abusee. We've called your ex-wife.

"Which one?" he asked.

"Get out," they said.

He fingered his gas mask and drank more beer sitting in his car underneath the magnolia branches beside a graveyard, then drove to the animal shelter to reclaim his dog. The clerk who told him someone else had taken it wouldn't look Gary in the eye, which Gary took to mean one thing: euthanization.

What the hell, he thought, and donning the mask, pushed his way through a flapping door and past the janitor in rubber boots and headphones. The room seemed foggy and every dog stood up, barking. Cage to cage and no familiar shit-eating low-esteem Asian-American-hating dog. Gary removed the gas mask and apologized to the janitor, who ignored him.

That night, when he clapped his hands for the light to go off, it sounded like the slap of a good woman.

BETH ANN FENNELLY AND TOM FRANKLIN

The Saint of Broken Objects

In Lloyd's twenty-sixth year, he became clumsy. He'd just made Level III Manager, and they'd bought their first house, a Queen Anne in a safe neighborhood with good schools. First, he shattered the smoke detector swatting a gypsy moth with the broom. Then, stripping wallpaper with a putty knife, he pushed too hard and gouged the plaster, revealing the dark, tender underskin. It surprised his wife, because she had always been the one to chip glasses, nick her underarm with a Lady Bic, back over the mailbox. Now, as the spackle hardened in the dining room, he frowned as he over-snipped the conical shrub by the rose trellis. Later he fell off the roof.

Because his family had a history of brain tumors, Molly took him to a specialist, a Dr. Moss, who never stopped talking—how little we know of the brain, its mysteries, machinations, its dark convolutions. "For instance," he said, "this one guy, about your age . . ." Molly clenched Lloyd's fingers.

"Outta nowhere," Dr. Moss said, "he starts getting hairy. In his ears, on his back, even his palms. Understand, this was a guy who'd had trouble growing a mustache. But now he has a five o'clock shadow by noon."

"What was it?" Lloyd asked. "A tumor?"

"Of course it was. It's always a tumor."

"What about Lloyd?" Molly asked.

"You?" Moss angled his computer screen toward them. "You got nothing."

That night, in quiet celebration, a wardrobe box for a table, Lloyd spilled his champagne on Molly's late grandmother's just-unrolled Turkish carpet.

"Maybe it's this," Molly said. "Maybe, subconsciously—"

"You're going to tell me I don't really want the house, so I'm being passive-aggressive."

"I'm just saying—"

"Well, don't."

* * *

Years to come, he broke windows, mirrors, ships in bottles, their daughter's kitten's spine, an antique crystal chandelier, a church pew, the binding of a first edition Alice in Wonderland, the lid of a piano. He broke a blunderbuss at a silent auction. He broke tennis racquets, fishing rods, luggage, a globe, his collarbone, an MRI machine.

Certainly there were moments where he wasn't clumsy, but these were not the moments he remembered. What he remembered was the skein of accidents, the stubs, the stumbles, the small explosions, the near misses, all of them exhilarating.

If, in the Far East on business, he tried to conjure Molly, her round face surfaced with a look of perpetual alarm, her voice a shrill yelp of warning. She never adjusted to his mishaps, as she called them, questioning his finger, for instance, which had slipped and forwarded the wrong email to the wrong people, costing him the vice-presidency in the firm where, over the years, he'd broken thirteen briefcases, twenty-one pairs of eye-glasses, fifty-nine umbrellas and occasionally the heart of Molly, who never learned to embrace the uncertainty.

Lloyd did, and grew to see his clumsiness as a kind of gift. To take a thing and use it showed failure of imagination. He took a thing and read its fault-lines, knew five ways it would break for him. When his great-grandchildren visited, they came gravely to his wheelchair, and when they left there were two toys in their hands where there had been one.

He had blessed them.

By now Dr. Moss had died, and Molly had died, and two of their children and even one of their grandsons. But Lloyd, Lloyd wasn't tired. How could he let his trembling hands fall empty to his sides? How could he leave the world before it was broken?

JONATHAN MILES

The Sadness of Windows

Because the sensation wasn't physical, she didn't startle or flinch or even shudder faintly. Her awareness of him came imperceptibly, like knowledge—which it was, to some degree, but then also something more: a kind of muted electricity, she thought, like the static of another presence just dimly perceived. The peculiar thing was that she knew it was him, because it could have easily been someone else: the ogre who lived next door, say, or the stammering old man who lived in the house behind hers and who sometimes in the summers offered her cold cans of beer in his lonesome, wishful way. But no—she knew instantly who it was. The ogre would have frightened her, and rushed her toward the curtains, and the old man would have filled her with a sickening dread, and made her angry, too, for he'd told her his wife was dying—in a slow, strenuous manner that he'd likened to a firefly perishing in a jar—and such behavior from him, even the urge toward it, would have been unseemly and sad; hot tears would have flooded her eyes, as if she'd seen an angel fall. But no, she was sure who was watching her: it was the boy who lived next door in the apartment above the ogre's, a boy of sixteen or seventeen—she didn't know precisely—who shared the apartment with his sister and their dog and who played his electric guitar so loudly in their attic that she'd once or twice been tempted to ask him to stop. She was wearing only a towel when she noticed him, and was just out of the bath, brushing her hair in front of the bedroom window unit, the air from the fan chilling the droplets of bath water on her arms and neck, still mottled pink from the bath's heat. She could have looked up to face him, to confront his stare with her own, but she didn't; she simply moved away from the window, a few steps toward the bathroom, and quietly out of sight. She wasn't upset, necessarily, but she didn't want to be watched. She changed into a t-shirt and shorts, ate her dinner in front of the television and, until the next time it happened, put it wholly out of her mind.

She was thirty-four, and people other than her mother said she was pretty. She'd stopped reading fashion magazines years ago so she didn't know if her hair or clothes were still stylish, and because she hadn't altered either very much since college she suspected they weren't. But this was of small and passing concern. She worked downtown in Cleveland at the county Chancery Clerk's office—a good job, steady if sometimes dull—and flirted regularly with the lawyers there, who often flirted back, and who sometimes asked her out. She didn't dwell on these dates, though typically she enjoyed them, much in the way she enjoyed television; they seasoned random evenings with warm noise and color but, like signals plucked from the air, flitted soon from memory. Like all mothers, hers wondered impatiently when she would marry, or more precisely fall in love, because her mother wished for her the kind of romance she'd had herself before marrying her husband, a round, hobbyless man who worked so faithfully at the Delco plant in Willoughby that when he died, in his sleep, he'd built up seven years of unused sick days. "He was beautiful," her mother would say, speaking of that prior romance, but her daughter always shushed her, as loyal to her father as he was loyal to his job. It bewildered her mother, but she was content by herself. She kept careful track of her retirement account and jogged ten miles a week. She liked watching *M.A.S.H.* and often laughed out loud, even at the reruns. Sometimes she slept with the lawyers and sometimes she didn't.

The radio in the kitchen was on the second time she sensed the boy watching her. The disk jockey was talking about the weather—the temperature had reached one hundred that day, and the Indians had lost, something the disk jockey was blaming on the heat. Her apartment, neither large nor small, encompassed the first floor of a prewar house of Victorian design just off Madison Avenue in Lakewood. All the houses on the street were more or less the same, with just the slightest of variances, as if the builders had moved up and down the block with seven or eight plans that they'd mixed indiscriminately, with unworried shrugs. She'd lived there for seven years now, since moving from a high-rise complex on the lakeshore. The high-rise had always felt to her more like a hotel than a home, with its infinitely-silent and sour-smelling hallways, plus the neighbors had felt so close, almost tangibly so, the steady hum of their lives drifting through the walls like cooking odors.

Not that she minded neighbors. The old man who lived behind her, with his slowly-dying wife, was a comforting if melancholy presence, waving to her from his overgrown garden behind the garage or from his stark green back porch, where he often drank cans of Pabst Blue Ribbon while watching his yard with an oddly expectant expression. Every now and then he'd pass through the gap in the low chain-link fence that separated their yards to offer her a beer. She'd accepted once, and though he'd offered again she'd always refused.

That first time he'd urged her to share a second beer with him, so she had, but then he'd offered another, which she'd declined, but he seemed so hurt by her refusal and so desperate for her company that it felt cruel, all of it, and she resigned not to put either of them in that position again. Next door, in the apartment facing hers, and below the one the boy and his sister shared, lived the ogre, whose name she didn't know, and didn't want to know. He made a lot of ugly noises—grunts and barks and yells, like an unmanageable circus bear—especially when the dog upstairs was romping on the hardwood floors, at which times the ogre would swing his head out a window and scream for them to shut up the dog's goddamn or motherfucking scratching, whichever variety it happened that day to be. The sister, a dark-haired woman close to her own age with whom she'd conversed on occasion, when they'd met coming or going with keys in their hands, once explained that the ogre was a cocaine addict and a drunkard, but she'd said this benevolently, with a gentle tilt of her head and a light, tapered laugh that seemed to ask what-can-you-do? This was somehow soothing, and made the ogre seem more harmless.

Then there was the brother. She was just out the bath again, roaming the bedroom in a towel, when she noticed, in the most upward corner of an eye, a flicker of shadow. At first it didn't register, and peeking sideways and up she saw a face in the upstairs window fly from sight, as quickly as a bird fleeing a hot wire. He'd been watching her again, his face partly obscured by what appeared to be a bookcase with a radio on its top. Maybe, she thought charitably, he'd been tinkering with the radio, merely fiddling with its dials. From her own radio in the kitchen, the disk jockey was forecasting more heat for tomorrow and bleak prospects for a doubleheader against the Yankees. She couldn't see much of the boy's room from below, save the blurred whirring of the ceiling fan, so she looked away, and went on with her business. She didn't want to close the curtains—hey were just cheap white sheers anyhow—because it felt prudish to her, and faintly paranoiac, and even, in a strange way, vain, for it presupposed that he was watching, and wanted to watch, and, worse, that she was worth watching, or that she thought she was. Instead she gathered her clothes from the dresser with one hand, the other clasping the towel to her chest, and changed in the bathroom, with the door closed. If he wanted to watch after that, let him. After all, she thought, there wasn't much for him to see: a thirty-four year-old woman watching television in bed while her hair dried, or rather refused to dry, the humidity being what it was. That night she watched a *Barney Miller* rerun and the news and didn't think much of the boy until she caught herself picking a toenail. With a prick of vanity, she stopped. She didn't want him to see her doing that.

A few days later, on a Thursday, she had a date with one of the lawyers. His name was Bob, and he'd played football at Ohio State; he talked about it a lot, perhaps too much, like a veteran overdefined by his war. But he was funny, with the gently-insulting wit of Midwesterners, and handsome in a thick, squarish way that reminded her of the men in JC Penney catalogs. They'd been out a few times prior, each date separated by six- or seven-week spans that neither of them seemed to mind, or ever comment upon. That night they had dinner in Little Italy and then drove to a bar in Lakewood, the same bar where their dates had always ended. At the bar, three of his buddies joined the pair without asking, as if it was perfectly natural, and drank pitchers of beer and talked about baseball at a small round table that was ashy and nicked and watered with rings from the beer mugs. She recognized a few names from what she'd read in the paper, but she didn't follow baseball, so she quietly poured herself beer after beer until she felt drunk, at which point she told the lawyer named Bob that she needed to go home, what with work in the morning, et cetera.

She could tell he wanted either to sleep with her or keep drinking with his buddies, but nothing in between, so she offered to walk; he wouldn't hear of it, however, and drove her home. Inside his car she thanked him for dinner, apologized for not inviting him inside, kissed him briefly, and then, alone on the sidewalk, watched him drive away. She knew he was returning to the bar but the knowledge didn't bother her.

Back in her apartment she turned on the kitchen radio and pulled off her shoes on the way to the bedroom. Unbuttoning her blouse, however, she paused—from the attic next door, she could hear the boy playing his guitar. She'd never really listened to him before. Usually, when he was playing, she shut the windows, or drowned him out by turning up the television, but this time she went to the kitchen, flicked off her radio and stood there, barefoot on the linoleum, listening. He was playing something bluesy and slow that brought to mind the Cream records she'd hoarded in her teens, but whatever it was, she thought, he was playing it quite well—it seemed fluid and thick all at once, like oil or molasses transfigured into sound. More than that, however, the music struck her as weirdly appropriate, as if, like a movie soundtrack, it had been programmed for her moment, and as she stood there in the kitchen, drunk, and listening to him play, her life seemed more dramatic, and she felt queerly and vividly more alive, as if nerves she'd never known were there had suddenly buzzed to life inside her. Wanting to prolong the feeling, she decided on a nightcap.

She almost never drank at home, so her choices were few, but below the sink she found an unopened bottle of scotch—a Secret Santa gift from an office Christmas party of maybe two, three years back. She wiped the dust from the bottle's neck and poured herself a drink in a plastic cup, swaying dreamily by the sink, then walked to the bedroom, where she stood beside the open window and sipped her scotch. She wished she could hang out the window but the windows had screens, so instead she gripped the windowpanes on either side, and curved her back, leaning gently into the hot dark. The slightest of breezes was blowing off of Lake Erie, and it fluttered her open blouse, lit weakly and opaquely by the streetlight.

She didn't know the next morning what time she'd gone to sleep, but she knew it was late, for she'd slept through her alarm. Yet she felt oddly satisfied that morning, hurriedly applying her makeup, as if she had awakened from a night of lovemaking of the sort she couldn't remember ever having. On the train downtown people smiled at her; she was unaware, however, that it was because she was smiling at them.

Of the boy she knew little. Back in the spring his sister had mentioned, in passing, that he was coming from California to live with her. Something about him not getting along with their stepfather—who was really more his stepfather than hers, she'd explained, as she was much older than her brother, having been twenty when their father died. The stepfather had moved their mother and the boy to San Diego, because he was in the Navy, or did something connected to the Navy—she couldn't exactly recall. She'd seen the boy, of course, but they'd never talked, or even exchanged waves. He walked everywhere, because he didn't have a car, but that was as much as she knew.

On occasion she'd heard him out on their upstairs balcony, playing an acoustic guitar and bending the strings to make the dog howl. The game never seemed to tire him, and it was usually up to the ogre to stop it. The boy was tall, and lean in a way that suggested his weight hadn't caught on to his height, with long brown hair that coursed smoothly down to a spot between his shoulder blades. Unlike most of the long-haired boys she saw, he never wore a cap, and too, unlike them, his hair didn't strike her as aggressive, or even mildly rebellious; it seemed natural on him, in an almost feminine way, and because of it, and also because he played so lovingly with the dog and favored mostly slow and melancholy songs on his guitar, she perceived him as gentle. In a way, she felt sorry for him. She imagined that he was lonely and confused, and that his stepfather had probably terrorized him for his long girlish hair and tender hours with his guitar. After a while, when she saw him walking toward Madison Avenue, she decided he looked sad, and found herself wanting to console him.

One Saturday she decided to lay out in the sun. This was something she'd never done before, at least not at home; on occasion she went to the beach at Lakeshore Park, but it was more for reading than for tanning. In the garage, where her landlord kept all the debris former tenants had left, she found a vinyl beach chair that was gummy with spider webs. She hosed it down, fetched a towel and moisturizer from the bathroom, and set up the chair on the driveway in a narrow spot where the sun wasn't obscured by the huge oak that draped the garage from the old man's backyard. She told herself that she didn't care if he saw her, but she couldn't relax, and, despite herself, feared she knew why. Shading her eyes with her hand, she peered up at the house next door, but the sun shone like metal on the windows and she couldn't see inside.

For that matter, she thought, she didn't know if the boy was even home. After a while she slipped into a sun dress and walked to the convenience store on the corner to buy a six-pack of beer. She didn't own a cooler, so she tucked the beer under her chair, hoping as she did that the old man hadn't spied her in the driveway with the beer. Even just one of the beers relaxed her. The pavement was radiating a dirty heat, and sweat beaded in her belly button and trickled between her breasts, fanning down her sides. After the second beer she felt calm, if not precisely good, and hummed to herself lightly.

Perhaps it was the beer, but she didn't think so—from one of those silvery windows above, she knew, the boy was watching her. Like an actress in a movie, every movement she made felt important, and imbued with meaning.

When she went to apply her moisturizer, however, she felt suddenly anxious, and stopped. The act of touching herself, no matter how innocently, seemed to her too unsubtle, too rife with suggestion, and after that, despite two more beers, the last of them hot as coffee, she found she couldn't relax at all. She gathered up the two remaining cans, the lotion, the towel and the sundress, replaced the chair in the garage, and went sulkily back inside.

At work the following Tuesday the lawyer named Bob asked her on another date. This was unlike him, for six or seven weeks hadn't passed, but he'd wrapped up a long case, he told her, and wanted to celebrate. She said yes, but then said no—her mother was coming by, she lied, finding herself stung by the lie, and unsure of its origins. Later that day she called him at his office to say that her mother had canceled and that, yes, she'd love to meet him later. They met at the bar in Lakewood, and though his buddies were there he ignored them, leading her past them to a quiet table in a dormant corner.

She couldn't believe how much she talked that night, much less the way she talked—loosely and wittily, with the flirty, hair-tossing poise of a starlet—and it wasn't long before they were at his apartment, a trail of abandoned clothes strewn from the front door to the bedroom. Their lovemaking was loud and humid, and at one point, atop him, and arcing toward climax, she screamed for him to fuck her. He gulped, and said okay. Afterwards he wagged his head in pleased disbelief, propped up against the headboard smoking a cigarette. She smoked one herself, even though she didn't smoke.

"It's so hot in here," she said to him. "Can we open a window?" He mumbled something about the air conditioner and his electric bill but she ignored him, walking nude from the bed to a window, where she peeled back the curtains and, with some effort, yanked open the pane. The small draft felt immense on her naked skin, and seemed to roll across her front like the vast winds she'd seen in movies of the Sahara. After a while, he asked what she was doing. She turned to him grinning.

She left work early the following day, on a whim, venturing to the east side to one of the used record shops on Coventry Road, where she bought Cream's *Disraeli Gears*, and then, back in Lakewood, to Russo's for some groceries. Inside her apartment she put on the record and opened all the windows and changed into a t-shirt and gym shorts. The sun was setting over Madison Avenue, and the sky's pink brushstrokes called to mind memories of her childhood, though she couldn't say why. She ate her dinner with a cloth napkin and one of her late grandmother's crystal goblets, into which she emptied, little by little, an entire bottle of middlebrow California chardonnay purchased just for the occasion. When darkness fell she walked through the dim apartment as if through a dream. Everything within it seemed to glow with sensuality; even the floor felt charged with current. She waited for the light to go on next door, in the boy's bedroom above her, and when it did she almost gasped.

Some of what she did next felt ridiculous; some of it felt rapturous. Leaning against the window frame, backlit only by the yellow lamp on her night stand, she listened to the dark: the throaty murmur of traffic on Madison Avenue, the glassy tinkle of the bell above the convenience store's door, mingled laughs and chatter spilling from the Irish bar across the avenue. Hesitantly, but willfully, after the boy had extinguished the light, and when she knew he was watching, she edged to the center of the window. There was no breeze. Her heart was thumping like something in a cage, her hands shaking like the old man's around his beer can, but closing her eyes, almost nauseated from the task, she began lifting her t-shirt. The sudden chill of air on her exposed midriff startled her, and she quickly pulled the t-shirt back down. "God," she whispered, composing herself with a long inhale, then lifted her shirt again, this time over her head, and cast it to the floor.

She felt his heart leap with hers, her pale skin blushing in the dampness of his gaze. The gaze didn't feel hostile to her, or perverse, or even invasive; instead, in an inexplicable way, it felt loving, and seemed to console something inside her. Backing from the window, her eyes still shut, she stepped toward her bed and lay on her back atop the sheets. She ran a fingertip down the outside of her thigh, to the edge of her gym shorts, but that was all, and she soon fell asleep with the lamp on, as if tucked neatly into a cloud.

For this and more she scolded herself the next morning. She was disgusted with herself, and felt not just pathetic but alone, terribly alone, which was a new sensation to her, and a miserable one. Even worse, she thought, the boy had probably been in his bed the entire time, or in the attic with his amplifier off, or in front of the television with his sister and her dog—anywhere but at that dark window, crouched beside his radio watching her strip trepidly behind the screens. At work, one of the lawyers asked what was wrong and she barked at him to mind his own business. He jumped a step or two back with his arms in the air, like a hold-up victim, and apologized. Softening, she apologized herself. "Rough night, huh?" he said, to which she nodded yes, then added, to herself as much as him, "Never again."

She might have kept that promise, too, had she not caught the boy watching her again three weeks later. By now it was August, and the heat had only worsened. The anchormen were leading nearly every night's news with stories of it: reports of the elderly roasting in their homes, advice from physicians on how to stay cool and breezy interviews with the heat's worst sufferers, like jackhammer operators, and largest beneficiaries, like ice-cream men. In those three weeks she'd tried putting the boy out of her mind. One afternoon, however, she spied him walking toward Madison Avenue, smoking a cigarette, and found herself disgusted by the sight of him—he was holding the cigarette cupped in his hand, like a cheap movie gangster, and it struck her as so staged and adolescent, and so in contrast to the naturalness of his feminine hair and smooth bony frame, as to be almost laughably grotesque. In the meantime, she'd been dating.

For the first time, she was asking out the lawyers herself; they acted startled and pleased, and she slept with nearly all of them. Usually she brought them to her apartment and had sex with them with the lights on and the curtains opened. This was spiteful, but she felt the boy deserved it. One of the lawyers, this one named Jim, complained about the lights. She knew he was self-conscious about his body, since he'd disrobed alone in the bathroom; pale and un-muscled, his body appeared to have seen minimal movement and sunlight, and he seemed all too aware of it. But in turning off the light she seemed to turn herself off, and the sex became dry and uncomfortable. After a while he rolled off of her, sighing into a pillow. "I'm sorry," she said, and he said it was okay. "Probably the beer," she added. He nodded dimly, but didn't stay the night.

When she finally caught the boy again she'd been at the bar, though not, this time, on a date; she'd just wanted to escape her apartment. On the answering machine, her mother's voice sounded worried and tremorous. "I can't ever seem to get you anymore," her mother said, adding hopefully, "Maybe you're out having fun?"

"Ha," she answered from the kitchen, two aspirin perched upon the end of her tongue. En route to the bedroom she slipped off her clothes, scattering them behind her in shallow piles. She wasn't even thinking of the boy when she passed the window. The drapes were drawn—as they had been for weeks, except during her dates—but even through them she spied something flit above her: the dart of his bony silhouette. Almost instantly the light in his bedroom went out, and she stopped, standing not at the window but not far from it, and stared up, for the first time, at his bedroom. They'd never met eyes before but she could tell they were doing so now, and she felt, angrily, as if she were staring down a rodent she'd caught in her garbage. "Fuck you," she finally said, turning to her bed.

But her resistance didn't last. For the first time, he came to her in dreams. They weren't sexual dreams—even awake, she couldn't quite picture sex with him—but rather sensual dreams: In one, they were together in a place full of light, like a heavenly sphere, her swathed in the sheer draperies and him shirtless, touching her hesitantly through the whitish gauze, his fingertips pulsing as they drifted across her shoulder. She awoke thrilled but weeping. "I hate you," she said to the dark. But no one was listening, and no one was watching. For a moment she wondered if that was what she wanted—someone to watch over her, like the God and His angels she'd stopped believing in when she was still a girl. Was that why we invented gods, she thought—to fill the dark with eyes, to assure ourselves, in that mute void, that we're alive in a gaze beyond our own? But then, in the boy's eyes, hadn't she had been God, a body, luminous and unmarred, to kneel obeisant before? "Fuck it," she said aloud, and rolled from the bed. In the kitchen she made herself some coffee and waited for the sun to rise. On the radio people laughed.

Later that morning she called in sick to work. She tried watching soap operas and tried reading magazines but found herself incapable of either, and passed the day foggily, in and out of sleep. When her mother called again she almost answered, but thought better of it. "Dear, please," came the voice over the machine, filling the apartment. "You're beginning to worry me. Please call me when you get this message." But then how could she explain it? Oh mother, do you remember that old saw about if a tree falls in the woods and no one is around to hear it, does it really fall? Mother, what if life is like that? What if we don't exist except in the eyes of others—what if loneliness and death are the very same thing?

When the sun set and the evening cooled the air, she poured herself the remainder of her scotch, drink by drink, and listened to the boy play his guitar. Her dry lips parted, as if to sing along, slowly and plaintively, but she made no sound. Instead she pulled a chair to the window and banked the side of her head against the screen, sitting there, listening, even after the scotch was gone.

After a while she saw his bedroom light appear. Raising her head, she watched the back end of his radio, with its glossy black tangle of speaker wires, and the fan whirring its circle against the ceiling. When he passed the window he was pulling up his t-shirt, and her heart leapt at the sight: his smooth hairless chest, his narrow angular arms. She leaned forward in her chair. For a while there was nothing, save the fan's vapory spinning, until she saw him pass again, and this time glance down. His expression, seen fleetingly, was puzzled, but in an instant he turned off his light. All at once she felt exhilarated and hopeless; she wondered vaguely if this was what dying was like, this queer hunger for a desperately unwanted end. As her eyes adjusted to the dark she found she could make out the outline of his head beside the radio. She could have seen it there the entire time, she now realized, if only she had looked closely enough.

And then, standing, with a deliberateness that was neither seductive nor timid, and without once taking her eyes from the window above her, she unclasped her bra and stepped from her panties. The shadow of his head in the window remained motionless. She was naked, but didn't feel it; she felt almost nothing save warmth, like that first pure sensation of a child in its womb. She tilted her head toward the bedroom behind her, but the boy's shadow stayed fixed. When she raised her hand it was pale and shivery. Still he didn't move. Her fingertips brushed the screen as she cupped her hand and drew her fingers in toward her, beckoning. "Please," she whispered. "Please."

Sitting on the edge of her sofa in the living room, she waited for him. She smoked a cigarette from a pack one of the lawyers had left, and then she smoked another. But the boy never came. After a while she sank into the sofa and cried from a broken heart she'd never known could break. Several months later she married the lawyer named Bob and installed metal blinds of many colors in every window of their new home in South Euclid. She loved the way they clinked faintly against one another when she closed them, like the click of soldiers' boots, like an army protecting her from everything she wanted to touch her.

Shay Youngblood

Triple X

The summer I was sixteen years old me and my Aunt Sofine took the number thirteen bus downtown to the Triple X theater on North Main Street every Thursday afternoon. This idea came to Sofine one morning early in June. We both sat on the floor in my grandmother's kitchen in our bra and panties, sweating in front of a loud table fan set on high and a bowl of ice. We dipped our hands in the bowl flicking our cool, dripping-wet fingers at each other from time to time. Sofine laughed low down in her throat, her big breasts decorated with black lace trembled when she came across the small black bordered ad in the movie section:

First-run features. High-Quality Adult movies. Air-conditioned. Thursday Ladies Free. Must be 18 years.

"Ladies free," she said. "Air conditioned," I repeated. I dipped my hands in the bowl of ice and water, then leaned forward pressing my palms to Sofine's face like she'd taught me to do since I was a little girl and we'd spent hot summer days in my grandmother's house. She closed her eyes and smiled in my hands. "This could be educational." Her long thick fingers selected a small piece of ice and began melting it back and forth across her bare buttery shoulders. My mother, when she left me at my grandmother's for the summer, insisted that I do something educational, that I think about what I wanted to do with my life. She and my father were not happy when I announced that I was thinking about dropping out of high school at the end of my junior year, just thinking about it. I was considering pursuing a career in acting, after knocking out the audience at Malcolm X High School with my original interpretation of Ophelia as a home girl in a contemporary staging of *Hamlet.* Mama said I was just acting myself and didn't seem to think the reviews I got in the Afro-American weekly newspaper meant that I was Broadway material. Parker Henderson, the cultural critic, said I had promise, that my Ophelia was the most original he'd ever seen. My father, although he said he was proud of my performance, said he hoped I'd go to college before making my final decision to be a stage actress.

I worked my behind off for that part. In Mr. Brandon's English class, the others were always laughing because I was a slow reader, but I fixed them. Mr. Brandon chose me to be Ophelia and he helped me to create my role. He stayed after school with me for three weeks straight helping me read Shakespeare. It might've been Greek, for all I understood in the beginning, but he took his time with me, and we cracked open the door to understanding.

"So you want to be actress?" Sofine didn't act surprised or even laugh at me like my mama had when I told her.

"I am an actress, I was Ophelia . . ." Then I stood up in my grandmother's kitchen, in front of the table fan in my underwear and gave Sofine and the kitchen cabinets all the drama of a mad Ophelia for the rest of your life. You are a black woman living in America.

"Maybe I'll make movies," I said. "As a back up career."

"Well, there's an original idea." She took down my grandmother's coffee can filled with change from on top of the refrigerator and counted out bus fare for the both of us.

"Let's go do some research," she said, filling my hand with dimes.

The first time we went to the Triple X, the clerk, a bulky black man with a wild afro and the mean gaze of a prison guard asked us for ID. Sofine started to flirt with him, talking about how hot it was. He smiled, showing a gold tooth left of center, and winked at her.

"We get a lot of ladies come in, just want to be cool," he said, looking at her driver's license through the thick, dirty glass. She told him I'd lost my license at a baseball game two weeks ago. Her story was beginning to get long and I was losing my nerve, shifting my feet nervously, but the clerk was disinterested and waved us in. The second time we came, he didn't bother to ask at all.

We lived in Atlanta then. My daddy delivered trailer homes cross-country. This particular summer he and my mama decided to use one of his long-distance deliveries to go on a second honeymoon. On their way out west they dropped me off in the small town in South Georgia where my mama grew up. I'll admit I was jealous, had already begged on my knees under the dinner table to stay home alone so I could rehearse for my audition for Juliet in the Atlanta Festival of Stars Dinner Theatre production of *Romeo and Juliet* in the fall, but they just kept piling meat and potatoes on their forks and shoveling it into their mouths. They were in love and what I wanted didn't matter at all. The only saving grace to a hot summer in South Georgia was that my Aunt Sofine was staying with my grandmother, and I knew she knew how to have a good time.

My grandmother was hard-of-hearing and spent her days piecing together quilts on the front porch when she wasn't watching afternoon soap operas and talking to the TV as if the villains could hear her harsh judgments of their sinful behavior.

Every Thursday all summer long, me and Sofine slept till 10 o'clock, took a cool shower and dressed in brightly colored tank tops and shorts and lace-up Roman sandals. We lotioned our bodies with cocoa butter, talcum-powdered between our legs and breasts, took three swipes of Mum deodorant under our arms and picked our hair into big curly afros that framed our faces.

I wasn't allowed to wear makeup at home, but Aunt Sofine put a thin line of black eyeliner on me and a little bit of blue eye shadow and pink lip gloss that made my lips shine like glass. I began to look glamorous. I had to look eighteen to get in the movies. Sofine let me wear her gold hoop earrings. I tried to give attitude like Lena Horne in *Stormy Weather*, I had to keep my glasses in Sofine's pocketbook until we got inside the theater. She said my glasses made me look like a square. It took Sofine longer to put on her face.

The first layer was a liquid foundation that made her face look like a flat dry pancake, then she painted on a thick line of black eyeliner making points at the corner of her eyes to emphasize their slanted shape. My daddy said she looked Chinese, which she took as a compliment. Her lips she outlined in dark rose and filled with Hawaiian Orchid, a kind of fuchsia color that matched her stretchy tube top. Me and Sofine walked slowly to the bus stop, so as not to encourage perspiration, and stood waiting for the number thirteen to take us downtown. We could have walked the eight or ten blocks, but it was hot, hotter than I imagined hell could be on a summer day.

A hand rests on a swollen breast, thighs spread open like a Bible. A man bows his head in prayer before them, holy. Her head thrashed from side to side, eyes squeezed shut. Small whimpers. Pleasure out of sight.

"You want some more popcorn?" Aunt Sofine whispers.

"No, I don't want no more," I cross my legs, shift in my seat, and let out the air I've been holding in my lungs, but I don't take my eyes off the screen. My mouth is dry and although the air conditioner is on full blast, my hands and crotch are sweaty. I try to memorize the expression for desire.

A wide, red satin skirt delicately above the knees. Thighs spread, lowered to the floor, hips dipping, picking up twenty-dollar bills. Smoke rings emanate from deep in her private parts. Perfect circles float in the air.

At home I take off my panties, squat down and try to pick up a dollar bill, but my legs get a ramp and I lose balance and fall and scrape my elbow against the bathroom door. I'm not allowed to smoke so I can't try the smoke rings. Miss Kitty makes it look so easy to be a movie star.

A pool stick aimed at the eight ball aimed at the center of a womanly body spread open a field of green felt.

My uncle High Five won't let me in the pool hall. He says I can't play pool and besides, "This ain't no place for skirts." He and his friends laugh and keep playing for quarters stacked on the edge of the pool cue rack.

"I ain't no skirt," I say. "And any way, blind Miss Lily could beat you shooting pool." I knew I could beat him too. All I had to do was use my imagination. When I see High Five leave the pool hall, I sneak in and rub my hands across the green felt, hold the smooth, cool white cue ball in my hand feeling the weight of it, wondering if my aim would be sure.

Practice . . . rehearse . . . make believe . . . make it look easy . . . make it look real . . . Eight ball in the corner pocket.

The frame is filled with moist flesh, steam heat, a white wash cloth makes trails in the water of her bath. The soundtrack is bland, nothing you could dance to, but my body is rocking on the beat.

At home I turn the volume on the radio up loud and sit in my grandmother's room in the dark, rocking in her rocking chair with my legs pressed together, a cool wash cloth wadded into a ball stuffed in my panties. I rock through the top ten soul hits before my Aunt Sofine bursts into the room and throws a comic book at me and tells me it's time to go to bed. My bed is a narrow single cot next to the bed she sleeps in with her one-year-old baby boy we call Honey because that's the color of his skin.

A man and a woman, both naked, gallop through a meadow on a white horse. Cut to interior bedroom. Day. The man lies still on his back. The woman sits still on his lap and rides as if he is the white horse.

My aunt is munching loudly on the tub of popcorn balanced on her knees. She slurps her orange soda and watches the screen as if it is a documentary on trees. She watches disinterested as if she has seen it all before and is reduced to looking at the background. Sometimes we see the movies twice if the temperature is over ninety outside. We like it cool. Sofine comments on almost every new scene, "I hope that horse doesn't have fleas," or "I would never sleep with a man had a butt bigger than mine."

A hand on my shoulder, a whisper in my ear.

"You don't want to go for a ride with me do you?" A voice inviting, whispers in the darkness behind me." His breath smells like licorice, his voice sounds like a little boy's, a boy who is afraid the answer will be no. "I'll take you to New York City. The Hotel Pennsylvania's got a room waiting on the sound of you calling my name."

"What you whispering in her ear?" Aunt Sofine turns around to look him in the eye.

"I'll whisper in yours, too, if that's what you into." He is eager to please.

"We're trying to watch the movie. Keep your comments to yourself soldier." She says without missing a beat. He gets up and moves two rows behind us.

Sofine can tell a soldier from two hundred feet in the dark. She should know. She's only nineteen years old, but she's been married twice, both times to Army men. Her first husband married her when she was just one year older than me. The problem with him was that he was already married to a girl in New Mexico. Her second husband was a short, chunky brick-colored sergeant from Pittsburgh, who was twice her age and expected her to cook dinner and make up the bed every day. She left him after two weeks. She say she didn't have to work that hard at home. Honey's daddy was in the Marines. Men liked Sofine and she loved men. She was sexy in a way that made them whistle, stop their cars in traffic and made them want to give her things.

I want men to give me things—flowers on opening night, shopping trips to New York City and diamond rings for each one of my fingers and toes. I want applause for a job well done.

The fourth Thursday in July, Sofine said she had a date with Honey's daddy. She gives me money to buy a loaf of bread, some slice meat and a carton of Coke at the grocery store. My grandmother was on a trip to the mall with a group of senior citizens. By eleven o'clock, heat rolls through the open windows of the house in thick waves. The fan just stirs up dust and blows dead flies onto the bed. I kept wondering what movie this week would be. If I'd learn some new acting technique. I am itching to learn something new.

I am nervous and sweaty at the thought of going to the Triple X by myself. I take another cold shower and decide to put on my Aunt Sofine's face and catch the bus downtown. One block from the theater I put my glasses in the pocket of my shorts and the world becomes a blur. I manage to wave in the direction of the clerk behind the window who barely looks up from the comic book he is reading. I am a regular. I open the door and a blast of cool air freeze-dries the sweat rolling down the back of my neck. With the money Aunt Sofine gave me I buy a tub of buttered popcorn and an Orange Crush. I sit in our usual spot three rows from the screen on the aisle. There are less than a dozen other people in the theater, scattered mostly in the back rows. The movie has already started so I can't see their faces.

Underwater. Bodies in slow motion. Graceful as dancers. Slow motion sex. Wet sex. Sunlight dances on their bodies. Two women kiss on the mouth. A man watches from a distance.

I wonder if they could drown underwater so long. Sofine would certainly comment on the man's hairy back or the woman's big feet. I squeezed my legs together, take a sip of Orange Crush and hardly blink at the images on the screen. I want to be kissed underwater like that. I want a man to lift me onto his lap. There is a sudden movement next to me. I don't look directly, but out of the corner of my eye, a large male body eases into the seat beside me. I sneak a look sideways.

Muhammad Ali handsome. My guess, Air Force. His elbow takes over the armrest between us. His breathing is labored as if he is out of breath. He leans in my direction, close but not quite touching me. He smells freshly showered and shaved. His breath is minty.

"I could do that to you," the mouth next to me whispers, cool in my ear.

A girl and a boy are sitting on a sofa, watching TV. The boy tries to kiss the girl. The girl says no, but she is smiling. The boy tries to touch the girl underneath her dress, the girl says no, but she is smiling. The boy is frustrated. He pushes the girl against the sofa and pins her down with his body. The boy rips open the girl's blouse. The girl says no, she is breathing hard, putting up a fight, but she is still smiling. The boy is so overcome with passion at the sight of the girl's naked breasts that he tears off the girl's skirt and panties. The girl resists, but the boy is stronger. The girl struggles for a while, but eventually she gives in.

My head thrashes from side to side, eyes squeezed shut. I am the girl in the movies who takes pleasure out of life. I am the girl who rehearses to become the woman who will win Academy Awards for her performances, the one who loves the sound of applause. I am the girl who takes the hand offered in the darkness. Small whimpers. Pleasure out of sight.

Ace Atkins

Bluff City

When the woman from Dream Weaver Foundation calls Zigzag up on his dog Tuck's c-phone, he got to fight back the urge to ask for a buck-ass naked woman. After all, he's about eleven years old and he know them Dream Weaver people don't think that way. When little Jimmy Jenkins got the cancer or some shit, all he got was a ticket to the Grizzlies games before that white woman in the Volvo drop him back at the corner of Poplar. Pat on the head. Little smile.

She afraid like hell to go into Dixie Homes.

Zigzag don't blame her. He don't blame nobody.

He just talks to the woman at the foundation about some man named Steve from Germantown who's really coming right into the damn projects to pick up his sick ass. He tell her he want to check out the Dirty South review, maybe see Eight Ball or go down to Pop Tunes and see what he can buy.

She says he can't buy shit. He gets some lunch, some fun, and something she calls fellowship.

"What?"

"Fellowship," she says. "May I speak to your mother?"

"She out."

"We need a release."

"You got one."

Zigzag flips through some papers that Tuck had signed last night down by the Circle K workin' that phone, smokin' that Newport. He knows it's a bitch to be sick when you ain't sick.

Tuck got them connections. Zigzag didn't tell him what it's for and he didn't ask.

When he hangs up, it's about eight and Zigzag is tired. He looks at his busted TV set, walks to the refrigerator, and opens it. His mama left some hot wings in there about two weeks back and things ain't smellin' too good. Half a bottle of flat Pepsi and a beer that exploded in the freezer.

Summer night. He sits on his broken steps of the projects and watches Memphis glow. That red light on top the Pyramid beat on and off like a tiny little heart, mirrored walls like a thousand eyes.

He watches a hoopty—some old Oldsmobile painted red and blue—float by and he sees the arm of a man flick the ash off a cigarette. Sky is orange and black. Man got a brand on his hand. Prison.

The end of the road stops at Dixie Homes and the man has to stop, reverse, and turn around.

Zigzag shakes his head and walks back inside. Them things makes his guts hurt.

* * *

When Steve picks him up on Saturday, he wants to tell him about that stripper he seen on a sign on Winchester. Woman's face was screwed up into some tight-ass look with her mouth wide open and head tilted back. The name of the club all in gold. Most Beautiful Women in the MidSouth.

Zigzag get into Steve's BMW and then they ride.

Steve asks Zigzag lots of questions about bein' a kid and if he like basketball. He say it's *aiight* and then Steve asks Zigzag if he like Eminem and shit tryin' to be all cool and Zigzag say he's *aiight*, too.

"Where we goin'?"

"Chuck E. Cheese," Steve says.

"Who?"

"Pizza."

"Man, pizza," Zigzag say. "You laughin' at me 'cause I'm dyin'? I don't want no goddamn pizza."

Steve smiles and turns down the beats on his radio. He got curly blonde hair and wears a shirt with a little horse on it. Zigzag know he smokin' cause he got a pack of Camels and the car smells foul as hell.

"There's a Redbirds game tonight," he said.

"Let's eat."

"You'll like Chuck E. Cheese's."

Steve click open his c-phone and press speed dial, he talks and smokes, and mutters like hell into the phone somethin' about a couple of hours, martinis at Automatic Slim's, and then he'll be done with it.

"You got to do this," Zigzag say.

Steve clicks off the phone and lights a cigarette as they skirt the edge of the Mississippi down at that park where his cousin got shot by those cops. His back to the river, Raven in his hand.

Steve looks at Zigzag and shakes his head, "It's not like that."

"What did you do?" Zigzag ask, twirling his baseball hat in his fingers and rubbing his dirty basketball shoes together.

"What are you talking about, bro?"

"Man, you a trip," Zigzag say. "Community service a bitch. Ain't it?"

* * *

Zigzag finishes up his pizza, talkin' about a whole pepperoni pizza, 'cause he ain't seen his mama in ten days, and still can't figure that shit out. There are these goddamn animals' heads on the walls and the lights get all soft when they want to sing and talk. Tell corny jokes. He watches a table of children about his age circle around a large cake frosted in pink icing. They have clean clothes and don't watch their backs as they get close to that flame.

"You gonna tell me what you done?"

Steve shakes his head and leans back into his chair. He runs his hand over his face and look at Zigzag in the eye like he's a man. "I got busted."

"Drugs."

Steve looks away.

Zigzag wanders over to the party and looks over a little girl's shoulder. She feels him breathe close to her ear and she turns to him, a Powerpuff Girl paper hat cocked on her head.

"You're not part of this."

"Yes I am," Zigzag say. "How would you know?"

"These are Adam's friends."

She tosses her head from side to side, her blonde hair whipping across his eyes and turns her back to him.

He takes a breath and turns away. Hands in his pocket, eyes on the floor.

Zigzag struts back to the table where Steve is talking on his c-phone again and he watches some sorry-ass bastard come out later in some gray rat's outfit. The fur is matted and brown. Stains on his paws.

He's running all round and tries to give Zigzag the high five.

The music is loud and electric. Kids are screaming and laughing.

Zigzag don't like him. Rats just make him think of shit that's crawlin' down at his feet while he sleep. And when he see the rat dancin' before him, blockin' his path, he kick that motherfucker right in the nuts.

The rat falls sideways.

Steve grabs Zigzag by the shoulder and they're back in the BMW.

"How do you top that," Steve says. "How about an ice cream and we call it a day?"

"Bullshit."

"Libertyland?" Steve asks. "They have this terrific roller coaster, man."

"Don't be man'in me. Come on, this is lame as hell."

"You're twelve," he says. "Your T-shirt has pictures of Fat Albert on it."

"My uncle gave it to me," Zigzag says. He pulls out one of Steve's Camels, slide down the window, and watch as that sky get all pink and black in the night. Swirls in the ceiling of a cave. Memphis is a room.

Steve doesn't say nothin' about the kid taking a cigarette.

"It's tough," Steve says. "I had a brother who died. He was sixteen."

Zigzag nod. "Yeah, it's tough."

"What's it feel like?" Steve asks, his face on that wide stretch of road ahead.

"What?"

"Dying."

Zigzag blows a smoke ring at a stoplight. Looks in both directions at a detour and more construction fuckin' up the interstate.

"Not a thing."

They drive for a while and when the man's c-phone ring again, he doesn't answer. The kid finishes the cigarette and they roll into a Baskin Robbins, Steve talkin' about getting some Butter Pecan and shit.

Steve shuts off the engine.

Zigzag says: "Titty bar."

"Excuse me?"

"I want to see some titties before I die."

Zigzag has this skill that no one can ever duplicate. He can cry like the world ain't never seen and that's what he does. Just as it start to rain down on Lamar, Zigzag cries watchin' the water slide down his windshield.

He breathes and sniffs.

Steve shakes his head, walks into the ice cream shop, and leaves Zigzag staring at the ignition.

The keys are gone. Even his doors locked.

He got to pop that lock up and down, just so he can breathe.

* * *

Steve hands Zigzag a cherry vanilla cone and they head down south on Lamar into South Memphis. Women wander down broken concrete sidewalks, pregnant. Shoeless. Men drink forties at carwashes where Escalades and Mercedes shine with a tight wax in the crime lights.

The man says he knows someone who knows someone who runs this place down by the airport. Zigzag seen it, too. White girls with big hair and red lips on billboards that been bleached like hell from the sun. He wonders if they are like the Most Beautiful Girls in the Midsouth.

The rain makes them drive slowly. It's gettin' late.

Zigzag puts his broken watch in his pocket.

The place is called Delphi. Place got these huge white columns out front of some old tin building painted pink. Neon signs flash in his eyes as Steve talks to some woman in a black silk robe by the back door.

She's got a tiger tattooed on her ankle. She nods, takes some cash in her hand, and rubs her fingers on the back of Steve's neck.

Steve waves at him. Zigzag squint into that white light and the man gives the motion for him to come on.

He does.

The girls aren't like the ones in the No Limit videos he's seen on BET. The women who are brown and perfect and rub their hands over the young brothers' faces don't live here. Zigzag can only see wrinkled butts, big stomachs, and women tripping around on stage.

The girls all licked up, eyes wide as hell.

Two of them sit in the lap of some white dude holding dollar bills in each hand like he's trying to squeeze the juice from them.

Then he sees her on a rounded stage, so high up he got to tilt his head and squint into the light that twirls from a mirrored ball and over his face. He can breathe. Ain't nobody crowded him.

Her.

She's lookin' down at him. Hair cut tight, slant eyes like a China girl and the smoothest brown skin. Her skin is polished and oiled; her nipples are brown and large and her titties fall like teardrops.

The girl only wears some red lace drawers that she twist down over her knees and place into his hand.

They so light, they feel like air. The DJ calls her Aphrodite.

He mouths the word as his heart beats quick. He wants to kiss her.

She smiles at him and he turns back to find Steve, get some of that cash money.

When he does, he bumps into a white man who looks like a toad. Blue dress shirt and red tie all cocked on his bulging neck. Zigzag push his drunk ass out the way and move through the scattered light and smoke and squintin' the whole way into dark at some table in the back.

Zigzag hears her laugh first.

Steve steps close to him—hand on his shoulder, a couple of red drinks in his hand—and Zigzag passes, crosses the floor and up the five steps, and through some long white curtains that float and brush across his cheek.

It's murky and clouded with smoke and feels like the edge of an early morning dream.

Two white men sit on pillow and play with a woman. They hold her. One got his hand around her throat, strokin' it like a street cat.

She jacked up. Eyes red. Voice all broken.

"Hey, honey," she say. "I got a boy look like you."

Zigzag watches her.

He makes his mama look him in the eye. Let her understand, he know where she been.

She don't see nothin', the men yellin' at him.

Zigzag turns and walks out the door and all the while Steve follows him, holding red drinks and wantin' to know what happened. Weeds grow in cracks on the sidewalks, a big oak tree over his head got diseased limbs covering up an old mansion rotted and broken like some kind of haunted house.

"What's up, bro?" Steve yells to his back.

He'll never know, Zigzag thinks, he's gone.

* * *

Two days later, Zigzag falls asleep with four lottery tickets, fifteen Coke bottle tops, and a pack of NBA bubblegum cards by his side. He twists a NBA card in his hand, imagines himself hittin' that three-pointer, and pulls up the blanket over his face.

People outside talkin' shit on his stoop; his mother jokin' with some crack head named Tony. He hears them walk to the end of the street to a weedy lot, where she'll work some favors for a rock.

Zigzag looks up at the ceiling and a large brown spot that spreads like a small mountain and drips with water. He dreams while awake. The stain is a mountain. The water is his river that takes him everywhere.

The river becomes a road and he's with that girl from the club.

They ride in his Escalade down Beale and up around North Parkway to see his people. She smells like strawberries and bleached clothes and sun and good cigarettes.

His people watch him and the girl throw money out of his car and he laughs at their silly asses.

Their feet stuck in concrete as he floats by, chrome rims blinding them with light.

In his mind, he pushes that pedal and is gone.

Anne Rapp

Snake Bit

As much as he tried, Jim Ed just couldn't figure out why his wife had gone so negative on him. She hadn't been that way at all eight years ago when they first hooked up. Hell, the day he'd met her in the Triple Crown Room at Oaklawn Park, and knocked her off her high heels he might add, she'd told him straight out that what attracted her to him was his sense of adventure, his willingness to throw caution to the wind, attack the unknown, live on the edge, roll the dice, ignore the odds, bet the long shot, and always look a gift horse in the blinders. He had no earthly idea what that last one meant, but who cared? He, too, was completely blinded. By her. And that was about the time she had turned those big caramel-brown eyes on him, like mints on a pillow at the Marriott, and looked straight into his soul and proclaimed that what turned her on the most was his unpredictability.

Unpredictability. He would never forget how she had pronounced it. Her inflection. The tone, the meter. Like two words, with a pause in the middle, emphasis on the un. Granted, how the heck could she predict at that moment whether he was or wasn't predictable? She'd only known him for about four hours, most of which were spent between a barstool and the fifty dollar window. And the next twenty between her designer sheets, he might add. So yes, he was fully aware, even back then, that her initial claims of admiration were mostly horseshit. But still, she didn't take the damn bugle player home that night, now did she?

That's what Jim Ed was thinking when he walked into the kitchen and found Susanna standing sad and motionless at the window, staring out at the grey-green Sabine River that was gently lapping against the green-grey deck down on the bank.

He walked over and stood next to her, checking out the new deck, his own handiwork from just last week.

"Jesus, look at the synchronicity," he said. "A symphony of synergy and symmetry. "

Susanna rolled her eyes, let out a little breath of annoyance, and turned toward a cereal box on the counter. Jim Ed grabbed a coffee mug off a hook by the sink.

"The exact words you once used to describe us, I might add," he added.

"Tell me, Jim Ed," she snapped, "why is it you always have to add something? Can't you ever just say the hell what you want to say and then stop there?" She dropped the cereal bowl a little hard on the tile and it made a few clattery rotations before settling. "Those last minute insights and explanations you throw in can be so irritating." She yanked open the silverware drawer. "Boring too, I might add."

Screw you. Not even worth a response.

Jim Ed carried his coffee with him out onto the screen porch, where he began to sort through an array of brand new ropes, hooks, snares and nets hanging on the wall. Benjamin, the border collie/Jack Russell mix, stood up from his faded L.L. Bean bed, slinked over and rubbed his wet nose across Jim Ed's pant leg. Jim Ed bent down and scratched his ear.

"Good morning, pardner."

"R," said Benjamin in complete comprehension.

"You know what I love the most about you, Benjamin? You don't give me a bunch of crap in the morning before I've even taken my own crap." He lifted the mug to his lips and savored the top inch of hot coffee. Coffee seemed to calm Jim Ed, rather than the opposite.

"I'm sorry."

It came from the other side of the screen door. Jim Ed turned to see Susanna standing there, mainly just a shape through the thick screen mesh.

"I had a bad night, that's all."

Jim Ed lifted his mug to her. "How many bad nights in a row is that now? Four?" He powered back another inch and a half. "And four last week too. I might add."

"Fuck you," said the shape of Susanna before it disappeared back into the grey-green unknown that was now her adventurous, edgy and unpredictable life.

* * *

"Careful what you ask for," Jim Ed laughed as Benjamin cowered away from the raccoon he'd been chasing around the cabin all morning. This coon turned out to be fearless and eventually decided he'd had about enough of Benjamin's crap. He charged him, swatted at his nose and displayed a mouthful of long, raccoon teeth right in his face. Benjamin yelped and retreated to the dock, where Jim Ed was already loading his flat-bottomed, fiberglass paddling boat, now tied to the dock post.

"Lucky that coon didn't take your nose off, pardner."

"R," Benjamin agreed.

As for luck, Jim Ed knew that he was personally blessed in that department. He was a lucky man, yes sir. Always had been, always would be. He just couldn't understand why everybody else didn't see it. Not even his own identical twin brother, Jim Ted, who had taken over the family business down in Beaumont right out of college. For fifteen years now, Jim Ted thought luck was the privilege of getting to oversee three Goodyear Tire franchises in Jefferson County, Texas, where he could spend all day learning, cataloging and keeping up with every single off-road and snow-traction and performance-ultra-grip-quiet-ride tire that came off the assembly line. Jim Ted thought luck was inheriting a business that, no matter where the economy stood, people would always need your product. Even in hard times, folks still have to get around. And yes, Jim Ted thought luck meant not having to take any risks to start with. And therefore, never having to even flirt with losing your shirt.

What Jim Ted didn't realize was that the true meaning of luck was never having to wear that same old shirt over and over again. Hell, losing your shirt just means you get to feel the air on your chest. And then you get the chance to put on another shirt, a better one. The world around you looks a hundred percent different in a different shirt. Put on a festive Hawaiian number and the sunsets are twice as orange. Put on some western fringe and the world is your corral. Put on a nice GQ blue one that matches yours and your momma's blue eyes and, boom, you win the heart of a girl like Susanna.

"On the spot. No questions asked. That's what luck is," Jim Ed finished explaining to Benjamin.

"What are you doing?"

Jim Ed looked up at Susanna who had wandered down the hill and was standing in the path about twenty yards away. She still hadn't found her smile this morning.

"Loading up."

"Loading up what?"

"My gear."

"Where are you going?"

"Snake hunting, my darling, snake hunting. Would you like to come along?" Right after those words came out, he wished they hadn't sounded quite so sarcastic. There was no reason for it, really.

Benjamin ran up the path to Susanna and licked at her ankles, but Susanna kept her eyes on Jim Ed. After a few seconds, she turned and looked around at the thick vegetation that almost completely camouflaged the cabin. She looked down river at the moss covered cypress trees that shaded the murky water, even though the sun was now getting high. She looked down into the boat at the arsenal of mean looking spears and snares and hooks.

"Jim Ed, what could you possibly know about snake hunting?"

Her tone was not sarcastic at all. It was a combination of confusion, fear, loathing and exasperation. With a silent call for help mixed in there somewhere.

"Enough to hunt snakes," he said, making a big effort to sound simply matter-of-fact this time. He reached for the only thing left on the dock, two large coolers. He dipped them into the water, one by one, until they were about half full, then he placed them in each end of the boat and put the tops on securely.

"Right," she said. "And does the Internet tell you what to do when you're out in the middle of a big river that's totally isolated and infested with God knows what, and you're thirty miles from any kind of paved road and an hour and a half from any town with a doctor or a rescue person, and something goes wrong and there's nobody around to help you out? Not even your wife because you refuse to listen to her and won't even figure out a way to get a goddamn telephone line out here!"

"Calm down, Susanna. I've got my cell phone." He held it up. "See, it's completely charged. I left it on the deal all night long."

"Fat chance that thing will even work where you're going."

He checked the display screen. The signal bars indicated a partial one.

"Why won't it work?"

"Why will it?" She looked off at the thick trees lining both sides of the bank. "You've never been down this river very far. So how do you know it's not gonna cut out the minute you turn that bend?"

Jim Ed shook his head. "Susanna, I love you, baby, but that's the difference in you and me." He whistled his best dog whistle. "Benjamin! Come on, boy, come on."

Benjamin immediately started running toward the boat, but Susanna was on him like a cat.

"Oh no you're not."

She snatched him up off the path, his legs still churning the air, and she held him tightly under her arm.

"You're not taking my dog snake hunting."

"What do you mean, your dog? Benjamin, get in the boat! Come on, boy!"

Benjamin squirmed and kicked and managed to free himself when Susanna tripped over an unfortunate vine that lazily stretched across the foot path. Before she could recover, Benjamin had lunged into the boat with Jim Ed.

"Good boy, Benjamin. Good boy, pardner, master snake hunter. You ready to go?"

Susanna was furious. She ran to the dock and tried to reach down into the boat and grab him, but he easily avoided her. Jim Ed already had the rope untied, and he used one of the oars to push away from the dock.

"Goddammit, Jim Ed, I swear, you are the biggest bastard I have ever known!"

Jim Ed turned the boat from the dock but remained about six feet away in the water. Benjamin settled down at his feet, tongue hanging out, tail wagging.

"Susanna, I don't know why you worry so much. Why don't you go back up there and relax. Take a nap or read or something. I'll be back by lunch time, I promise. You can make me a ham sandwich. With mayonnaise."

"Your brother was right! You don't know shit! You're an embarrassment and a hazard!" Susanna looked around at the swamp again. Every time she checked, it threatened to engulf and smother her more and more until she knew she eventually wouldn't be able to breathe.

"I don't like being left here alone," she said, a little quieter this time. "I mean, what if something happens?"

"Nothing's gonna happen."

"Well, what if some, some deranged hillbilly or some axe murderer comes up here while you're gone?"

"You know where the shotgun is. It's loaded, just like always. Put it by the door if it makes you feel better." He almost laughed, but thought better of it. "I can promise you, Susanna, no axe murderers are gonna come around here. Axe murderers like to work at night. And hillbillies, most of them now have jobs during the day, thanks to Sam Walton. So you're safe."

"I hate you, Jim Ed! I hate you!"

Jim Ed stared at Susanna standing barefoot on the dock, wearing only her white ribbed undershirt and draw string cotton capris that she'd taken to sleeping in. God, was she gorgeous. A vision. Perfect perfection. Her creamy brown eyes, now filled with tears, reminded him of two big bottomless vats of pure milk chocolate that he could easily just dive into and swim around in with his mouth wide open and never come back up for the rest of his life. He had never loved her more than he did at this moment.

"If there's a word worse than hate, that's how I feel about you!" she cried. A cloud moved overhead, allowing a ray of light to hit her for just an instant, then it immediately cast her into shadow again.

He was one lucky man, Jim Ed Barnes.

"And if you're not back in two hours, two hours, I'm gonna take that gun and shoot myself!" she yelled. "I'm gonna blow my brains out all over your dead computer!"

One lucky, lucky man.

* * *

The Sabine River was the only river in East Texas that still had long isolated stretches like this one, and Jim Ed considered himself fortunate to have staked his claim here. Who could ever imagine this kind of beauty existed only two hours outside of drab, tiresome Beaumont? This river was almost six hundred miles long. The northern part flowed through pine woods, then it eventually formed the boundary between Texas and Louisiana. The word Sabine came from the Spanish word for "cypress," referring to all the stately trees that were thick along these southern banks. Only two roads crossed this particular sixty-mile stretch, and aside from a few sandbars that sometimes attracted campers, it was mostly deserted.

"I only had to buy four acres, and look what came with it!" Jim Ed bragged to Benjamin. He was gesturing with wide, outstretched arms but he quickly pulled them in and ducked under a series of low hanging branches. Spanish moss clung to his cap when he straightened back up. "I might as well own the whole damn river!"

Benjamin didn't answer. He was preoccupied looking into the water at the reeds that moved in a wiggly pattern just under the olive green surface.

"Something special about this place. You know that and I know that. Now all we have to do is convince your mother." He cut into the still water with his oar and navigated the boat on down stream. "She'll come around," he added.

Benjamin suddenly started jumping around and barking at the water.

"What you see there, buddy? Those snakes starting to follow us already?"

Jim Ed looked just in time to see a catfish swimming next to the boat. It was larger than Benjamin. It tracked them for a few seconds, then disappeared under a large patch of algae. Jim Ed looked back up at the gnarly cypress tree that had suddenly appeared right in front of them. He quickly paddled the boat sideways to avoid it. A fog was starting to descend, obscuring his depth of field a little, but it only added to the magical quality of this gloriously uncertain place. Jim Ed was ecstatic. After maneuvering the next bend, he stopped paddling and put his oar down.

"Okay, Benjamin, it's show time."

Benjamin's tail was now rotating like an oscillating fan. He sniffed at the rope that Jim Ed was knotting and testing.

"Remember what we practiced yesterday, and the day before? On our trial runs?"

"R."

"Good. Because that was just a scrimmage. But now, my friend, it's time for the real deal."

He looped the rope around Benjamin's neck and midsection, not too tight, not too loose. Benjamin patiently waited as Jim Ed picked him up and moved to the back end of the boat.

"Okay, sport, let's go swimming. Don't worry, Daddy's got your life line." He tightly clutched the other end of the rope in his free hand.

Benjamin hit the water with a big splash for such a medium-sized dog. He went under just briefly, then surfaced and immediately started swimming, staying fairly close to the boat, occasionally looking up at Jim Ed but mainly just sloshing around and enjoying the cool water.

Benjamin was a champion dog paddler. He followed the boat obediently as Jim Ed began to slowly steer it down the river again. Jim Ed's senses were now sharp as a knife. He divided his attention between the course ahead of him and Benjamin swimming behind him.

"Good boy, Benjamin, atta boy."

It was no time before the system started to work. Within minutes, Jim Ed noticed the wavy patterns that began to appear in the water just a short distance behind Benjamin. He calmly stopped paddling and put the oar down. He stood up and began to bring in the rope, little by little, pulling Benjamin closer to the boat. He keenly watched as the wavy lines closed the distance between them. Benjamin was completely oblivious to the half dozen cottonmouths following him. He swam like a pro, watching Jim Ed in the boat as a player might watch his coach on the sideline from the playing field. Not only for further instructions, but for any ounce of praise or encouragement that might be tossed his way.

Jim Ed now had about half of the length of the rope back in the boat, and Benjamin was only four feet away in the water. Jim Ed slowly reached back and grabbed the pole with the net attached. He balanced himself, then in one big motion, he pulled Benjamin forward with a fast, strong tug and swung the net out over the water behind him.

"In, boy, in! Get in the boat! Get in the boat!"

With the help of another yank, Benjamin was able to leap up onto the back end of the boat just as Jim Ed dunked the net over the top of the snakes. He quickly turned the net over and then pulled the pole out of the water.

"Hot damn! We got 'em, boy, we got 'em! Look what we got!"

Inside the net were about four or five angry cottonmouths, wiggling and squirming and trying to get out. Benjamin started barking furiously at them. In no time, Jim Ed had the cooler open and was able to dump all the snakes into it and put the lid back on without losing a one. He secured the lid tightly with a bungie cord that he connected to the handles on both ends.

Benjamin continued to bark at the cooler. He could hear the snakes knocking around on the inside. Jim Ed was thrilled. He threw his arms around Benjamin and gave him all the praise a coach could ever openly express for his star player. A snake-hunting team was born.

* * *

An hour and a half and three runs later, Jim Ed had one cooler full of snakes and the other half full. He was beside himself with the victory of this outing. He and Benjamin had decided to take a little rest and were just letting the flow of the river carry them down stream. An osprey flew by overhead with a fish in its mouth. Herons and egrets perched on snags along the shoreline and watched them as they floated by. They saw frogs, woodpeckers, ducks and warblers. More catfish and gar swam by, and mullet jumped all around them. This was like Disneyland without plastic. The Pirates of the Caribbean without a ticket line. Jim Ed wished Susanna was here to enjoy it.

"We'll bring her next time we come," he said, swatting a mosquito on his neck. "She'll love it once she gets out here."

Benjamin, still wet from the last go-round, was reclining with his chin on Jim Ed's left boot.

"She didn't really mean all that stuff she said back there, you know. No more than Jim Ted meant all that stuff he said either. Yeah, he does seem to lose his cool every time I get my fill of that damn tire business and decide to go try something new. His problem is, he never sees it like that, you know? Trying something new. Jim Ted only sees it as failing, instead of opening yourself up to the opportunity of the next thing. Sad way to live, isn't it, boy?"

Jim Ed removed his cap and brushed off some of the dried moss.

"That greyhound business back in Florida, that was a nice little run. Wouldn't do one thing different. Well, maybe I wouldn't invest quite so much in that line of Susanna dogs." He stopped for a second and chuckled. "Oh Susanna, boy, she was the worst D dog in the whole kennel, wasn't she? Maybe even in all of Florida. Couldn't stay with the pack if she tried. But I just kept throwing money at her, didn't I? I mean, how could I not? With her name and all. You would've done the same thing."

"R."

They passed by an egret on the bank that was stabbing at shad as it swam past.

"Pt. Arthur would've worked out too if it hadn't been for that bartender stealing me blind. Then torching the place to the ground." Jim Ed shook his head. "Never saw that one coming. I trusted her, you know. Only guy in Jefferson County willing to give a two-time arsonist fresh out of Huntsville a third chance, and who does she end up burning?"

He looked down at Benjamin, who was as peaceful right now as the setting itself.

"But you know what? That, too, was a blessing in disguise. The bar business wasn't for me. And if that hadn't happened, I would've never been able to spend that next year racing my Triumph all over Mississippi and Arkansas, now would I?"

Benjamin lifted his head and watched a V-pattern of ducks fly overhead.

Jim Ed was certain that the Pt. Arthur incident was about the time Susanna had started to go south on him. He couldn't believe she had actually sided with Jim Ted on the motorcycle racing issue. Just didn't seem right. I mean, your wife is your wife.

He reached down and stroked Benjamin's head. "Jim Ted had no business telling her she was foolish and crazy to move out here with me in the big middle of nowhere, with nobody around and nothing to do. He scared her, dammit. No wonder I threw that tire iron at him. You would've done the same thing."

"R."

Something suddenly scraped the bottom side of the boat. Jim Ed looked down at the water. Dead vegetation probably. The fog was getting thicker around them, and Jim Ed started to steer the boat around a huge stump in the river. Benjamin perked up and sniffed at one of the coolers.

"This snake deal is gonna work out, though. That Texas A&M professor down there in Kingsville is paying big for venom these days. And damn if this isn't just about the easiest work I've ever done."

Benjamin was now standing at the front of the boat, looking down into the water. His tail was moving fast again, whipping the air behind him.

"What we're doing here means something, little buddy. For society. They use this venom for research, you know. Cancer, heart attacks, osteoporosis, hell, even nicotine addiction. Good grief. We're not just capitalizing here, we're saving lives."

* * *

Jim Ed had just tossed Benjamin into the water again when he heard the gun shot. He whipped around in the boat. His muscles tightened and his skin started to tingle. Benjamin was oblivious, just enjoying the cool water. A few seconds of silence went by. Jim Ed eased himself down onto the seat. He looked at his watch, then shook his head.

"Two hours exactly. Benjamin, your mother has a very sick sense of humor."

The boat scraped over the top of something again. Jim Ed looked around at the fog that had pretty much surrounded them by now. Maybe they should think about getting back to the cabin, he thought for the first time. He had caught plenty of snakes for one day. There'd be more tomorrow and more the day after. Hell, give him a week and he'd have a whole truckload to haul down to Kingsville and sell to the National Toxins Research Center.

Jim Ed stood up in the boat just as the second gun shot went off. The adrenaline rush hit his chest like a busted pipe. He had just started to gather the rope and pull Benjamin toward the boat, but this second shot distracted him. Confused him. He was suddenly disoriented. The boat was now drifting sideways down the river, and the fog had gotten so thick, he wasn't sure which direction was which. He frantically tried to get his bearings. There was another scraping noise underneath the boat and that's when he heard Benjamin's loud yelp. He turned to the back of the boat just as the alligator surfaced a few feet away. Jesus Christ, that sucker had to be twenty feet long! The Internet site said fifteen max in this water, but this was no time to be measuring.

"Benjamin! Benjamin! Get in the boat! In the boat, boy, in!"

Jim Ed began pulling the rope in as fast as he could, trying to drag Benjamin out of the water. Benjamin was now starting to panic. He dog paddled quickly to the back of the boat, but just as Jim Ed was about to yank him out of the water, the alligator opened his jaws and clamped them down firmly around the lower half of his body. Benjamin began howling for dear life, and the commotion stirred up the birds on the banks and in the trees. They all began to caw and screech, and eventually they instigated a cacophony of swamp noise.

Benjamin was now writhing in pain and helplessly kicking his free legs in the air. Completely horrified, Jim Ed grabbed an oar and started punching the nose of the alligator. The boat started rocking and he lost his balance, falling hard into the bottom. He landed squarely on his shoulder and immediately felt a fierce pain deep in the socket, but he was right back up again, tugging at the rope and punching the gator. The gator had Benjamin tightly locked in his jaws, and now it became a tug of war with Jim Ed. The gator tried to turn and go under, almost pulling Jim Ed into the water.

"Benjamin, kick! Kick! Come on, Benjamin, get loose! Kick him hard!" He could hear these words in his throat, but he wasn't certain they were coming out.

Jim Ed lost his balance and fell again. He grabbed onto the edge of the boat, but this time the force of his own weight, along with the power of the gator on the other end of the rope, pulled him into the water. He took the boat with him. It ended up next to him, upside down and twirling around in the current. By the time he surfaced and got his bearings, the oars were already floating down stream. Jim Ed managed to grab one of them. The coolers were now bobbing up and down in the water too. Both were upside down, and the top to one had become askew in the turnover. Snakes started finding their way out.

Jim Ed was coughing and spitting up water, but he continued to pound the gator with the oar. Benjamin was still struggling in the gator's mouth, but the yelping had turned into a paralyzing, haunting plea for mercy. The chorus of the swamp life changed from chaotic clamor and distress to more of a death dirge.

Even though it seemed to Jim Ed like hours passed by, it took less that a minute for the alligator to bite through the rope, free himself and disappear under the water with an already dying Benjamin clutched in his vicious overbite.

Jim Ed's first instinct was to dive into the river after him. But the half dozen cottonmouths that now circled him persuaded him otherwise. Dizzy with fear and shock, he made a mad, desperate swim to the east bank, not wanting to acknowledge, not now not ever, that this fifty feet would be the longest, most agonizing retreat of his life.

* * *

Clinging tightly to the branch of a cypress tree, Jim Ed inched his way hand over hand to a place where a stretch of solid bank was beneath him. The acute pain in his shoulder had turned into to a numbness equally excruciating. When he finally dropped to ground, it was oddly the first time in his life he'd ever set foot in the state of Louisiana. Unbelievable. All those years of growing up in East Texas, and then subsequently spending many months in Arkansas and Mississippi and Oklahoma and a few other states on numerous escapades, and being the explorer and adventure-man that he was, who would've ever thought his first actual arrival onto the rich, black soil of Louisiana would be under such circumstances?

This geographical fact never entered Jim Ed's consciousness, however. Instead, his mind was a blur. He was unfocused, with no sharp edges any more, but with ten times the heartache he'd left Susanna with back at the house. And Jim Ed's silent call for help wasn't silent at all. He was crying at such a primal gut level, the swamp chorus raised its own to that of a hundred-piece bongo drum concerto in an echo chamber. The trees actually shuddered, and moss shimmied in perfect rhythm. Jim Ed had made it safely to ground, but Benjamin was probably still in celestial limbo, somewhere between Jim Ed's new sixty-mile paradise down here on the Sabine River and the ultimate paradise of his new happy hunting grounds up there.

The thought of Benjamin was unbearable to Jim Ed. The only thing that kept his head from either exploding or imploding or both was his concern for Susanna. She had infiltrated every cell in his brain, and she was all the survival motivation he had left in him. He must get home to her. Now. Fast. He must get there and never again leave her, not even to just turn away and look at something she might be looking at, something on the horizon in her future, in their future, that might make her smile again. That might even allow her to forgive him.

* * *

The mile and a half trip back up the east bank was a trek so jaggedly surreal that only God, and his new friend Benjamin, could be fully cognizant of its specifics. They watched together as Jim Ed slashed and clawed and flung his way through the snarls of trees and roots and soggy swampland and quicksand bars that stretched into what seemed like infinity. They watched him swing from branch to branch like the injured yet determined primate that he was, over the spots where the hard ground was too far inland to reach, and over the murky water below that held any number of fatal menaces and show stoppers. They watched, almost amused, as he dodged the dozens upon dozens of copperheads slithering around on the banks and in the trees. These copperheads blended in with the classic tea-brown colored soil, a result of tannic acid produced by all the dead vegetation in this river. Exactly what that Internet site had promised. Funny how, at a time like this, Jim Ed actually recalled that fact, and also another one he'd picked up on that site. That the venom of a copperhead was not as potent as that of a cottonmouth. Which was the reason he had initiated his hunt in the water. Go straight to the good stuff, he had figured. The best, the biggest payoff, regardless of the risk. Always his method.

Jim Ed was only instinctively aware of the feral hogs that snarled at him from the bushes mere yards away from the deep boot tracks he was leaving in the rich Louisiana clay. And even less aware of the friendly frogs and woodpeckers and ducks and warblers that had earlier convinced him his life was near perfect. A snapping turtle snapped at air as Jim Ed splashed past him. This large, half-submerged creature didn't care much for human intrusion, but in Jim Ed's peripheral vision, he was only a big rock. All Jim Ed could think about, obsess about, were two questions that curled around in his brain, intertwined like these knotted and twisted cypress roots he kept tripping over: Was Susanna all right? And if so, how on earth was he going to explain what happened to Benjamin?

He couldn't stop hearing the gunshots in his head. They continued to rattle his senses, a constant hot prodder from behind, a stinging switch on his flank, screams and ultimatums from the crowds on both sides, the mechanical rabbit just barely in sight ahead. He had to go faster. He had to get to Susanna.

What were those gun shots? What had she done? Was this, in fact, just a sick joke she was playing on him? Or was she in real trouble? Was she actually serious this time about turning the gun on herself? Jim Ed mustn't think about that right now. He should just keep running. Running, running for his life that was somewhere inside hers.

* * *

It only took Jim Ed twelve minutes to make it back up to the spot across the river from his property. The Sabine was a good eighty feet wide here, and he could see his little house sitting over there in the trees, exactly as he'd left it. He didn't pay any special attention to how good it looked. How well-constructed, well-designed it was. All this little house represented to him right now was hope. Hope for the next card to fall his way. One time, Mr. Jones, please. Deal the card. The one that will give me my life back.

Jim Ed dove into the river and was halfway across the river before he felt the sting of the jaws clamp into his right calf. He stopped and began to furiously kick with his left boot. Both boots at this point were filled with water and they felt like they weighed a hundred pounds apiece. Jim Ed took in a noseful and immediately began choking and coughing, but continued to kick like a mad bull. He grabbed onto a cypress stump and clung to it desperately as he tried to shake his right leg, all the while continuing to pound it with his left boot. After a few seconds, he felt the grip of teeth loosen on his calf. One last hard kick revealed the big, ugly river rat that had just released himself from Jim Ed's leg. The rat paused and looked Jim Ed straight in the eye, as if to say, 'Just a warning, pal,' then turned and defiantly swam on down the river. Jim Ed had no time for ego-saving stare downs. He took only a second to get his breath, then turned and powered his way to the hallowed Texas bank.

* * *

To say Jim Ed emerged from the river looking like a creature from a first rate movie lagoon was an understatement. Moss clung to his entire body, obscuring the number of places his clothing had been ripped, snagged or torn off completely. Blood and mud, mixed together, formed burgundy-colored patches on his face and hands. But nothing quite covered his being like the aura and aftermath of a near death experience. He had looked it square in the face and it had shaken him to his bones, and he only hoped that death's shadow had now left for good too, left the premises, without any intention of hanging around to teach him one more lesson.

He looked up at the house. Sure was quiet. Yep, too quiet, he tried not to think. He crossed the dock and started moving up the foot path. Will she, please God, will she be on the bed with a book on her chest and a smirk on her face? The Browning automatic lying on the floor next to her? What's going to happen to that smirk when she notices Benjamin isn't tagging along?

Now that Jim Ed was out of the peril of the river, and everything seemed so calm, taking a couple of seconds to gather himself didn't seem like a bad idea. He stopped in the path, closed his eyes and inhaled a few times, then looked up at the house. That's when he saw the glint of light just behind the south corner. Sunlight on something metal. What the hell was that? Not his truck. His truck was in the new carport behind the house. So was the lawn mower, the two Triumphs, the half-constructed hand glider, and all the other tools and equipment.

Jim Ed stepped sideways through the area he had just cleared for a vegetable garden. He could feel his heart still pounding in his chest, like a man accidentally buried alive might pound on the coffin. His head pounded even harder. As he stepped over the far edge of the garden space, the champagne-colored sports utility vehicle came into view. Jim Ed's knees turned to liquid. He melted down onto them with relief. It was Jim Ted's jeep! The jeep with the brand new Performance Ultra Grip Quiet Rides. Jim Ted was here! Oh, dear brother dear brother. The card had been dealt and it had fallen for him. His older and wiser brother Jim Ted was here, and everything was going to be all right.

Jim Ed stayed on his hands and knees, watching blood, sweat and mud drip into a puddle on the ground. Maybe Jim Ted even had an apology prepared, an apology for all those mean things he'd said. That stuff about Jim Ed being worthless. Being the very definition of bad luck and too stupid to even realize it. Maybe Susanna would come around, too. And be loving and understanding again. Loving and understanding enough to forgive him for Benjamin. One more thought of poor Benjamin put Jim Ed over the edge and sent a stream of vomit shooting straight out of his throat. It hit the ground with a splatter and added bulk to the same little puddle, causing it to run downhill between his knees. He caught his breath and wiped his mouth with his sleeve. Okay, Jim Ed, it's show time.

* * *

The brand new porch boards were so perfectly cut, aligned and nailed down that they didn't even creak when Jim Ed stepped up onto them. As he made his way down the porch railing, he finally heard the first sound. Something from inside. It was a low moan. He was immediately relieved. It was unmistakably Susanna. He'd heard that moan, and variations of it, for eight years now. It was definitely Susanna.

Jim Ed couldn't quite wrap his mind around the tone of it, though. It wasn't necessarily a moan of pain, or that of a last breath. It did have some desperation in it. But what kind of desperation? And where was Jim Ted right now? Why hadn't anyone around here even noticed his return?

Jim Ed entered the back door quietly as if someone else was in control of his body now. Someone else who was going to take care of him for a while. An angel, hopefully a good angel. A lucky angel. He moved through the front room without making a noise, then turned toward the bedroom. As he approached, he noticed the Browning leaning against the wall just inside the bedroom door. Without even feeling his last few steps, Jim Ed was suddenly standing inside that bedroom, the one he had built less than two weeks ago.

How had he made it here so quietly? How had he managed to survive the past half hour, and then get all the way up river, up this hill and into this house, and be standing here looking at them without either Susanna or Jim Ted knowing he was even on the premises?

It didn't take very long for all his senses to sharpen again. The first thing he saw clearly was Susanna, of course, lying on the bed, on her back, her legs spread, her pretty bare knees up in the air. The drawstring capris were on the floor, right next to her dog-eared self help paperback. Her eyes were closed, her mouth open, slow moans and whimpers coming out almost rhythmically. Her breathing was quick and gaspy. Enough to make his own stop.

The second thing he saw clearly was Jim Ted. Only the back of his head, of course, since his face was buried between Susanna's legs. He was kneeling at the end of the bed and the muscles in his bare back were tensed. Beads of sweat had formed between his shoulder blades. The burnt orange shirt that Jim Ed had given him last Christmas was in an uncharacteristically careless heap on the floor next to Jim Ted's knee.

Jim Ed had no idea now long he stood there. How long he watched them. He had no idea exactly when his right hand, the one connected to the throbbing arm, reached over and picked up the shotgun. Nor when he lifted the butt end of it to his chest, the barrel pointing straight toward the bed.

He had no idea how long he listened to Susanna's moans and quick breaths, nor how long he watched the back of Jim Ted's head move up and down with such purpose. No idea how much time passed before he finally spoke.

"Susanna?"

She jerked up from the bed. Her big chestnut eyes met his and shot through him like dark honey fired from a cannon. Full of surprise, they were completely void of the bitterness that had filled them at the dock earlier this morning. A little frightened, maybe, but almost free of all that hate. She was still breathing in small, panting bursts. She opened her mouth but the only sound that came out was something that vaguely resembled his name.

His hands started to tremble on the gun barrel.

"Susanna, oh Susanna . . ."

By now, Jim Ted had whipped around and was fixed in horror on Jim Ed. His face was flushed and wet, especially around the mouth. Moisture formed into bubbles at the corners when he tried to speak.

"Jim Ed, I –"

"Shut up, Jim Ted."

"No, please –"

"I said shut up!"

Jim Ed might as well have been looking at his own face. His own blue eyes, the exact same nose, same chin and eyebrows, everything the same with the exception of the tire iron scar on the forehead. Even the exact same frown that, quite frankly, Jim Ted used a whole lot more often than he did. Jim Ed wondered briefly if that's how he looked when he was in the act of pleasing his wife. Surely not. Most certainly not.

Jim Ed's attention now returned to Susanna. Her bewilderment was crumbling into something else. Defeat maybe? Jim Ed wasn't sure.

He tightened his grip around the gun and aimed.

"Jim Ed! No!" Susanna had finally been able to assemble a few words.

He leveled the barrel at her.

"Your dog Benjamin is dead. An alligator ate him."

She barely had time to let out a cry before the blast of the gun hit her. She flew back onto the bed hard and was instantly motionless.

Jim Ted screamed and immediately began to crawl around the end of the bed.

"Jim Ed! No! Wait!"

The gun was already leveled at him before he could raise his hand. Just as Jim Ed pulled the trigger for the second time, Jim Ted's left hand pointed at the opposite corner of the room. His chest exploded and he flew back against the wall with his arm still in the air. He landed in a heap on the floor.

Jim Ed lowered the gun slowly. Tears had started to clean some of the caked mud off his face. The sounds of the swamp rose again and everything went blurry. When he focused again, it was on Jim Ted's left arm on the floor, dead but still outstretched. Finger still pointing. Jim Ed followed it, followed it down the line of the perfectly laid hardwood planks, followed the straight shiny boards to the far corner of the room. And there it was, the East Texas timber rattlesnake. The body of it, anyway. With a bloody stump where the head had been, before being blown off and splattered against the wall.

Jim Ed knew the East Texas timber rattler all too well. The "Don't Tread On Me" snake from the Revolutionary War flag. The Internet had taught him more than he needed to know about this one. Grey background, dark cross bands, tan stripe along its vertebrae. With potent venom, but not as potent as that of the cottonmouth or the copperhead. This kind of rattler could maim you in a heartbeat but probably wouldn't kill you. Less dangerous, also less valuable.

Jim Ed quickly turned back to Susanna on the bed. He threw down the gun and ran to her side. She was covered in blood from chest up, but her legs were still spread. He now saw for the first time her white cotton underwear still in place. And the burnt orange sleeve of Jim Ted's shirt, torn off and tied like a tourniquet around the very top of her leg where it converged with her torso. And the snake bite high on the inside of her thigh. The indention of Jim Ted's mouth print still around it.

Jim Ed wondered for a brief second if his own mouth print would've been identical to Jim Ted's. But no, that would've never happened, because anyone knows that trying to suck the poison out of a snake bite is an old and outdated remedy that's no longer recommended. It doesn't take the Internet to tell you that. What are the odds that both Jim Ted and Susanna didn't know?

Jim Ed fell against the wall and crumbled into a ball.

Somewhere out in the Sabine River, a satiated alligator and a few dozen cottonmouths, even under water, heard a high, tragic, bone-chilling swamp sound like nothing they had ever heard before and would hopefully never hear again. If they were lucky.

Jamie Kornegay

Words May Never Hurt Me

I've spent the better part of my new life in the passenger seat of this bucking doolie, the one with a fine cherry-red finish you can only see when the mud is washed off. The man driving is wanted in several states—and I, as an accessory, in two—so he likes to take it off-road every chance he gets, leaving behind a trail of angry land owners and terrified livestock. The windshield looks like an impressionist's canvas, all smeared up with mud and bug guts. Wherever we're going tonight, I won't be able to walk out of there.

I strayed from the safe path of righteousness and conformity about a month ago when I accepted a hitch from him, Rubarb McElhaney. I have not once in our acquaintance met his eyes, for they're perpetually obscured behind mirror lenses. He smells like groin sweat and woodsmoke, like I imagine pioneers smelled. People cower before him, as if sensing his troublesome nature, for he does not cut an imposing figure, barely as high as his tires and clad solid in denim with sprouts of wrankled, cigarette-smoke hair escaping his crisp Stetson.

He shifts gears with an angry hand and will not discuss our destination. Always we are just driving along and then, in a flash of maniacal inspiration, caught up in some mischief—setting billboards on fire, beating up rest area attendants, scaring stranded motorists with a 12-gauge and a goalie mask—and then we are off just as quickly, red and blue lights diminishing behind us, the bitter taste of menace in our cheeks. It is a taste to which I am yet accustomed and one he must feed like the bloodthirsty vampire.

About tonight, he will only say, "I am ending a grudge."

I am all ajostle by the end of our ride. My neck and shoulders are in bad need of rub.

He parks in the woods, along a wooden fence. There are probably 200 trucks and sports utility vehicles parked in chaotic fashion up, down and around the span. We get out, and I whiz on the mud tires. The world becomes a creaking black forest.

These secret get-togethers of redemption seekers are never held at day, nor in public, he says. To me, the mystery of this is not appealing.

In the distance a man speaks. Over the crunch of our hike, I can't make out a word. The voice is calm and unstuttered. I haven't eaten since last night and hope there will be refreshments. Cold beer maybe. Sausages. Is this too much for a stranger to ask?

As our careful strides carry us closer to the voice in the dark, I divine a weak light in the distance and stupidly point it out to my compatriot, who has crawled inside a hollow log some ways back. I forge ahead, somewhat relieved that he is gone yet nervous of where he'll turn up next. It will be impossible to find him in the bitter pitch. Not a single star shines. Were it not for the light ahead, I would be lost in a maddening blindness.

As I get closer and the light grows, I can just make out mingling human forms. The action is still a blur, but I swear I see a clown marching around on stilts. It's lucky spotting this humanity, all hunkered and shifting under a pavilion, listening to a man talk forthrightly—a minister, a politician? Creeping up on the periphery, I encounter another man leaking on a pine. I startle him, and he farts. I laugh and keep moving.

My eyes scan the crowd, sitting tight together in what looks to be an old barn with no sides, and similarly the men along the outskirts study me. I return their nods, their curious glances. They are all men, not a woman in sight, and they are all several years older than me. I am made to feel both welcome and unwelcome, but such is the suspicious nature of close-knit social groups. I relish my outsider status none the less.

Quite frankly, I'm on the make for fried meat. A beer, some tacos. It doesn't matter much. Chips and store-dip will suffice. And there, on the back of several pick-ups, are the remains of a spread. Big tin foil pans with various lingering juices and crumpled napkins. In one there is a stray wiener, a little too black, which I swallow whole and remember someone who once tried to convince me that a wiener is cooked and until then it is but a wienie. I nab a couple of dill spears before an old man in an apron snatches the jar and screws the lid on and takes it away. I wipe my hands on the seat of my pants.

The voice I'd heard previously comes from a scarecrow of a man trapped in jeans and flannel too large for him. Under the barn's bright hanging bulb, he paces and relates tales of his father's brutality and how, later in life, he appreciates it, though at the time, his mind still unformed, it seemed cruel and unwarranted. Then he sits down and the men clap and shift in their lawn chairs and on their hay bales. Another man gets up, a coach of some local team, and begins delivering a pep talk, making excuses for last season and forecasting better prospects for the coming year.

I stand under a spotlight before the famished truck beds and watch the proceedings and the men around me. It smells of pine needles and tamale butane. There are equine beasts moving in the shadows of the stable behind the coach. I am dizzy by the subtle action.

"Where's the clown?" I ask a nearby man teething boiled peanuts.

"Do what?"

"Has he left?"

"Ain't been no clowns," wheezed the man, peanut steam venting from his lips. "Feller played the banjo while ago."

I have some musical proficiency, but only on instruments that require me to be seated, I explain to the man. The sliding Dobro goes either way, of course. It's in the truck, but the hay is too dry to risk a spark from the rusty strings. My mind flashes back to Barny Suds, a ridiculous drive-thru beer store shaped like a barn, where they only sold hot beer due to some antiquated local ordinance. Upon learning this, Rubarb damned the barn and the town and pounced on the thick, back-talking attendant, then set the barn on fire. As flames climbed into the rafters, he made me take twenty cases while he filled the truckbed with sacks of looted ice.

"Who're your people?" the peanut-eater belches.

My parents are retired. They ran me off with their middle-America values. One worked himself mad for a kitchenware company, always in futile pursuit of the better loaf pan; the other produced a series of audio cassettes on bird and fish mimicry. Today they sit during daylight on Naugahyde couches drinking protein beverages and trading word jumbles. They argue about the miscreants on daytime TV and plan vacations they'll never take.

He says the Lord will help me find my way back home, and I tell him I doubt it. I try to explain that I'm just here with a friend to help settle a grudge.

"Friends are good," he replies.

I step back from the small talk and admire the trees. They rise up like columns into the blanket night, their tops invisible. The stars are asleep. Mules bray in rally with the repentant coach, and I am wary that Rubarb may be lurking in the stagnant night.

Coach wraps up his talk and would-be ministers scramble over themselves to reach the pulpit where increasingly innocuous jokes are related, tales of humble folks stumbling along the path of righteousness. They wash over me, not half the jokes Rubarb has told over the weeks, jokes so vile and hilarious they made me, an unrepentant runaway teen, turn a startled crimson.

"There's nothing funny about this!" my mind screams. "These are weak people doing the best they can for chrissakes!"

The men turn and look. Good Lord, I've really hollered it.

A tall, official-looking gentleman in black polyester grabs my arm forcefully, relaxing his grip almost immediately.

"Who brought you here?" he asks in a fried catfish whisper.

I lick my lips. "I was lost in the woods," I tell him. "I'm starving."

He leads me to a cauldron of simmering potlikker and offers a straw. I slurp the gamey broth as he rubs my deltoids.

"Brother Mayes," he whispers. "What's yourn?"

"I'm embarrassed to say," I say, rising from the brine.

"Taint nothin to be shamed of out here. This is a friendly gatherin."

"I lost my friend in the woods," I confess. "He went after a squirrel and got sucked into a log."

"Who is he?"

"Who, hoo-hoo-hoo," I call. It's an owl impression I picked up from my mother. It's dead-solid perfect. Some of the joke-listeners crane their necks toward the wilderness.

The man is doing math in his eyes. I am seized by a cruel desire to spit soup at him, but it's too fine, too substantive.

"How many animals's lives went into this?' I ask him, nodding at the cauldron.

"Just a few," he says. "You'll have to contribute to the fund unless you tell me how you got here."

I despise this incessant need for evidence, yet the game has me feeling good, so I confess. "Rubarb McElhaney brought me."

The man considers this, kneading his jaw like a ball of dough. He takes me by the collar and walks me around behind the pavilion, near the stables, where the equine shapes sniffle and stamp, and the anecdotes deplete into mumbles as we get farther away. He leans me against the clapboard, then turns his back to me and unfastens his trousers, drops them to the ground, and waits for his anemic trickle to rise. In the meantime I consider his bare, drooping ass, full of myriad cracks and fissures like a busted windshield, and I lament my future. Not just the physical wears of age, but the fear of getting further from what matters, further from truth and empathy, so far you have to come to a pavilion in the woods at night, hustle strangers for their names and acquaintances. He finishes his business and bends to pull up his trousers, then I catch a glimpse of what Jonah must have seen in that turgid sea. It upsets my sloshing guts.

The man puts his hand on my shoulder. He doesn't ask my name again, and I don't remember his, though I guess it's Burgher.

"You should know why he brought you here," Burgher says.

"Is there beer around, or only sodas?" I inquire.

"Has he cursed you yet?"

"Do what?"

"He will. He's mean. Got a wicked tongue."

"I don't know him all that well. Said he'd give me a lift into town after we made some stops. That was last month."

"Well, this is one stop he shouldn't never have made."

He leans in, his nose brushing against my ear, and I spin away, but he sticks with me like a boxer.

"Put a curse on Polie, he did," Burgher says. "Said something to him one time that embarrassed hell in him. It's mortal sin just to think it."

"Who's Polie?"

"Polie Richards, givin this here get-together. It's a friendly gatherin. Supposed to be anyhow. Polie finds out he's here . . ."

"What'd he do, tell him a dirty joke or something?"

"What's the vilest thing you ever heard?"

I think about this. When I was a baby, my parents put on a Richard Pryor album every night, hoping the conversation would lull me to sleep. My first word was pussy. I like to think I've heard everything, that words may never hurt me.

"You ain't heard nothing like what Rubarb said," whispers the man. "Touched Polie to the fire with those words. He ain't been the same since."

"What about you then?" I ask. "What's the worst you've heard?"

"Polie never told me. He's too good a man."

"Where is this goddamned Polie?"

Burgher leads me back around to the scene of comedy, which has now shifted to a demonstration on pitching horseshoes. After a few trick throws by a pair of elderly twins in overalls and tennis shoes, the scarecrow figure from earlier reappears, his eyes red as if he's been weeping. He brings the applause down by stretching his arms out and lowering them. Like a well-trained orchestra, the crowd decrescendos.

He nestles into the hay-strewn pulpit.

"Gentlemen, I want to thank you all for coming this evening. You are the finest men I know, and therefore I have asked you to convene with me here tonight because I have a confession to make to you all."

The barn grows still and quiet. Even the runners, hiding the remnants of the truck bed feast, stop to listen. I don't know about them, but I'm hoping he has a heinous crime to share, or marital shame with loads of spicy detail.

"I'm scared. Fearful! The world is crumbling around us. Our leaders are going insane. Nations are falling, divided by bloodshed. Our mothers and wives are tripped out on booze and pills. Negroes are the only ones they'll let make music. Heathens are fornicating in department store dressing rooms. Our children are being issued firearms at school. You can't go out in public without fear of being shot from a bell tower or set ablaze by flame-throwing bank robbers on the lam. And that's not all. It was ninety-five degrees today, in the dead of November! The seas are roiling, turning black from disease. The earth has leapt its orbit and is careening into the sun, something the newsfolk won't tell us. I know because I've got a meteorologist friend who's in on the cover-up."

The men gasp and stroke their chins nervously, some bravely, others relieved that their time may be drawing near. Their sudden, concerned rectitude disgusts me. My mind unreels its own sermon, and I can't help but shout out, "Listen to you, blaming your children for carrying out what you started, the society you raised out of your vast depression!"

"Ho now, nobody's blaming anybody. This is a friendly gathering!" Polie cries. "Who goes there, anyhow? Who invited you, son?"

"Rubarb McElhaney!" I shout with pride, and the old men set to ruminating. Several of them scamper off, followed by the distant sound of cranking trucks.

"I see."

In an effort to save the evening, Polie changes gears and divvies up the party favors, electing a few front-row men to help pass them out. Long-distance phone cards and pencils for everyone. A sheetcake as big as a car hood is wheeled out. 'To All My Friends, Happy Life' is written in blue icing, hemmed in with pink roses.

The men attack the cake, and in the maelstrom, Polie scampers over to me and my escort. From a distance, Polie looks like a scarecrow. Up close, he has the soft, dignified hue of an ill celebrity. I figure he'll ask my name, and I'm feverishly dreaming up an alias.

"Is Rubarb here?" he asks. There is no anger, only a sliver of embarrassed anxiety.

"Not at the moment."

"How is he?"

"He is very tired."

"I suppose the end is near for both of us."

Something clicks at this mention, and I start to see what's going on, and it may be out of some subconscious concern for this man's life that I relate to Polie my past several weeks with Rubarb, how our trail has been decided by old scores in need of settling. The bull-whippings, the hair-pullings, the brake-tampering and hot-greasings. I watched a man being tied down and smeared with jelly on a fire ant bed, and overheard a possible castration, though I'm not certain, for I was occupied in the adjacent bathroom stall. He even cut one man's vacant summer cabin into quarters with a chainsaw, a careful procedure that took him about six and a half hours. All the clues suggest a man putting his business in order before the end.

"Well," Polie replies, "it's good he's settling down. I only hope he can repent before he's delivered to the grave."

I open my mouth to suggest a gun duel, but instead ask, "Why do you hate him so?"

"I hate no one," he replies, then folds, all at once. He shudders, as if he is crying from the neck down.

"I loved Rubarb like a brother, I did," he says in a cracked whimper. "But now I hate him. Okay, I do. And I will spend what's left of my life paying for that, and not only that. I must also live with the voice of a demon that echoes in my head. He poisoned my heart, young man who wishes to remain nameless. He polluted my soul with one sentence, spoken in jest, I presume, though I cannot imagine what sort of person could dream up such a sentiment. Only the devil. Only a rare enemy."

"He likes you," I lie. "Maybe he came here to make peace with you."

He pleads like a child to me, clutching my shirt. "I have bathed in the scriptures. I have shouted praise until my throat bleeds and my eardrums burst. I have begged forgiveness from God, but the curse on Him that resounds in my skull is too sharp for even Him to touch."

He stares at me, and I see it in his eyes, that he's about to say the one thing that will freak me out completely. He's going to spill it. He's going to poison me.

Instead he lets go of my shirt and runs to the hay. On a bale rests an electric guitar rig, which he snatches up and strikes a violent chord.

"Alright, we're gonna have our sing-a-long now!" he yells, and launches into an upbeat and frankly bitching version of "Victory in Jesus." He yowls and thrashes as cake tumbles from their jowls. In the middle of the third verse, he calls for his fiddlers and pickers, who are scattered among the crowd. They scurry up front and grab their instruments and file in one at a time. By the last few bars, it's a glorious noise.

They bring the song to a rousing finale, and a smattering of confused applause rises around the barn. The mules shuffle between the slats.

"This is an original! It's called 'I Hear You Ringin But You Can't Come In,'" Polie announces, then rips into a difficult figure. There's anger in his strum, something of the young and hungry Chuck Berry. His eyes ravish the fools at his side.

"It's in E minor, goddammit—and put some pepper on it!" he yells to the players, who have only modest talent and so fumble over themselves to create ordered noise. It sounds like a child's jamboree.

Polie belts out his homemade lyrics:

Heresy and harlotry
are hiding in the hearth for me;
Uh-huh ... Lord please gotta pick up—
Buggery and skullduggery
never made a fugue to me;
Nuh-uh ... Lordy, please pick up!

Polie's eyes roll back in his head and he struts around, then strokes out a killer rockabilly solo and the boys finally pick up. It's rocking along so well I get out and scoot around in the hay a bit, waggle my hips. I do a few Presley turns that seem to spark delight. Polie, meanwhile, leaps atop the picnic table and kneels in the cake, just wailing away on the guitar. I consider running after my Dobro, but then realize it would be a selfish gesture. There's no escaping this moment.

We plead for another verse, and Polie doesn't disappoint:

Don't know no song, know no pray'r
can help stave off the devil's doomsayer
Nuh-uh ... Lord take my call —
A fiery tongue spake hell to me
And now my brain's been burned by blasphemy
Uh-huh ... For eternity!

Polie gestures to the fiddler, who steps in without missing a beat and screeches out a solo. He's a young cat, though, and gets indulgent, loses himself in his own syncopation. The harp player steps up and toots him out of the way. Several of the old ones dance a fine jig as the banjo player picks his way forward, frolicking up and down the fretboard, all apluck with twinkling fingers. Polie grinds against the amplifier, teasing out feedback. He turns around with a great, broad grin on his face and pink frosting on his shins. The old boys are transformed into blathering heathens.

Caught up in the spirit, Polie screams in a rock-n-roll falsetto, "Connect me to my La-hord!" a couple of times in rhythm, then raises his guitar over his head and smashes it down on the picnic table top. It shorts out and sparks fly from the amplifier. The spotlights go down and the haybales go up as if they were doused with diesel. I run to let the beasts out, rip down chickenwire, and a fleet of thankful mules scurry forth. A minute longer and they'd have been cooked. Then I turn to pull out Polie and the fiddler, still in the throes of his bitching solo.

"Song's over," I yell, and with that we careen into the night of topless trees and old rot-gut gas and grudges that are never forgiven. We roll and roll and roll, laughing like kids the whole way. The flames billow and the last image I see before passing out is a volunteer fireman with a sore prostate stumbling out of his sweaty dream.

I wake up the next morning caked in dust and soot, sprawled out in somebody's driveway. My head is throbbing. I'm hungover from my spiritual high, beside a brown house in the woods. Who lives here I haven't a clue. The sky is morning lavender. The birds and squirrels are chirping their forgiveness. The pine trees have heads now, but just barely, through the haze.

The forest coughs up Rubarb, who walks up waving his hand in front of his face, as if to say, 'Who farted?'

We all did.

"Where the hell have you been?" I ask.

"Be polite," he answers. "Is there beer around, or just stinking sodas?"

He reaches into the beds of pick-ups, but there are only empty cans and pine straw and old tires. He is parched, like these scorched woods. I offer to take him inside where surely there is someone who is either thinking or will think very soon of breakfast. He tells me I look like a savage, and offers to beat the dust out of my vest with me in it.

"I'm beginning to think you really are the devil," I propose.

He puts down on the tailgate of a pick-up, and I can't believe it when he takes his shades off and rubs his eyes. I hear a storm door's distinct screech. Polie appears from the house in a long flannel night shirt. He looks about ten years older.

Polie walks over silently, his pristine feet gathering dirt.

"You're gonna need bleach for them nice socks," I whisper, desperate to add my two bits.

It must have been years since these two last saw one another up close. Polie considers his old acquaintance, who sits with threadbare resolve on the tailgate. His hair is a nest of pine needles and bark. His chest heaves so it tuckers him, his mouth quivers and strains to keep his breath from seeping out. His eyes are pale, the ire bled from them long ago. Whatever hell had kept him going in his youth, it has been subsumed by the contents of countless bottles. Whatever trust he once held had diminished every time someone turned their back to him.

Polie's eyes swell up and quietly sprinkle. He sits beside Rubarb and runs twig fingers through his old friend's smoky hair, massaging his mush scalp, searching for wood ticks, which he says are hell this year.

George Singleton

What If We Leave?

It would be easier to explain past breathalyzers, and littering, and obstructing justice charges to the local television station than it would be for me to admit what we did to sad, blind—though beautiful and tanned—Mrs. Swift. I wouldn't even tell a therapist, the first time around. Mrs. Swift lived behind my parents' house, and thus my house, in the late 1970s, and she and her childless husband built a swimming pool back there.

Every afternoon, between about one and five o'clock from mid-March until late-October, she toddled her long white cane out to one of those green woven and aluminum lounge chairs, stretched out, and sunbathed. She wore those extra-large sunglasses, like regular blind people always sport. What blind person cared about a suntan? I thought even back then at the age of thirteen. Who told her that a white woman needed to have some color to her skin in order to stand out at a dinner party? Wasn't being blind enough? Mrs. Swift, I'm sure, stood out from everyone else when she showed up clanking her cane against end tables and lamp stands, half of her face covered in a way that suggested opthamological dilation, or the rare afternoon of witnessing a solar eclipse.

Mrs. Swift didn't keep a wind-up alarm clock beside her chair. More than once, though, I took note of when she flipped over from stomach to back, then back to stomach. She had one of those internal clocks, I guessed, that told her when thirty minutes was up. Not that I was ever a perfectionist, but I used a stop watch to make sure that she, indeed, turned better than barbecued rotisserie chicken at the local Piggly-Wiggly.

Anyway, I watched her endlessly through the largest crack in our cedar plank fence. Later on I figured that my father kicked himself for going to such an expense for privacy, only to have a blind woman move in behind us. Mrs. Swift stood five-ten at least, wore a pink rubber bathing cap at all times outdoors, and had the body of one of those large-chested beauties on Hee-Haw. My father never talked about her, but more than once I noticed how, on Saturdays and Sundays, he found ways to slowly pull crabgrass and weeds back there at the base of our fence. Me, I possessed Mrs. Swift all summer long while my mother and father worked their respective first-shift jobs—Mom at the hospital as a nurse, and Dad at Graywood Mills trying to come up with new and better fabrics.

She wore a flesh-colored one-piece bathing suit every day. I wondered if Mr. Swift knew how naked she could appear from a half-acre away, viewed through a one-inch crack between eight-foot-high one-by-sixes. He wasn't blind at all. He was a barrel-chested man who owned a sand and gravel company. Word was that he used to own a lye-making factory that Mrs. Swift worked for him, and that's where she got blinded. Word was she got her tits stuck in a steering wheel one time, and wrecked, and that windshield glass punctured her eyeballs in a way that made her a walking kaleidoscope.

"We're trying to come up with a fabric that'll never stretch or shrink at all, and we're trying to come up with a cotton fiber that'll easily expand or contract up to six sizes on men's pants," my father said at one time or another during every dinner conversation.

"It's a lot harder than it sounds. Rubber—if we made rubber fabric—we could do that. But what would rubber clothes do to a normal human being, I ask you."

My mother never looked up from her Chicken Buenos Noches!, a dish that she made up herself and served about five nights a week. She always said, "For women, it would give them yeast infections. For scuba divers it'd be perfect."

"You goddamn right," my father would say. "And not everyone's a woman or scuba diver. Or lady scuba diver."

Then we'd look back down. I'd drink my milk and pretend that spicy food didn't bother my esophagus. I was an only child who spent his day thinking up what excuses I could use when my father or mother asked how I spent my day. As far as they were concerned, I pretty much read all of O. Henry's stories before I went to eighth grade, and kept a collection of model airplanes hidden beneath my bed. My best friend Andy Agardy—the only Hungarian in Graywood—and I spent all day perfecting our chess acumen, from what my parents knew.

"We can't seem to get a decent phlebotomist from the technical college," my mother said inevitably. "I'm having to show girls veins, once, twice an hour. It's as if the only thing they're teaching in schools these days is sponge baths."

Sometimes at dinner I would think that I felt a splinter stuck in my eyebrow from staring at Mrs. Swift so long. Sometimes when a twitch took off in my eyelid I daydreamed about winking at Mrs. Swift, and that she winked back even though she couldn't see.

"Next year you need to go get a job," my father said this particular summer toward the end of every meal. "I don't know what the legal age is for social security cards, but it's time. Fourteen's when I got my first job. Well, hell, actually I was five when I got my first job, but it wasn't for real, you know. My father had me out there selling his cantaloupes and watermelons. We went door-to-door down to the rich people in Columbia, people who didn't have to keep gardens or know directions to the farmer's market."

Chicken Buenos Noches! wasn't anything more than boiled breasts, thighs, and legs slathered with paprika and jalapenos. It went well, my mother always contended, with rice, mashed potatoes, macaroni and cheese, turnip greens, Brussels sprouts, beets, stewed tomatoes, or—on special occasions—jellied cranberry sauce. I always said that I thought so, too.

"I shouldn't complain," my father ended every dinner conversation. "If no one lost or gained weight they wouldn't have to go buy new clothes to cover their bodies. At least I'm not trying to work up new fabric at a nudist colony out there in those nudist colony places. Hell, the only thing those people would need would be flesh-colored, I guess."

At this point I should've told myself, "Uh-oh. Get that thought out of your head, get that thought out of your head." It was as if my father wanted me to think up a trick on Mrs. Swift.

Dad wore a crewcut his entire life. He wore seersucker shirts and khaki pants when we went on vacations to Myrtle Beach. Both of my parents believed that anything in the house out of place might tilt the Earth one way or the other. My mother's spice shelf always stayed in alphabetical order, as did my father's tools. Melvil Dewey himself would've been ashamed of his decimal system had he met my folks.

Unfortunately, I'm now able to admit, they never took the time to make sure I hadn't misplaced any of the various Magic Markers that they bought me as a set, after I made an A in seventh grade art class. I don't want to sound the victim, but I'm sure that if my parents catalogued my possessions and kept track of what I actually did with them, I wouldn't be the mean, guilt-ridden, ex-pervert that I am today.

* * *

Andy Agardy came over one mid-June day at five after nine in the morning. My mother and father had left for work thirty minutes earlier, as had Mr. Swift. I had already taken to my spot in the backyard, even though it would be another four hours before Mrs. Swift appeared. This occurred daily for the rest of the summer. It seemed logically possible to me that, for some unknown reason, she might decide to change her routine, and I didn't want to miss it. What did she do in the mornings anyway? I wondered. What could be so important? Maybe she painted her toenails, or listened to the TV set. Maybe she had Braille books in her house, and read about skin cancer.

"Hey, Louis," Andy Agardy said after he snuck up. "What're you doing out here?"

I jumped. I hadn't told Andy about Mrs. Swift's routine, and up until this point in the summer had told him that I couldn't leave the house from one until five because my parents expected some phone calls. "Keep it down," I said, and stuck my index finger to my lips.

Andy looked through the second-best crack in the fencing. He said, "What're you looking at?" I sat down on the ground and told him everything about Mrs. Swift's daily sunbath. Andy said, "Word is she lost her eyesight when she found her first husband doing it to her own sister. This was back when she lived in California. She used to work as a stewardess, after she quit being a movie star."

I looked back through my crack and said, "That's not the truth. She was never a movie star. When she lived in California she worked for Walt Disney himself, as some kind of advisor."

Andy looked through his crack and said, "Is that the bathing suit she wears?" He pointed. I'd been so enamored with the sliding glass door from which she always appeared that I'd not noticed the clothes line, and that her bathing suit dried there amidst blouses, Mr. Swift's blue pants, and some T-shirts.

I shifted to Andy's crack and looked. "Yeah, that's it. That's what she wears. I swear to God she looks almost naked if you squint your eyes enough."

We must've stared at her limp one-piece for fifteen minutes in silence. Andy said, "She doesn't walk out here naked and put it on, does she?"

"No," I said. "No. I've never seen her even walk past the pool. She just lies out in the sun, and turns over. That's it."

Andy said, "Hey, I got this idea." He stood up. "You're sure she's blind, right?"

I said, "Uh-huh."

"Watch this," he said, and took off out of the side gate. I looked through the crack in the fence and saw him tiptoe into Mrs. Swift's backyard. He didn't turn and look at her house until he reached the clothes line. Then, slowly, he uneased the wooden clothespins to her bathing suit, draped it across his left forearm, and began running back over. I watched the sliding glass door most of the last part of this escapade, certain that Mrs. Swift would regain her eyesight and nab him.

I took off running for the inside of my own house, as a matter of fact. When Andy Agardy came in he laughed and said, “Maybe she’ll go out there and accidentally put on one of those T-shirts, and be naked down on the bottom.” He sniffed her one-piece, then placed it on my parents kitchen table, where we ate our Chicken Buenos Noches!

I said, “You have to take it back. This is too mean. She’s a blind woman.”

Andy shook his head. “You have to take it back. I got it, Louis. If you want to be in the club, you take it back. Hey, do y’all have a camera? We should take pictures of us doing crazy things like this. That’ll be funny. I could take a picture of you putting it back”

I didn’t ask what club. And I had a camera of my own that my father won for saving his company something like a million dollars with an idea he had for saving the company money. The previous year, he got a pocket watch, but he gave that to my mother.

I don’t think he won that set of Magic Markers, but for some reason I found it necessary to go unearth the cardboard box in which they came, bring them to the kitchen table, and draw perfectly circular brown nipples and V-shaped black pubic hair on Mrs. Swift’s flesh-colored one-piece bathing suit.

I did. And when I was done I said to Andy Agardy, “Oh, I’m in the club. Let’s see what you can do to top that.”

I don’t think he ever closed his mouth. He shook his head, and didn’t blink. “You’re going to Hell, Louis,” he said. “I won’t tell anyone. Unless they ask.” And then he took off running for home.

If I’d’ve thought things through I would’ve gotten on my bicycle with Mrs. Swift’s bathing suit and thrown it in a Dempsey dumpster behind the Quik-Way convenience store. Or I would’ve buried it in the woods back behind our subdivision. But I panicked. Before my Magic Marker pornography had time to dry well I carried it back over to the Swift’s house, and stuck it back on the line. I averted my eyes from their back porch. If caught, I planned on saying how our dog must've drug it over. We didn't have a dog at the time, but I figured that Mrs. Swift wouldn't know the difference.

It wouldn't be long before I howled at night anyway.

* * *

The few times I've told this story—outside of when I had to explain it to my parents, Mr. and Mrs. Swift, and this overeager child psychologist—every damn person thought I would be stupid enough to take photographs of blind Mrs. Swift, fake-nude, then run the roll of film over to a Jack Rabbit, Eckerd's One Hour, or wherever. Then, upon development, the processor there would call the authorities, and when I came in to get my 3X5 glossies a cop would jump out from behind the counter and arrest me. I wasn't stupid. I went to the library and checked out a number of books on photography and so on. I planned on making straight As in eighth grade, then asking my parents for a film tray, chemicals, an enlarger, and paper. I planned on promising my father straight As and a washed car weekly for the rest of my life if he would convert our basement into a personal darkroom. Meanwhile I stored the completed rolls in my hollowed-out O. Henry book.

Mrs. Swift, indeed, went outside and gathered her dry clothes that first day. She went back inside and returned wearing her graffitied one-piece, and looked as naked as any celebrity photographed from afar on a French nude beach. I took pictures through the crack in the fence for a while. Then I got out my father's step ladder, stood on the last step before the Danger! sign, and took unobstructed shots. I turned the camera sideways, then off-kilter. I changed the shutter speed to get ghostly effects. I saved up my allowance, and bought both color and black-and-white rolls of 35 millimeter film.

If I didn't get the darkroom I wanted, I figured, I could hold off until my junior year in high school, where I could volunteer for the yearbook, and get free use of the tiny art department's dark room. Then I could go in there after hours, develop Mrs. Swift, and somehow get a commendation for the hardest working yearbook staff member of all time.

I never thought about how Mrs. Swift might go check the mailbox. What blind person worries over mail? I never thought about how she might wander into the front yard, and how every housewife up and down Calhoun Lane might look out their front windows daily—either expecting or dreading salesmen and Jehovah's Witnesses—and see her fake naked self slowly edging down the driveway. I'm sure that, being tolerant folks that surrounded us, they gave her three chances before finally calling the sheriff's department to report indecent exposure from a blind woman. And I'm sure the sheriff's deputies gave Mrs. Swift about three times, and that they, too, took photographs for evidence.

Listen, if you put dark glasses on Eve herself, then took away the fig leaf—that's how beautiful Mrs. Swift looked. I don't want to brag any about the drawn-on figures on her suit, but it proved that I deserved that A in art class, plus another in geometry.

"Our neighbor got arrested today," my mother said to my father right before the Fourth of July. "June Chandler called me up at work to see if I left the iron on. She said that fire trucks, and county cops came by."

My father took off his clip-on tie. "Which neighbor? That peckerhead who runs the sand and gravel joint?"

"His wife," my mother said. "His blind wife. She was walking around naked in the front yard, from what I heard. June Chandler said that she was drunk, and not wearing a stitch of clothes. Word is she's been senile for more than a few years. Word is she might be the youngest woman in the history of medicine to go senile, and that Hollywood's thinking about doing a movie about her life, just like *The Three Faces of Eve*. And she was doing cartwheels."

My father went to the cupboard and pulled down a bottle of Jim Beam. He said, "Why would a blind woman do cartwheels? Turn on Walter Cronkite, Louis. Maybe scientists have found a cure for blindness." I raised my shoulders high to see if my hair touched them yet. I raised my eyebrows.

I said, "I didn't see anything. I don't know anything about Mrs. Swift walking around her backyard naked. Y'all know her better than I do. I don't know anything about it." I felt like I might cry, and I could feel my face turn red—a sure sign of when I lied to my parents.

My father looked out the den window and said, "I thought you said she was in the front yard. Hey, why is the ladder set up against the fence?"

I wouldn't have known exactly how things turned out with the Graywood County sheriff's department deputies had my father not, finally, gone over to Mr. Swift's house to say that he had a good lawyer friend in case the Swifts needed one. I'm not sure what conversation took place between those two men, but the next thing you know here come the Swifts over for cocktails. These people had been living behind us without either party ever making an attempt to act neighborly. Now, because of me, my mother got out her fancy crystal glasses and a blender. She made up some concoction called Tequila Buenos Noches! which involved limes, salt, and everything else required for what most sane people called a plain margarita.

Mrs. Swift came over wearing a backless sun dress. She didn't have her cane with her, and relied solely on her husband's elbow. He wore a bow tie.

I watched all of this from the cracked hallway door. I'd told my parents that I needed to work on a model airplane that night because my tube of glue was about to expire. A half-hour into their visit I heard Mr. Swift say, "It was the damnedest thing, Lou," to my father. "Evidently I left a pen in my pocket from work, and the way the ink washed out in the machine it came out looking just like nipples and pubic hair. How could Evelyn know? She's blind as a bat."

My father, who never cussed in the house, said, "Shit. Damn it to hell. Nipples and a wedge."

"I'm so sorry that we didn't meet earlier," Mrs. Swift said. "I've just found that I make people too uncomfortable.

No one knows how to act around the blind. When I go into town I can hear people in wheelchairs trying to roll away from me." She laughed in two short spurts, like a tugboat leaving the harbor.

My father and Mr. Swift went out in the back yard to smoke cigars. My mother said, "You know, I guess if we could educate people at an early age, they wouldn't be scared of people with limitations. Louis! Louis, come in here, please and meet Mrs. Swift."

I waited for what would be a normal time for me to get from my bedroom to the hallway door, then entered. Mrs. Swift had her naked back to me. She wore those big sunglasses. I said, "Yes ma'am?" to my mom.

Mrs. Swift held up her left hand. "I've already met your son indirectly," she said. My mother looked at Mrs. Swift, then back to me. It took seventy-five minutes for all of this to occur, it seemed. "In the afternoons when I take my sun, I am always aware of a cologne coming across the breeze. I believe it's British Sterling. One time I was at Belk's walking through the men's cologne section, and I smelled this particular brand and asked the saleslady what it was. British Sterling."

I didn't shave yet, of course. But I was known to fog up a room with British Sterling, Brut, and/or Old Spice. Aqua Velva. Williams 'Lectric Shave. I said, "Hello."

My mother made the proper introductions. Mrs. Swift said, "Yes, that's the smell. Have you been spying on me when I take sun, Louis? If you have, I must commend you on your stealth. Usually I can hear the slightest movement within a hundred yards." She cocked her head. "Did you hear that ladybug fly by just now over on the other side of our lot?"

I looked out the window, like an idiot. This time my mother joined Mrs. Swift in two short pulls from their tugboat horn laughs. Seals from the zoo in Columbia probably perked up. Geese probably U-turned going north.

My father and Mr. Swift came inside. "This is my boy, Louis," my father said. He pointed at me. "Louis, shake hands with Mr. Swift."

I started to do so—and was glad that the subject got changed—when Mrs. Swift said, "On weekends I smell that cigar wafting over our way, too."

The doorbell rang, my mother went to get it, and then Andy Agardy came slumping in as if he'd carried a bag of rocks over. He said, "Hey, Louis, you want to go catch some bats tonight?" He looked over at Mrs. Swift and pulled the tendons in his neck tight. My mother, I think, started making introductions again, I don't know.

Maybe I had seen too many *Candid Camera* episodes as a child. That program can make an entire nation wary, I'll go on record as saying. With the Swifts over all of a sudden, and Andy showing up—with Mrs. Swift recognizing my after shave and my father's brand of cigar—I knew that a giant practical joke was being played on me. So I went ahead and blurted out, "You didn't have an ink pen go through the washing machine. I painted those things on Mrs. Swift's bathing suit, and y'all know it. Y'all know I know it, and I know y'all know it. So the joke's on you. Ha-ha." I did a good impression of Mrs. Swift's laugh. "Ha-ha."

Andy Agardy left when my father said it was time for him to go home. Mr. Swift stared at me in a way that could make wet cement flow back up a truck's trough. My mother went into the kitchen, and Mrs. Swift said, "I bet I know what Louis was doing on the other side of that fence every afternoon. That'll make you go blind, you know."

I didn't laugh. A noise came out of my throat, but it could never have been taken for laughter.

* * *

My second wife doesn't believe this entire story. She says that a book came out about that same time wherein parents were encouraged to test their children, to out-and-out play tricks on them.

"It was called *What If We Leave?* Louis. My parents had the same book. They used to fake splitting up all the time. The next day, they'd be giving each other shoulder rubs and asking me which babysitter I liked most so they could go out on a date."

Claudia and I sat in Tryon's new Korean restaurant, waiting for our friends, Drayton and Louise. Dray and I used to work together for a fundraising organization. He quit when he got diagnosed with diabetes, and when he couldn't get workman's comp. Dray felt sure that he'd contracted the disease as a result of eating too many pecan logs, World Famous Chocolate bars, and Blo-Pops that we sold to high school glee clubs, pep clubs, PTAs, church youth groups, and Shriners.

I said to Claudia, "This kimchi stuff isn't so bad with the right beer. What is it again?"

The eighteen-year-old white waitress had brought it out and said, "Now this is kind of like salsa in a Mexican restaurant, but you don't eat it with chips." She leaned down and said, "From what I understand, this is really the only real Korean food here. It's complimentary." She put down tear-apart chopsticks. "So are the fortune cookies."

"Pickled cabbage," my wife said. "I don't think you want to eat much anymore. It'll kill you."

We'd been there a good hour. Claudia asked to change seats right away so she could look out of the plate glass window to see if Dray and Louise passed the restaurant by accident. She said, "Sometimes with diabetes in the advanced stages, a person will lose his eyesight."

That's what got the whole Mrs. Swift-and-her-special-bathing-suit story started. Claudia and I hadn't been married six months yet. We had both thrown up our hands and gone to a justice of the peace before knowing each other, more than likely, as well as we should've. Claudia's first husband left her one day when he decided that he wanted to live off of the land. On a houseboat with his secretary. I'd been divorced for six years. Claudia worked as a cheerleading coach at Polk County High, they needed giant lollipops, I came in at lunch time, and we married four months later.

The waitress came up and said, "Y'all still waiting on your friends?" She wore a high school graduation ring on her index finger and another one on a chain around her neck.

I said, "They'll be here." We sat at a four-top and, because it was a new restaurant, prospective diners waited in the small, Pier One Import-inspired lobby.

"Would y'all like to order an appetizer? We got boneless spare ribs on special. We got crab rangoons and shrimp toast."

I pointed at the kimchi and said, "I like this slimy stuff. Bring us more of this cabbage. I'll tip you well, I promise."

My wife closed her eyes, and I thought about how, in most real-life stories, the Swifts would have never come back to our house. And they wouldn't offer any invitations to theirs, either. They would either move out of town presently, or construct a privacy fence of their own—maybe out of brick, or cement block, and eight feet high. Maybe my parents and they decided to go from conservative, upstanding members of the community to free-for-all live-and-let-live swinger types in the matter of one evening's batch of Tequila Buenos Noches! I know this: no one ever brought up the incident again directly. The Swifts and my parents took to visiting each other once or twice a week. My mother called Mrs. Swift almost nightly, and took her to doctor's appointments, grocery shopping, and the movies. My father and Mr. Swift went fishing and bowling. They played poker with some other men twice a month.

One time Mrs. Swift said to me, "Hey, Louis. Come on over here and feel my face. I don't have one wrinkle. Do you know why?" I walked over and stuck my hand on her forehead. "Because I don't squint, and I don't laugh or smile very often. Now quit looking down my shirt. Ha-ha."

Claudia said, "Drayton and Louise are having marital trouble. I can feel it. That's why they're late. Why wouldn't they call? They have your cell number, don't they?"

I said, "It affected me, sure. You can count on that, believe me. No one involved acted like anything was wrong—not my parents, and not even Mrs. Swift. She got to where she'd tap on over to our house in the middle of the day when she knew my parents were at work. And she'd say how she just wanted to know how I was doing. Nothing else. I wouldn't ask her if she wanted to sit down or have some iced tea or whatever, but she'd just come right on in and get her own iced tea and sit down.

Claudia kept her eyes closed. "Did you tell this story to your first wife? What did Patti think about all this?"

I picked up my chopsticks by the wrong end, pretended to know what I was doing, and pulled more kimchi from the white ceramic bowl.

"Andy Agardy quit coming over to my house altogether. I can't even remember his talking to me again all the way until we graduated from high school."

"He might've been in on the trick. Maybe your parents paid him money to prod you toward drawing those nipples and pubic hair. I'm promising you that these kinds of tricks and guises are in that book I mentioned. That book my parents had. I finished it, too. I'm thinking about making it required summer reading for my cheerleaders."

When I graduated from high school Mr. and Mrs. Swift gave me a check for a hundred dollars and told me that I had to use the money to buy books in college. Mrs. Swift handed over a horrendously-wrapped box and said, "This might help you out in college, too. With the coeds." When I opened the package—it was a pair of fake X-ray glasses, like the kind ordered out of a comic book—Mrs. Swift laughed and laughed and said she had no idea if they worked or not. "I don't know if they're as good as my X-ray glasses," she said. "I hope so."

The waitress came back. "Our manager said y'all need to probably go ahead and order. We have some reservations for people coming in later." She set down two margaritas and said, "These are from some people over there." She pointed at the bar. I looked, expecting to see Dray and Louise. Hell, I imagined to see Mr. and Mrs. Swift, even though I knew that they still lived in Graywood, that they had retired, that they spent most of their time down on Kiawah Island.

I said, "Who? Who sent these over?"

No one from the bar looked toward us. "That man. That man right there wearing the hat." She pointed again. I'd never seen him before, but he turned and lifted his own drink our way.

"He comes in here all the time. Well, he's come in here for two weeks, seeing as we ain't been open but that long," our waitress said. "He's my little brother's psychologist. I forget his name. He's supposed to be good, though."

I lifted my margarita. I told myself over and over that he must've heard me tell the story to Claudia, that he overheard the word "margarita." I wished that I had a box of fundraiser candy out in the car to give him. My second wife ordered the Happy Family. I pointed at the menu, for I couldn't pronounce anything that looked good, and knew that I would slaughter anything I wanted. Our friends never showed up. Later, I paid.

VERSE

BETH ANN FENNELLY

Bite Me

You who are all clichés of babysoft
crawl to my rocking chair,
pull up on my knees,
lift your delicate finger to the silver balloon
from your first birthday,
open your warm red mouth
and let float your word, your fourth
in this world, Bawoooooon –
then, delighted, bite my thigh.
I practice my stern No. You smile,
then bite my shin. No, I say again,
which feels like saying No, Wind! when it blows.
But how to stop you? This month
you've left your mark on me
through sweatshirts and through jeans,
6-teeth-brooches that take a week to fade
from my collarbone, hip, wrist.
What fierceness in that tiny
snapping jaw, your after-grin.
You don't bite your teething rings,
don't bite your toys, your crib,
other children, or your father.
It makes us wonder.

Daughter, when you were nearly here,
when you were crowning
and your father could see your black hair
and lifted in his trembling hands
the scissors to cut your tie to me,
when a nurse had gone to the waiting room

to assure my mother Just a few more pushes,
when another had the heat lamp
warming the bassinet beside my cot,
then held up the mirror
so I could see you sliding out –
you started turning. Wriggling
your elbows up. The mandala
of your black hair turning and turning
like a pinwheel, like laundry in the eye
of the washer, like the eye of the storm
that was just beginning
and would finish me off, forever,
because you did it,
you got stuck, quite stuck,
and so, they said, I'd have to push
head-shoulders-elbows out at once.
And Lord did I push, for three more hours
I pushed, I pushed so hard I shat,
pushed so hard blood vessels burst
in my neck and in my chest, pushed so hard
my asshole turned inside-out like a rosebud,
pushed so hard that for weeks to come
the whites of my eyes were red with blood,
my face a boxer's, swollen and bruised,
though I wasn't thinking then
about the weeks to come
or anything at all besides pushing and dying,
and your father was terror and blood splatter
like he too was being born
and he was, we were,
and finally I burst at the seams
and you were out,
Look, Ha, you didn't kill me after all,
Monster I have you,
and you are mine now, mine,

and it is no great wonder
that you bite me –

because you were crowning
and had to eat your way out of me,
because you were crowning
and developed a taste
for my royal blood.

I Need to Be More French. Or Japanese.

Then I wouldn't prefer the California wine,
its big sugar, big fruit rolling across my tongue,
a cornucopia spilled across a tacky tablecloth.
I'd prefer the French, its smoke and rot.
Said Cezanne: Le monde – c'est terrible!
Which means, The world – it bites the big weenie.
People sound smarter in French.
The Japanese prefer the crescent moon to the full,
prefer the rose before it blooms.
Oh I have been to the temples of Kyoto,
I have stood on the Pont Neuf, and my eyes,
they drank it in, but my taste buds
were in the beer line at Wrigley Field.
It was the day they gave out foam fingers.
I hereby pledge to wear more gray, less yellow
the color of the mockingbird nestlings' beaks,
that huge yellow straining open on the delicate,
wobbly necks, trusting something yummy
will be dropped inside, soon. I hereby pledge
to be reserved. When the French designer learned
I didn't like her mock-ups for my book cover,
she sniffed, They're not for everyone. They're
subtle. What area code is 662 anyway? I said,
Mississippi, sweetheart. Bet you couldn't find it
with a map, and a brain. OK: I didn't really.
But so what if I'm subtle as May in Mississippi,
my nose in the wine-bowl of this magnolia bloom,
so what if I'm as mellow as the punch drunk-bee.
If I were Japanese I'd write about the magnolia
in March, how tonal, each bud long as a pencil,
sheathed in pale green suede, jutting from a cluster
of glossy green leaves. I'd end the poem
before anything bloomed, end with rain swelling the buds,
the sheaths bursting and for a day capping the budtips,
then falling to the grass like a fairy's cast-off slippers,

like candy wrappers, like spent firecrackers.
Yes, my poem would end there, spent firecrackers.
If I were French, I'd capture post-peak, in July,
the petals floppy, creased brown with age,
the stamen naked, stripped of its long yellow filaments.
The bees lazy now, bungling the ballet, thinking
for the first time about October. If I were French,
I'd prefer this, end with an image of the red-tipped filaments
scattered on the scorched brown grass,
and my poem would incite the sophisticated,
the French and the Japanese readers –
because the filaments look like matchsticks,
and it's matchsticks, we all know, that start the fire.

Once I Did Kiss Her Wetly on the Mouth

Once I did kiss her wetly on the mouth
and her lips loosened, her tongue rising like a fish
to swim in my waters
because she learns the world
by tasting it, by taking it inside.

I desired it – her learning my tongue that way.

Yes, I wanted to soul-kiss my daughter,
to lather, slaver the toothless gums
and the cat-arched back of her palate,
to sniff the bouquet of baby's breathe
all the way to the vase of her throat

Look at her, in her highchair,
wearing her yam goatee

I like to take her whole foot in my mouth

Look at her, in her bib
slung backwards, like a superhero's cape –
beware, small villains everywhere

Oh, that first day
when the nurses returned her to my cot
so newly minted, her soles were black from ink
they laid her, naked, on my naked chest
so she could swell my breasts with milksong,
so I could warm her skin with my skin,
and so, next to my more regular heart,
her skittish beat would steady –
though I swear when she latched on
all meter, music changed

I whispered in her see-through ear
I'd keep her safe forever –
I, her first lover.

We Are the Renters

You need no other names for us than that.
The good folk of Old Taylor Road
know who you mean. We are
the renters, hoarders of bloated boxes,
foam peanuts. When the welcome wagon
of local dogs visits our garbage,
we're not sure which houses to yell at. So
what if we leave the cans there a bit too long.
We have white walls, a beige futon, orange
U-Haul on retainer, checks with low numbers.
Scheming to get our security deposit back, nail holes
are spackled with toothpaste. Yes, our modifiers
dangle. Our uncoiled hoses dangle, but the weeds
in our gutters do not, they grow up,
they are Renters' Weeds, they are unafraid.
An old black one-speed leans against the carport.
So what. Maybe we were thinking about riding
past these houses with posters for Republican governors.
We have posters too: Garage Sale. "Can I hel–"
"No, just looking." We are just looked at, we renters.
Are we coming soon to your neighborhood?
We're the ones without green thumbs,
with too many references, the ones
whose invitation to the block party
must have gotten lost in the mail. If we're still here
come winter, tell the postman not to bother
searching our nameless mailbox for his Christmas check.

Why We Shouldn't Write Love Poems, or if We Must, Why We Shouldn't Publish Them

How silly Robert Lowell seems in Norton's,
all his love vows on facing pages: his second wife,
who simmered like a wasp, his third,
the dolphin who saved him, even "Skunk Hour"
for Miss Bishop (he proposed though she was gay),
and so on, a ten-page manic zoo of love,
he should have praised less and bought a dog.

We fall in love, we fumble for a pen,
we send our poems out like Jehovah's Witnesses –
in time they return home, and when they do
they find the locks changed, For Sale stabbed in the yard.
Oh, aren't the poems stupid and devout,
trying each key in their pockets in plain view
of the neighbors, some of whom openly gloat.

We should write about what we know
won't change, volleyball, Styrofoam, or mildew.
If I want to write about our picnic in Alabama,
I should discuss the red clay earth or fire ants,
not what happened while we sat cross-legged there
leaning over your surprise for me, crawfish you'd boiled with
–
surprise again – three times too much crab boil –

Oh, how we thumbed apart the perforated joints
and scooped the white flesh from the red parings,
blowing on our wet hands between bites
because they burned like stars. Afterwards,
in the public park, in hot sun, on red clay, inside my funnel
of thighs and skirt, your spicy, burning fingers shucked

the shell of my panties, then found my sweet meat
and strummed it, and soon it too was burning, burning,
burning,
and then my burning juices dyed that clay a deeper red.

Ah, poem, I am weak from love, and you,
you are sneaky. Do not return home to shame me.

Claude Wilkinson

The Enduring Night – after a painting by Michael Crespo

Still in the beginning
before order and purpose,
without cushions of moss
or tumbling rivers,
without swallows dropping
from palm fronds into flight,

moon and rabbit
are stacked like
porcelain objects d'art, float
as if models for creation
in the black chiffon of space.

Certainly this is that time
that Roethke meant
when he said, "I weep
for what I'm like
when I'm alone."
Moon, rabbit, dark.

Who among us hasn't stood
in the same empty
square of canvas,
as unhappy as God, overlooking
swaths of new-mown grass
and shell pink azaleas,
unmoved even by lagoons of stars?

Who hasn't blended into
the one infinite night,

and with raucous crickets,
a death owl's quavering whistle,
waited for silver morning
to bleed through?

Staples

Bread or aspirin,
or whatever desire
had me out so late,
brought me to him
waiting at his Bethesda,
not asking alms,
nor to be dipped
that the buds of his legs
might be restored,
but for a six-pack
of Busch talls.

Outside the store,
As I hand him his change,
He tells me as he goes by
"Frank in the wheelchair,"
that he likes zydeco and jazz.

I tell him I teach
at the university
ask if there's
anything more he needs,
wishing he'd confess
some hope to have
an incorruptible body,
share everlasting wealth,
and then, we send hosannas
to the lambent vault.
"Nope," he says smiling
and patting his sack,
"just a buzz . . .
like everyone else."

The Barbershop

With the jawbones of asses,
we enter rank and file to join
shaggy allies already thick
in their smoke of fretting and cigarettes.
From huddles of two or three
scattered against the walls,
politics, bits of debts or sex
rise and fall through the drone
of freshly oiled shears, a phone
ringing with appointments
till someone's magic phrase
knots us into one heroic chorus.

As the Romeos among us
finish laying waste
women's arts of controlling a man,
another is summoned to our inner sanctum
of attention to be cropped,
shaven, anointed with pomade.

After the gardener makes me vow to try
His prescription for killing nut grass,
I over hear one's smothered scheme
For cheating with a girl half his age.
When the farmers settle
that one's indifferent bull is strictly
a liability, that at eight hundred pounds
and puzzle unbroken, he should
be more than willing to fill a pasture
with calves, we conquer what remains
of secret philistines till nothing
is left but that utopian lull
we fear most, till the last of us tramples out
over the dingy fleece of our strength.

Blackberry Fools

Devil's shoestrings, walls of woodbine,
Snakeskins crumpled like silver code,
Barbwire, now and then an angry bull.
We hardly noticed the biting flies.
We took them all on, waded branches,
scrambled down ravines – in early morning;
best of all, in the afternoon;
light forays just before dusk.
We wanted them, like something taboo,
sought them out and keep tabs on
their times of ripening from a strict
inedible red to the lavish black
that bled across trails, plumped
to the dark thimbles that would fill
all our empty lard tins, cookpots
and any Mason jars we could manage.

The earth gave under our load.
This when the world was young
And blinder, or holier, but more.
We always seemed within reach
of something: jeweled birds
that just flitted away in time,
a hive of places we liked believing
no one had ever found. The hills
rang with names and nicknames
as grown-ups shouted for our whereabouts.
This when the sky was blue
as a trance, when cool welts left
by briers harvesting our arms
meant no more than a necessary pain,
when bushes blazed like dark sayings,
heaving their priestly bait.

The Men's Hunt Club

They came down from Memphis, friends
of my uncle and co-workers of theirs
driving pickups, wearing camouflage coats
gorged with deaths, bird shot or buckshot
depending on the season, armed with
pumps and a few double-barreleds.

They brought speckled bird dogs
or a knot of motley hounds
depending on the season, fifths
of Wild Turkey wrapped in paper bags,
then wandered behind the house
for a ritual of swigs

before starting out. We walked
for hours under a gloomy haze,
me halving their man-steps—for hours
worming through puffs of ragweed,
crunching into sometimes calf-high snow,
watching the best dogs solve networks

of thorns. You could tell the best dogs.
Those were the ones that weren't gun-shy,
that wouldn't wince as shot blazed
right past their heads. They were
the ones that hardly made a sound
while being whipped into shape.

There was a camaraderie in how
the group finished one's whiskey first
before opening another fifth, in how they
traded mysteries of women they'd known
and glanced back to see if I'd grin, the way
they mirrored poor creatures they hunted—
both trying to escape the dangers
of their worlds by the only familiar means.

Behind, I followed the rubies of blood
as they leaked through game bags, the fresh
dangle of trophies, beholding my reflection
in the frozen gaze of a quail's eye.

Carly Grace

Southwest Georgia Haiku

Pabst Blue Ribbon Beer
Under shady magnolias
Spring tastes like heaven

What is this tin roof?
Mobile home that covers me
Rain tickles its back

Duct tape binds my shoes
Cracker ingenuity
Fixed my toaster too.

Fishing pole, my friend
Bamboo cane preacher of church
Find me a lunker

Melancholy Pabst
Johnny Cash plays on repeat
Another day gone

Goddamn bream buster
Broke dick line snapped smug fishing
Scrappy little fish

Sunday cold beer drive
Shadowed pin guide red clay roads
Tastes good to be alive

Honky-tonk angel
Painted on jeans dance close to me
Prettier than life

Winding gravel road
Lead me back to my real friend
Blue tick howls at me

Boone's Strawberry Hill
Drank too much and puked all night
Sweet light pink rhine wine

Honeysuckle vine
Seduced my copper head friend
Sure is puttin' off

Burned down bar last night
Uneasy rider playing
No more Dew Drop Inn

Rattle snake round-up
Mama sells scrap metal
Daddy wrestles snakes

Possum creeps across
Gasps like he's still here
It ain't though, it's dead

NON-FICTION

Larry Brown

Discipline

I saw a black guy knock the cold shit out of a white guy at Parris Island in 1970 because the white guy called him nigger. It was an unusual event. It was winter, December, and we had to get up before dawn every morning to march over to the mess hall, a hungry green herd of us, and if we were good we might be allowed to smoke a cigarette sometime after breakfast. The smokers among us hoped fervently for that at every mealtime. It almost never happened.

I don't remember where the white guy was from, but the black guy was from Nashville and his name was Clarence. The white guy was small, the black guy was big. The outcome was not surprising.

Joining the Marines is like serious camp for adults. The admission fee is a couple of years out of your life. In return you get to eat and sleep out in the field and shoot those big chattering M60 machine guns, which is a hell of an adrenaline rush, throw fragmentation grenades, blow up things with TNT and det cord, learn how to knife fight, and how to survive for a while alone in the Atlantic ocean, or how to kill a man by crushing his larynx through an ingenious use of your elbows and forearms and hands. It's chillingly simple. You make a lever and get it around his neck and then . . . squeeze. And in a knife fight, you will be cut. The only question is how much.

If you don't act the way they think you ought to, they treat you shitty, plain and simple.

Our senior DI was a bad motherfucker. There's no other way to say it. He was a black guy named Staff Sergeant Green who had finished the Marine Corps marathon way back before running got so big. He had been wounded in combat in Vietnam and had the ribbons to prove it. He wasn't very big, but he had great arms, and a way of talking to you that put the fear into your heart.

He was a Rifle Expert. He wore a brown flat-brimmed campaign hat like the one Smokey the Bear has, and a wide black leather belt, spit-shined just like his boots and his shoes. He even spit-shined the little leather strap on his hat. He had his shit together. We walked on eggshells around him, snapped to, didn't "eye-fuck" (their phrase) the entire area. Except once in a while I would and he'd catch me, and when he came over he would do this thing that turned him into a frightening man and not only because he had the power to send me home.

He'd get right up in your face telling you what a miserable piece of human work you were and you couldn't say anything. Well, you could say something, if you were really stupid, no matter what else you were, but then you'd wind up over in the brig, where they had a ghost named Herman the German, left over from World War II, and they'd whip your ass regular over there if you mouthed off any of your old tired rap. Either that or they'd make you go swimming in the sedge lagoon all day, bring you back covered with actual liquid human shit from head to toe, and then make you stand in front of your whole platoon in the squadbay with shit dripping down your legs and all over your face and testify to the heavens at the top of your lungs that you were now motivated and weren't going to give anybody else any lip. All kinds of lovely things like that went on. But you have to understand that the Marines are involved in the fine art of killing. How to conduct warfare as well as ceremony, and administer large doses of discipline. And if there was one thing we had, it was that.

You couldn't go to the head without permission. You could go all you wanted when the lights were out, between the hours of 10 p.m. and 5 a.m., which were reserved for sleeping, but any other time, like in an emergency, you just couldn't depend on it.

Sometimes you could go. Sometimes you couldn't. There were naturally some unfortunate accidents sometimes. I almost had a few myself. I almost had a bowel movement in my utility pants once when I was marching back to the barracks in the middle of my platoon. It took all my intestinal fortitude to hold my butt cheeks clenched together while keeping time.

I found out early on that people were not made the same. Some were soft, some were hard. Some who looked hard were actually soft. And it went the other way as well. Some were weak sisters or simply maggots. We all had various identities and different looks when we came in, some with beards and beards and mustaches or long hair, but it only took about one hour to remove all that from all of us and then we looked alike: a bunch of scared weirdoes with pale shaved heads walking around in tennis shoes and new green clothes with creases still in them. Except for the ones who wore glasses. They were the only ones who looked different. It turned out somehow, in our platoon, anyway, that lots of the ones who wore glasses were also fat. That usually always meant that they couldn't climb the rope.

They had terms of endearment for everybody, Four Eyes, and Fat-bodies as well, and if you could not climb the rope you were in world of shit. That's what they told us. It was awful to see those fat bald boys with their steamed-up glasses trying to hoist themselves off the ground, up a hanging fifty-foot rope, the sweat-soaked DIs after them like terriers on rats in an empty barn. They'd make short work of them. The fat boys would fall. Sometimes they were soft and they cried.

The DIs would get them up it again. They'd fall again. Lucky that I was quick and small, I could go up and down it like a monkey, and for that part of it they left me alone. One hysterical day when we were running, some who couldn't run were dragged, an upheaval orgy of mud and rain and screaming mud-spattered veterans still earning their paychecks among hundreds of frightened young men and boys.

But that's what it's all about, breaking you down so they can build you back up. What they build in you is unquestioning loyalty, so that you in theory will devote yourself to the Corps and the officer who leads you, and follow their orders, whatever they are. If those orders are in fact charging a machine gun nest, then that's what they expect you to do. And I had discipline, by God. I had it. I loved my Marine Corps. The uniform. The history that went past the halls of Montezuma. Tarawa. Tripoli. Iwo Jima and Ira Hayes raising the flag. Semper fidelis: Always faithful.

Some boy was unlucky enough or dumb enough to try and walk through the ranks of another platoon early on in my time at the island. Bad move. They beat him almost to death in just a few moments. It was a killer dog attitude kind of thing. They wanted you to be vicious. And unless you got sick, or badly hurt in training, or died, there was no early escape from the island or that world except through a path of dishonor.

They were truly some tough sons of bitches. I was scared to death the whole time I was down there. Later on, after I got through with all my training and schools and got stationed on a base, it was cool. Cigarettes were thirty cents a pack, and you could get a beer in an NCO bar for a quarter. Three square at the mess hall, anything you wanted, breakfast every day, ham and eggs, hash browns, all the fruit and juice you needed. Uncle Sam feeds good. All you want: I loved the food every day. By the time I got out in 1972 you could go into the mess hall and get sandwiches and desserts and coffee at night.

But trying to get to that place was hard back in the winter of 1970. At eighteen I'd gone for my physical in Memphis and had been classified 1-A. I bought cold beer at Johnny Zanola's across the river in Marshall County plenty of times on my draft card. My birthday, July 9th, was drawn first in the lottery the next year, and like a dumb ass I joined up before Christmas and got to spend it down there, my only solace was Jesus and the church services we were allowed to attend, because a lot of scary stuff was going on. One lieutenant stood up in front of us in the same place we met for church and told us what a great glory it would be to the history of the U.S. Marines if we all got blown to Kingdom Come in Vietnam. My funky bunkie from Knoxville had rotten teeth with terrible breath and VD. His breath was so bad I couldn't understand how he'd gotten close enough to anybody to get VD.

He'd have to go on sick call all the time for his hurt peter and we could all tell it really disgusted Staff Sergeant Green, because even though he was a bad motherfucker, he was a pretty straight arrow and even had a sense of humor, albeit all at your expense. You had to bow and scrape to go on sick call even if you were really sick. I mean they had to let you go, hell, but they always had to fuck with you first. I never did go to sick call but I watched a lot of them do it. It didn't matter what you did, they were going to fuck with you first.

We lived in this old wooden barracks up on the second floor, a real fire trap. We had to take turns walking fire watch at night with a silver helmet and a flashlight, just like Matthew Modine did in *Full Metal Jacket*. They also made us get down on our hands and knees every morning before breakfast and scrub the floor with soap and hand brushes and then pour hot water on it and squeegee all the water out the door with our shower shoes, what we now call flip-flops. Then we'd have our day. Sick call was at night.

My bunkie would be shaking with fear but needed to see the doctor really bad because I think he had something leaking out of him, the way he talked he did, and he'd have to scream out for the whole platoon to where he was going while he was standing at rigid attention in front of Staff Sergeant Green, and why he needed to go: "VD, sir," and being of the same race had nothing to do with it. Staff Sergeant Green held my bunkie in about the same level of dog piss.

He'd say, in this big nasty whisper that everybody could hear, since it was deadly quiet and fifty privates were listening to get every word, "Get your disgusting self away from me, Private."

And off into the darkness my shade bunkie would go, to return later that night and speak of medical miseries from the lower rack once the lights were out. Guys talked about cutting their throats to get out of there. One guy in our platoon just stayed in his rack one morning with his eyes tightly shut, and his whole body stiff, after they turned on the lights and started throwing shit cans around and screaming like they did every morning, and the guy wouldn't get up at all until a couple of corpsmen from the hospital came over, and loaded him onto a stretcher like a board, and hauled him there before breakfast. We never saw him again because they stamped him Rejected and shipped his weak sister ass home.

I knew I could never go home if I failed to pass recruit training at Paris Island. The shame would be too great. I knew I was there until it was over. Whatever it took to stay. Mostly without regular cigarette breaks.

Getting picked up is when you get off the bus from Charleston still in your civvies from your airplane ride from Memphis. It's a nightmare bus ride through the hanging gardens of South Carolina, all that stuff that's up in there, the moss that hangs down in great beards. There is a causeway you cross going onto the island and after you get on it you begin to see out the windows what is waiting for you.

There are a lot of yellow footprints painted on Panama Street, and long rows of barracks on each side, and when you get off the bus you go and start standing in those footprints while a bunch of drill instructors who have worked themselves into a froth, I mean actually foaming at the mouth, come out and get you and spit on you and shriek curses from hell at you while slinging their slobber on you and just generally make you feel weak and forsaken in your soul and real sorry you left the warmth of the soft world your mama had so carefully created for you. I can see now that the DIs had jobs to do. If some goober from Mississippi broke down weeping at a little verbal harassment in South Carolina, what the hell would he do in a firefight in Southeast Asia with incoming bullets ripping the shrubs to shreds? It was their job to see that the weak and unfair got weeded out and sent home, and that the strong got pruned and nurtured into fighting shape.

The only bad thing about that is that some of them were sadists and you could see that they got off from watching you sweat in pain. Green wasn't like that, but some were. We had three of them altogether who stayed with us in shifts and lots of times all three of them with us at once. You had to get your mind right. You had to decide that you would be as strong as what was called for. You had to decide that you would survive.

That morning, it was still dark, like it always was after breakfast, and we'd all eaten, and were coming out of the mess hall, going back into formation. The white guy pushed Clarence, and said, "Out of my way nigger," or something like that. The N word was definitely used. The answer sounded like a pistol hot. The solid crunch of fist connecting against jawbone, a WHAP that was heard by all. The white guy fell out with arms flopping, and some other guys caught him before he hit his head on the pavement, and dragged him across the street and into the formation, and then they slapped him around some and got him back into some semblance of standing consciousness before Green came out of a mess hall no wiser to march us back to the barracks and the coming day of training, pop, snap, pop.

Later, in one of those small private moments we sometimes got, where it was possible to talk a little, the white guy kept professing his innocence. He said that he didn't say what he said, and he swore on his mother's grave that he didn't say it. Which just made him even more of a maggot. We told him to blow it out his ass.

And I stayed in a guard company at Camp LeJeune, North Carolina, for a long hot summer in 1971. My nephew Glen was born then and Paul and Linda McCartney had a popular song on the radio, something about hand across the water.

One smoking August day around noon, when the big fans were blowing hard in the squadbay, and people like me were trying to sleep between brutal shifts of guard patrol, and radios and talk and dirty jokes and laughter were preventing some of them from doing it, an asshole who had duty and therefore was in legal possession of it put a load clip into a semi-auto Colt pistol, chambered a .45 round and cocked it, and walked around pointing it at people and giggled like a stoned lab monkey while they cringed. I watched it from my rack with sick fear and revulsion in my stomach.

I didn't say anything. But it was a damn good thing for him that he didn't point it at me. I was raised around guns and nobody in the Marines had to tell me that you never point one at something or somebody you don't intend to shoot. And, too, the way I felt back then, being hardened then, seeing so much violence in an all-man's world and having to adjust to it, I know what I would have done if he had pointed it at me. I would have waited until he stopped playing around and put it down, and then I would have picked up something heavy and hit him in the head with it.

But then I would have been in the brig. You had to try and consider your actions in there because the punishment was so harsh. They just brooked no bullshit at all. That's how they kept us in line. Mostly.

A sergeant in the NCO bar at camp Geiger held a little advisory seminar for all of us before he'd let us buy our first beer in over five months, I mean those of us who had gone to the bar that beautiful May afternoon of first freedom after a whole winter of infantry training and schools and general military bullshit, and that was most of us.

We were all waiting for orders, waiting to find out where the Marines were going to send us. We were just standing in a group around a patio. The sergeant seemed like a nice guy. He had a cushy job. He said we were welcome to come there and encouraged to come there because being in the Marines was like being in a big family, but in the case of a fight between some of us or anybody else inside the club, whoever threw the first punch would pay for it with one hundred dollars out of his hip pocket. And we were only making about ninety a month, so it was a sobering thought.

But I wasn't planning on misbehaving anyway. After all that time and that crawling in the mud with real bullets going over your head and running in a raincoat with a rifle and a full marching pack for nine miles sometimes, it was nice to be able to put jeans back on, buy a regular shirt at the PX, go out and have my first beer in all that time. I wasn't going to mess that up.

I don't remember too many altercations in that particular spot but I saw fights in enlisted men's bars, over and over, on every base I was on. It was just something that happened. People with a couple of old bullet holes in the arms are not shy about getting into fistfights. People would get to drinking and start talking shit. But pure acts of violent meanness occurred too. At one time there were gangs of black Marines who roamed the dark areas of Camp LeJeune and found lone white Marines and beat them senseless. It happened to a young friend of mine, a boy who was seventeen. Back then, back when the war was going on, the Marines would let you in when you were seventeen if your parents signed for you. He wore glasses and they broke his glasses with their fists and drove glass splinters into one of his eyes.

He had to wear a patch over it for a long time. Kept having to sick call. It was a bad thing to see. I heard black gunnery sergeants refer to white Marines as swine. American Indians got called Chief. Boys from Texas seemed to not like Mexicans. I had black and Mexican friends at LeJeune, but still there was prejudice floating around. Things between the various got so bad in 1972 that the Commandant ordered every enlisted man in the entire Corps to start taking human relations classes, where we sat down in classrooms and faced each other, black and white and red and brown, and talked about what pissed us off the most about each other.

We learned amazing stuff. And it got better before I got out. But if you ever got in any serious trouble over fighting, you were really in a world of shit. I found that out in Philadelphia.

I worked in that guard company all that summer, wanting to get home, not able to. I rode in Jeeps and carried a 12 gauge pump shotguns and .45s, checked door, roads, buildings, walked a post for four hours at a stretch with an M-14, big heavy bastard that weighed eleven pounds, rested and wrote letters between shifts, drank beer, read.

I was stuck on a huge base with a few thousand other guys and I didn't have any wheels. Didn't know anybody who had any. I didn't know what town looked like because I never went out there. I think it's called Jacksonville. I know there were girls in bars with Polaroids who charged ten dollar for a picture of you with them that you could send home because I saw guys with those pictures. But that seemed pretty sad to me even back then. Pay some chick to pose with you? Nah.

There were big herds of deer all over LeJeune, thirty and forty and fifty of them at a time. We'd see them out at night on our patrols when we were riding from one post to the next. But there was nothing really to do except watch television or movies or read or drink beer in the PX with your buddies, unless you devoted yourself to the Marine Corps and the service of it.

That's what I did, except I just couldn't help being a shit bird. I didn't want to be a shit bird. I tried not to be one. I ran. I lifted weights and shined my boots, but none of my inspections were completely good. I could spit shine fine, but I couldn't make up that bunk exactly the way they wanted me to. I could get my rifle clean, but then I'd display my underwear the wrong way. I was never on time for 4 a.m. mess duty, not one single time in two weeks, and kept getting yelled at by the cooks. The shit bird just lived in me.

The only fun thing I really did in North Carolina was catch a ride one weekend to Columbia, South Carolina, to visit my aunt and uncle and my cousins. They took me to Myrtle Beach and I swam in the ocean for the first time. We had cold beer and they fed me well. I spent that good weekend with them, and then I went on back to LeJeune to walk some more posts and write more letters to friends and family back home, try to save a little money to send to my mother, who needed it badly, since she was trying to get my little brother into college so that he could stay out of the shit I was already in.

Everybody wanted to get a Med cruise and they were hard to get. You'd get to go on a ship as a guard and sometimes you'd get liberty in these overseas ports whenever the ship docked. And the troop strength of the Marines in Vietnam was already winding down. Too much blood had been spilled and America had seen the faces of one week's dead and the names of their hometowns in *Life* magazine and America was screaming No more! There wasn't that panic like before. We knew it was going to end. We heard lots of real stories from plenty of guys who had been there, though, and were still just doing their time. A lot can happen to you in four years in the Marines. But I was only in for two. My recruiter was honest and told me the Marines offered a two-year enlistment. I also met some pretty bitter guys whose recruiters had lied to them and told them they could only get in if they signed up for four.

I guess the recruiter got a better grade that way, or more money that month, or something. I don't know. I don't know. I don't know why anybody would lie about something like that, something that involved a couple of years of somebody's life. But it seemed in there sometimes that the natural inclination of at least a considerable amount of people was to fuck over his fellow man as quick as he could, be an asshole to him to show him his power, however small it was in the scheme of things. It might just be a guy supervising some other guys peeling potatoes.

People would just take exception to things. Sometimes people would take exceptions to my face, as in, "I don't like your face." That was said to me more than once. I was young and strong and pretty fast, didn't think death could get me then. It would always happen in a bar, while we were drinking. My response was always the same, "Then why don't you try and change it?"

I had to choke a guy from the Navy one night, but it really wasn't my fault. He sat down at my table and started bothering me. I'm not proud of it and probably wouldn't do it now. But I was young then and I was drinking. He kept bothering me and he wouldn't stop, even after I told him a bunch of times, nicely.

I even went over to the bartender, this sergeant I knew, and told him what was taking place, that I didn't want to get thrown out of the bar because it was the only one I had, but that if the guy didn't stop bothering me there was probably going to be some trouble. The sergeant wore granny glasses and long-sleeved paisley shirts with puffy sleeves when he was off duty and he said, "Back up and regroup, baby."

The reason I choked him instead of hitting him was because instead of the rule being whoever threw the first punch paid a hundred dollars, in this bar the rule was that whoever threw the first punch got thrown out of the bar for a month. That was a really sobering thought. So I thought maybe if I choked him instead of hitting him, if he bothered me some more, they wouldn't throw me out of my only watering hole for thirty days. I went back and sat down and he started bothering me again and I choked him until some of the other guys made me stop. But they didn't throw me out. They threw him out.

And one night, in their bar, the Navy threw our asses out. I guess it's true that what goes around generally comes around.

I got offered orders to Marine barracks Philadelphia in the early fall of 1971. Gunny West called me to his office and showed them to me and said, "It's good duty, Brown, you ought to go."

It is the oldest post in the Corps. It's where they were founded in 1775 at Tun Tavern. It was dress blues duty, white cap and white gloves, all spit and polish, all pomp and ceremony like the ads on TV. It was going to be a big city instead of something that was strictly a military base. So I signed on. They offered me some leave and I took thirty days. I was glad to be leaving LeJeune. I had some friends there yeah, but they were about as unhappy as I was, and like me just waiting to go somewhere else, or get out. We had no wheels, we couldn't get out of town, we couldn't get any women.

I bunked next to and hung out a lot with Felix, a skinny kid from Memphis who had two gold teeth and favored Hendrix a little. He'd sleep with a stocking over his head to mash his 'fro down for inspection the next day and then when he went off duty he'd fluff it back out with a pick and put on his cool duds.

But I cut them all loose and left, and flew back home. Back then the airport in Nashville was a cracker box, and you could smoke on the plane while you were having cocktails, and the stewardesses liked Marines in their snazzy uniforms and bright shoes, and would sit on the armrest of your seat with their good legs rubbing up against you and talk to you. I've noticed that they never do that now.

I squirrel-hunted all the time I was home. One golden uninterrupted month of beautiful fall. My old friend Sam Jones and I went out and killed fox squirrels and grays every day. I spent time with my mother, my brothers, and my sister, saw her son, my nephew for the first time. I think my family was drawing a sigh of relief since it looked like I probably wasn't going over to the meat grinder that had taken so many, that had caused all the mamas' tears that are still being wept even now.

My friends at home hadn't changed. One or two had different cars. They were all glad to see me, and it was that way for me, because I'd missed them. We played our eight-tracks and rode our old routes on smooth sand roads through vast holdings of timber that had proper names like the Big W and the Crocker Woods, and drank beer and talked and listened to a radio station out of Chicago at night, and they had their jobs, but all I had to do was get up every morning and put on my old clothes and get my gun and hunt.

I could roam the old hardwood forests then, the ones that are gone from around here now, back in those deep hollows of shade and towering trees, the banks of the creeks crowded with huge beeches gray as smoke, their tops riddled with smoothworn holes, squirrel dens, some the homes of coons. A wonderland I used to walk in my youth that is no longer there.

The time at home was sweet, but I had to go back. I still owed Uncle Sam another year or so. I had no idea what I was going to do with my life. My daddy had fought on the worst killing fields of WWII, and a picture of his uniformed father in WWI at some tender age stands on my desk, and my great-great-grandfather, Samuel L. Paschall was buried in 1862, in Richmond, where he still lies, a Confederate lieutenant dead of "disease" at twenty-one.

He contracted something in a hospital while tending to his brother, who had been grievously wounded, and who had died in his arms. Samuel wrote a letter to their mother after that said: I am now brotherless, and I fear that soon, Mother, you will be sonless. And he was right.

So it was okay with me to be a soldier. Tarawa. Okinawa. Iwo Jima. They'd shown us the color films taken by combat photographers who were part of the assault that day. The Navy had parked offshore and heeled for two weeks before the first waves went into the water with their rifles and charged the beach. The sand was black, the uniforms green, the sky full of gray smoke and red fire.

Three thousand U.S. Marines died that first day under Japanese guns. We saw what that looked like on film. It was just exactly like a movie except that it was real. It was murder and mayhem and death and I was ready to go rejoin the herd, maybe stay with them forever.

I still had time to be a good Marine.

DAVID MAGEE

Understanding Oxford

When I was young and growing in different directions near the town square in tiny Oxford, Miss. my closest friend was a Faulkner descendant. William, by then deceased, was his great uncle. I spent unreasonable hours at my friend's house during the 1970s, often wondering why his parents were still home at ten in the morning on a Monday or a Friday or any day.

I knew that his mother, Dean Faulkner Wells, was a writer. Same for her husband, Larry Wells, though I was not sure what that meant in either case other than they spent most of the traditional work day at home and often had house gatherings at night with an ever-changing list of guests who did not talk or act like the typical Oxonian I knew. They were usually loud, always funny and sometimes swaying in the night. I remember bumping into Jimmy Buffett at the house, long before I knew about *Coconut Telegraph.* And I first met a writer there named Willie who drank too much but truly got funnier with each passing hour and played the meanest game of *Trivial Pursuit* I had ever seen.

But I was not unlike most residents of the small college town at the time in that my appreciation and fascination was with the people and not their published works or those that were in the making. Oxford gracefully abutted the University of Mississippi, affectionately known as Ole Miss. And Ole Miss meant football, not literature. It was the mighty Rebels that we hoped would prevail and not merely endure another rugged Southeastern Conference season. Archie was a bigger name than William and most adults I knew joked of having never even read Faulkner, but remembered the score of the 1969 Sugar Bowl.

My sixth grade English class took a field trip to the grocery store to learn how to read receipts. We drove in the yellow school bus down Oxford's tree-lined North Lamar Boulevard to get there and passed the turn to Faulkner's home, Rowan Oak, without notice or mention from the front seated, megaphone holding teacher.

Oxford's town square was sleepy in those days and angling easily toward the unavoidable transition we've all seen southern towns make as forces pull and stretch painfully outward. The square barely came alive even when Ole Miss played a home football game on campus, despite the fact that the 30,000 fans quadrupled the town's population for one day.

Football so dominated Oxford's aura that in 1979 most residents and University students were already in Memphis on the evening of September 14, drinking and gathering at the Peabody hotel, waiting on the season's opening game, Ole Miss versus Memphis State, to be held the next day at the Liberty Bowl. Back in Oxford a small but enthusiastic crowd, including Dean and Larry Wells, gathered for the opening of Square Books, owned by Richard and Lisa Howorth. Richard, who grew up in Oxford and graduated from Ole Miss, and his wife, Lisa, spent two years in a self-apprenticeship at the Savile Bookshop in Washington, D.C., before returning to Oxford to open their own independent store.

The day after Square Books opened Ole Miss beat Memphis State 38-34 in a night game that had electric moments and saw Buford McGee rush for 160 yards on 11 carries. I was there and was sure that Oxford and Ole Miss would never be the same from that day forth. McGee, a freshman playing in his first game, was on his way to the Heisman and the Rebels would return to the Sugar Bowl, finally.

Days later my Faulkner friend and I were back at home and knocking around Oxford's square, still basking in victory and aimless about everything else in life. We climbed the stairs and went into Square Books, Oxford's newest retail establishment, looking around briefly. We made a half-hearted crack about stealing a book, but didn't, probably unsure of what to do with it, and left.

I write all of this not as a beginning to a personal essay about a time and a place that I remember, but as an attempt at an accurate answer once and for all to the question that almost everyone who lives in Oxford or visits Oxford or knows about Oxford asks, and usually more than once. Just more than ten thousand residents, dozens of published writers who live in the area full-time, dozens more who consider Oxford a part-time home, and a memorable handful who once did but have now gone away. The names, when placed together, are far bigger than the place, which usually appears on the map with only a single small dot. William Faulkner, Willie Morris, Barry Hannah, Larry Brown, John Grisham...

How did this happen?

Local wisdom has it generally as this: First there was the Faulkner Thing; then came Dean and Larry; Square Books opened in 1979; Willie Morris came to town as a writer in residence at the Ole Miss in 1980; Hannah arrived in 1981; the University, Oxford's fraternal twin, began to actively shake its stuffy image by the late 1980s; and finally, John Grisham moved in the early 1990s and the Grisham Thing happened.

None of this will be disputed here, except for adding mention of the obvious. Football is not a part of the time line. Buford McGee got hurt and while he had a good, but oft-injured college career, he did not win the Heisman or ever get a single vote. Ole Miss went on to lose seven games in 1979 and has still not returned to the Sugar Bowl. There have been periodic moments of gridiron glee and occasional minor bowl game appearances and negligible winning records and the stadium has grown to accommodate more fans and even ugly losses still garner bigger than necessary headlines and inches in the local newspaper. But Oxford, as a municipality, is known today by and large more for its writers than nearby running backs and Square Books, with its gravitational forces giving cohesion to these oft-wandering souls, is the center of this universe.

The tall and bespectacled Richard Howorth says the arrival of Willie Morris to Oxford shortly after Square Books opened in a small, second-story location in 1979 helped the store get started and recalls the early days when the writer moved to town. Morris' book, *The Courting of Marcus Dupree*, was released by Doubleday in 1983. Howorth says Willie was sure it was headed for the bestseller list, a first for him. In reality it only did just okay in sales nationally, but Willie was buoyed by the fact that Howorth told him that his in-store signing event, with more than 300 books sold, was Square Books' largest in its short history. Morris became consumed with how the book sold at the store and called Howorth weekly for a sales total from the previous week. The Yazoo writer went on to brag for years before his death almost 20 years later at parties and among friends when in the company of Howorth that his was the all-time best-selling book at Square Books.

This was true in 1983, but, of course, by the 1990s and John Grisham, and countless others, it was not. But Morris did not care. Neither did Howorth, especially since Morris shared his passion for Oxford's independent bookstore in the early days with friends he brought to town for visits and signings like William Styron (not long after *Sophie's Choice*, marking the first time people actually lined up to buy books at the Square Books), John Knowles, Peter Matthiesen and George Plimpton. Howorth, a community minded sort, worked to make this literary influence become a reflection of the town and the folk by integrating the writers and the works in subtle ways. He treated small local writers published by the university press or even self-published writers with some of the same shelf appreciation the noted writers received, avoiding the local interest corner that plagues so many chain stores and belittles well-intentioned writers. Howorth also promoted the works of the bigger writers to many residents who had never before read them by specifically explaining to long-time friends and acquaintances why they would like a work.

Square Books expanded in 1986, moving to a bigger two-story corner location on the Square. This bigger, yet approachable literary atmosphere, coupled with the explosion of the locally beloved, but now geographically departed Grisham, and the development of fireman turned author Larry Brown, became in the 1990s one of the nation's top independent bookstores. A key reason was unique personal service and attention to readers fostered by Howorth. Or, as author Richard Ford once said in reference to Square Books and Howorth, "bookselling is no less an art than writing," and writers and readers seemed to understand this about the store.

Others in the trade wanted in on the secret and Howorth, who got actively involved with the American Booksellers Association, began teaching ABA sponsored classes to prospective booksellers on this unique art of personal bookselling. One of his students during a four-day session in Oregon in 1994 was an unknown student named Jeff Bezos, who announced to the class he wanted to start something called an Internet bookstore. Bezos took Howorth's class, based on his personal customer service principles. Bezos listened, apparently well, and used the lessons as the cornerstone of his new business, Amazon.com.

On the local front, Square Books was becoming such a staple for its blossoming group of local writers that the store began serving as their unofficial office. When I was the news editor of the local newspaper and wanted to get in touch with Grisham I simply left word at Square Books that I needed to talk to him. The telephone always rang within a couple of days.

"I hear you've been looking for me," he would say.

Grisham's home telephone number sat handwritten on a small piece of paper in the top of my desk drawer at the newspaper and I knew I was free to dial it at any time. But routing these calls through Square Books seemed more natural. In fact, everything began to seem more natural with Square Books. The store developed such a grounding feeling on the Oxford Square that writer Josephine Humphreys proclaimed, while sitting outside on the store's second floor balcony and looking out over the town square, "this is the center of the universe." Nobody knew whether she was referring to Oxford or Square Books specifically, but it made no difference. The two were becoming synonymous.

Howorth took his bookselling prowess beyond Oxford and the ABA classrooms, serving two years as ABA president and traveling the country as one of the book industry's most powerful forces. When his term was up he felt it was time to refocus his energy on the Oxford community and became an outspoken critic of local government, pushing primarily for controlled development, long-term planning and funding for the arts. When municipal elections rolled around in 2000, he lobbied others to run for mayor against the incumbent, believing strongly that change was needed. Nobody stepped forward.

Howorth called a neighbor at 4:45 p.m. on deadline day for candidate qualification, hoping to talk the person into running for mayor. Oxford's city hall would close at 5 p.m., just 15 minutes away, and Howorth was distressed that Oxford residents would have no alternative in the mayoral race. The story goes that Howorth gave momentary pause on the telephone and it was apparent what he was thinking.

"It would not be fair to be a critic if I am not willing to serve myself," Howorth said, quickly hanging up the telephone to make the short but quick dash across the Square to city hall from the bookstore, in time to fill out required paperwork before the doors closed.

A few months later Howorth took the oath of office on a hot, first day of July. Football season was still months away and most University students were home, or elsewhere, but the town square was vibrant with activity amid the festivity. I knew at that moment the town I grew up in had changed.

Oxford had become a writer's town, with a bookseller as its mayor.

Dick Waterman – Photos and Text

Journey of the Blues

How long does it take to get from Itta Bena, Mississippi, to the John F. Kennedy Center in Washington?

A little over 70 years . . .

* * *

B.B. King, born dirt poor in the Delta on September 16, 1925, celebrates his 70th birthday on Saturday and he'll mark the occasion by doing what he has done for almost half a century. He'll get on stage at Chastain Park in Atlanta and show thousands of people why he is the most famous singer/guitarist in the history of blues music.

If these are good times for Mr. King, few people have worked longer or harder to get their little piece of the pie. When B.B. King started out, there was no pie at all. He moved to Memphis in the late 1940s and soon was on the air at WDIA as "The Beale Street Blues Boy." That nickname was shorted to "B.B." and it wasn't long before he decided that he could probably play the blues as well as the music that he was spinning on the air.

He combined some Louis Jordan, a little Django Reinhart, a pinch of Lonnie Johnson and a whole lot of T-Bone Walker. He mixed it together with some Delta roots and came out with a sound that has influenced musicians ever since.

Some of his early regional hits were "Sweet Little Angel," "Three O'clock in the Morning" and a string of others that kept him out on the road playing over 350 nights a year, a staggering number considering that King and his band traveled country roads in an ancient bus. One old itinerary shows him playing eight different states in as many days (i.e. Florida, Georgia, Alabama, Mississippi, Louisiana, Arkansas, Oklahoma, Texas).

Years ago in Boston, I used to see B.B. play a place called Louie's Lounge in the Roxbury section of town. It was under the elevated tracks on Washington Street and the whole building rumbled whenever the trains came through.

In the spring of 1968, I was asked to book some music at a "McCarthy For President" rally in Fenway Park. I invited B.B. King to perform and, to my surprise, he accepted. The crowd was huge, far beyond the 40,000 capacity of the ball park, and they erected speakers in the street outside for thousands more.

B.B. played for about 30 minutes and was just taking his equipment off stage when word came that McCarthy was running late. I rushed back to the stage and told B.B. to start playing again and keep going until McCarthy arrived. He ended up doing an extra hour and got his first opportunity to show a white audience just what he could do. It certainly didn't hurt him at all that McCarthy's speech was stupefyingly dull and people left talking about B.B. King.

Having the opportunity for success is one thing but taking advantage of it is something else entirely. But B.B. King had the talent that had been waiting all those years for the door to open. He had a huge commercial hit with "The Thrill Is Gone" and followed that with "Why I Sing the Blues."

What English kids named Jagger and Richards and Clapton had known for years was finally apparent in the country were B.B. King was born. He is a national treasure and we are blessed to live in his time.

I was disappointed in his Ole Miss concert in April but consoled myself with the memories of the many great shows that I'd seen him do in the past. Then I went to Mud Island to see him again last Friday, and I was thrilled by a performance that was exuberant and energetic. After an hour with the full band complete with horn section, he sat on a chair surrounded by only bass player, organist and double drummers.

He proceeded to play an hour of music that was nothing less than an artist in passionate commitment to excellence. It transcended blues as a genre by elevating artistry into pure communication with every member of the audience.

He was cooking. He was on fire. He was almost 70. God bless him. Every June, B.B. King comes home to Indianola and plays a series of concerts for the local folks at a low ticket price. He wants the children of the Delta to know that it is possible to come from poverty and still aspire to greatness.

I have always suspected, however, that B.B. needs that trip to his native soil as much as the audience needs to hear him. It gives him the continuing reminder of from where he came and how far his journey has been.

B.B. King is very privileged to be named at the John F. Kennedy Center's

Honors List.

And the Kennedy center is no less honored to have him as one of their distinguished honorees.

Happy Birthday, Mr. King.

JOHN T. EDGE

My Life as a Lucky Dog: No one wants to kiss the wienie man

"Anybody can be a Lucky Dog vendor," Jerry Strahan promised. After spending the better part of the past twenty-six years managing the fleet of wienie wagons immortalized by John Kennedy Toole in his comic novel about New Orleans, A Confederacy of Dunces, Jerry should know:

We've had transvestites, transsexuals, homosexuals, and just plain old eccentrics. You name it. We've employed them all. And as long as they stay somewhat sober, they work out fine. Almost anybody can sell hot dogs down in the French Quarter.

But, as a pall crossed his jowly face, Jerry added, "Well, okay, anybody but mimes—mimes just won't work out! Anybody else, we'll take them. Hell, we could even put you to work."

That was a while ago, back in December of 1996. At the time, standing amidst the clutter and clamor of the dank, cement-floored offices of Lucky Dogs, Inc., I did not take the offer of employment seriously. After all, I had come not in search of a place to work, but to see the workplace of Ignatius J. Reilly, the corpulent, flatulent, over-educated, antihero of *A Confederacy of Dunces*, who, when forced by his mother to find a job, sought solace in the employ of "Paradise Vendors," Toole's fictional equivalent of Lucky Dogs.

As if things were not odd enough, on my way out the door, Jerry mentioned that he had written a book about his experiences as the manager of Lucky Dogs. With what I fear was probably a smug cordiality, I acknowledged the accomplishment but inwardly dismissed the possibility of it being published. In fact, I forgot all about Lucky Dogs until my phone rang one fall morning. Jerry was on the line.

"Remember the book I told you about, *Managing Ignatius*?" he asked. "Well, LSU Press bought it. It's due out in March and I was wondering, since you live in Oxford, if you could help me out a bit."

Before I realized what was happening, Jerry popped the question. I guess I should have looked upon it as some sort of rite of passage—recognition of my status as a citizen of Oxford, Mississippi. "Do you know how I might get in touch with John Grisham?" he asked. I replied that I could be of no help, but Jerry did not accept defeat easily. "Look, I'm not looking for an autographed book," he explained. "I just want to send a copy of my book to him—maybe get him to write a blurb for the back cover."

Five minutes and five thrusts and parries later, Jerry said goodbye, but not before promising to send along a review copy of the book for me to read—and not before renewing his offer of putting me to work as a Lucky Dog vendor.

"Read the book first," he teased. "You may not want to work a cart after reading it."

In *Managing Ignatius*, Jerry, a self-described "conservative redneck" born in Sullivan's Hollow, Mississippi, recounts his progression from high school student body president, to doctoral candidate in history, to manager of Lucky Dogs—a sort of inverted, perverted Pygmalion tale of his awakening to the aberrant. By the time I reached his description of the attire of one of the veteran vendors, I was hooked.

Smitty came in the shop wearing red hot pants, fishnet stockings, pink ballerina slippers, a ruffled tuxedo shirt, a bra, a Prince Valiant–style wig, and smoking a pipe. He insisted on working his cart like that. I told him absolutely not. Board of Health regulations dictated that the pipe had to go.

The seed Jerry had planted months before began to take hold. I began reading *Managing Ignatius* more as a manual of preparation rather than as a series of voyeuristic vignettes. Soon after turning the last page, I was on the phone to Jerry, arranging to take him up on his pitch. We decided that I would work a cart for two or three nights around New Year's Eve. "With New Years and Mardi Gras, we always have two vendors working a cart," he explained. "You'll be able to work with a veteran and get a feel for what it's like on the street. You know, a reporter from the Chicago paper tried this once. He lasted four hours."

December 30, 1997

And so it was that, approximately one year after my first encounter with Jerry, I found myself back in New Orleans. Attired in a red-and-white-striped shirt and an official-issue Lucky Dog cap, I stood in the heart of the French Quarter at the corner of Bourbon and St. Louis streets, listening to a fellow vendor's harangue.

Drink up you slobs! You know the routine. Drink. Stumble. Dance. Eat a Lucky Dog. Go home . . . What's the matter with you people? You're sober, you pitiful pieces of shit! Drink tequila. Smoke dope. Get the munchies. Eat a dog! Let's go!

It is a little after nine o'clock on a frigid Tuesday night and Adolf, a former Ole Miss student, is just a wee bit upset. With New Year's Eve only a day away, he had hoped to be raking in big commissions on the sale of quarter-pound Lucky Dogs at $4.25 and smaller, regular dogs at $3.25. Instead, business is down. According to Adolf, it is all because the crowd is too sober. Lucky Dog vendors pray for drunks like farmers pray for rain. Drunks do not normally debate the relative merits of paying $4.25 for a turgid tube of offal meat, fished from the steamy depths of a hot dog-shaped cart, and cradled in a gummy bun that threatens collapse under a molten mountain of mustard, ketchup, chili, relish and onions.

For drunks, Lucky Dogs are not so much food as fuel, and drunks need fuel if they are to survive a night of debauchery in the French Quarter, an area that Ignatius, perhaps the most famous vendor ever to peddle a dog, claimed "houses every vice that man has ever conceived in his wildest aberrations, including, I would imagine, several modern variants made possible through the wonders of science."

With business still at a crawl, Adolf, a onetime Nazi who says he has mellowed and now just likes to think of himself as a racist, asks me to look after things as he goes in search of a bar that will let him use their bathroom. I begin poking around inside the cart. Self-contained restaurants of a sort, the carts are equipped with sinks, steamer compartments, iceboxes, propane tanks, and prep tables—all enclosed within a seven-foot-long, 650-pound metal wienie-on-wheels. As I peer into the inner workings, I begin to understand Igantius' befuddlement when he exclaimed, "These carts are like Chinese puzzles. I suspect that I will continually be pulling at the wrong opening."

When Adolf returns, I wander up the street in search of a bit more on-the-job training. At the corner of Bourbon and St. Peter, I find Rick. Nattily attired, pleasant and well spoken, Rick is the antithesis of Adolf. As drunks stumble out of the Krazy Korner Bar, Rick jingles the change in his pocket and calls out, "Lucky Dogs. Get you Lucky Dogs here. Buy one at the regular price, get a second one at the same price!"

While we are talking, a black man in a white satin jump suit stops in front of us and screams out, apropos of nothing, "That Tom Jones is a bad white muthaf—a!" His attempt at doing a split in the middle of the street is unsuccessful. When he topples, I move on.

I wade deeper into the Quarter. At the corner of Bourbon and Orleans, David is sporting a soiled Santa hat and barking like a carny. "I don't want your first born!" he shouts. "I certainly don't want your ex-wife! And I probably don't want your college grades! But I do want your tips!"

Like many of the twenty-odd vendors working Bourbon Street on a typical night, David, a veteran of two weeks, sees Lucky Dogs as a way station, not an occupation. "I'm a commercial fisherman by trade," he says. "But I've done my share of street vending. Worked the carnival circuit too. I love it out here . . . Out here I'm just David. No past, no future—just passing through."

It's now about 11 o'clock and though I am enjoying the spectacle, I am not doing much work. Most carts are already fully staffed by two vendors. Fortunately, soon after I leave the corner of Bourbon and Orleans, I meet up with Jerry who tells me that Alice is in need of help and is willing to share her cart with me for the next few nights.

When I first encounter Alice, a woman of great girth but few teeth, she is standing at the corner of Bourbon and Conti, opening and closing the cart's steamer compartment, fanning wiener fumes across the street in hopes of luring passersby. She is having little luck.

"It's still a little too early. They're drinking now, but they're not quite drunk enough. They'll come around; they've got to . . . I only cleared 65 dollars yesterday," she says, a touch of desperation in her voice. "We've been waiting too long for this—suffering through December, waiting for New Year's and then Mardi Gras."

After more than fifteen years on the job, Alice, knows the street. And more importantly, Alice knows her drunks. Over the course of the next few hours she shows me the ropes and mentally prepares me for what will happen tomorrow night. "It's gonna be hell on New Year's Eve," she warns. "This isn't a party; this is a job. And you damn well better treat it that way."

Alice runs a well-stocked cart. In addition to the company-issued condiments like mustard, ketchup, chili, onions and relish, Alice offers her patrons a little Tony Chachere's Creole Seasoning—"for a taste of New Orleans"—as well as pickled jalapeño peppers. And, for those in search of still more heat, Alice will douse your Lucky Dog with her own special blend of hot sauce. "It will light your ass up," she says, her face creased by an enormous smile.

During the lulls between customers, Alice and I gaze at the slovenly promenade. The few customers we serve retreat just a few feet before trying to stuff the oversized dogs in their mouths. I watch, disgusted, as chili and relish plop from the back end of their buns and onto the sidewalk like dung from the business end of a horse. But, as one o'clock passes, the lulls become shorter. Soon a line has formed and the rush is on.

By two in the morning Alice and I are working as one. I make the dogs. She makes the change. And when she flails away at a gawky drunk who dares curse me for being too slow, I attempt to hold her back. Fortunately for the drunk, the crowd parts and he vanishes into the lurch.

Meanwhile, with the horde pressing down upon us, Alice and I scramble to keep up with the orders. In a rush of syllables and slobber, two college freshmen, down to their last dollar, plead for a bun full of chili, and then, as if by divine intervention, scrounge together the $3.25 needed for a regular dog. With my back to the crowd, I lean into the cart, reach for the tub of relish, and begin spooning it on their dog. I grab a pair of tongs and begin to pile on a mess of onions. When the soberer of the two leans in and mumbles "Gimme more chili on it will ya?" I feel the spray of spittle and liquor on my nape. Rather than break the rhythm of work to wipe away his request, I ladle on the chili and turn to take the next order. Alice collects the clump of bills that he shoves in her face.

By half past two, our pockets are bulging from the night's take. When the pizza place across the street closes at three o'clock, we suddenly have six customers in line. "They've got no choice now!" Alice cries with delight. "Now we've got 'em." We may well have them now, but thirty minutes later the street is starting to clear. At a quarter 'til four, Alice decides to call it a night. Ketchup splattered and bone tired, I head on.

New Year's Eve, 1997

When I arrive at the corner of Bourbon and Conti, Alice is already on the job. Standing at the prow of the cart, she surveys the crowd. "It's comin'," she warns. "I can just tell it's comin'. Some little sh– is gonna piss me off and I'm gonna have to whale on 'em. I've got too much at stake to put up with any sh– tonight!"

Though it is only eight o' clock, foot traffic on Bourbon Street is heavy. Friends lock arms and sway down the street, sloshing their way through stubbed-out cigarettes, dumped daiquiris and draft beer. Above it all ride the mounted police patrols, searching the crowd for prone bodies, pickpockets and bare breasts.

Alice and I begin laying in supplies for the long night ahead. "No regular dogs tonight, honey . . . they'll take what we give 'em," she says, dumping bag after bag of Lucky Dogs in the steamer. As I work to stuff the packs of Evangeline Maid buns in the cart, Alice runs down the street to stock up on a little bourbon.

In the five minutes that Alice is gone, I sell five hot dogs—three alone to a pack of barely post-pubescent kids. "We were gonna go to a titty bar," slurs the tallest of the three, "but we didn't have enough money for titties *and* Lucky Dogs."

Alice returns and a dapper, seemingly sober, young man wearing a black turtleneck, black pants, and blue sunglasses approaches the cart. When I ask for his hotdog order, he strikes a match, then lights his entire pack with it and stands back to admire the flame. The flame flares and then fizzles, yet he stands transfixed. I ask again for his order. Instead of replying, he tries to hand me the blackened book of matches. When I let them fall to the street, he screams out, "Damn that was pretty! Wasn't that pretty hot dog man?"

He walks off.

As the clock heaves toward midnight we enjoy a hard won breather, though Alice takes time to do business with a rag-tag pack of young tap-dancers who have been working the street for tips. After an evening of bucking and scraping, their pockets are heavy with quarters and Alice cashes in a couple of twenty-dollar bills with the smallest of the four, a cute, brown-eyed girl who looks like she should know more about Sesame Street than Bourbon Street. I knock back a finger or four of bourbon and begin cleaning up around our cart. With neither a trash can nor a cop in sight, I sweep everything—half eaten hot dogs, broken beer bottles, sticky plastic drink cups, gaudy plastic necklaces, even a spent condom—under a police car that is parked hard on our bumper.

At the stroke of midnight I drop my broom and join the drunken revelry in the center of Bourbon Street. As the sky above the French Quarter blossoms with fireworks, I search for someone to kiss. But no one wants to kiss the wienie man. My red and white striped uniform, smeared with mustard and ketchup has, in the words of Ignatius, "stamped me as a vendor, an untouchable." Before I have a chance to feel sorry for myself, Alice calls me back to the cart.

"They're comin' now," she promises. "And if anybody messes with me, they're gonna get it. I'm gonna whale on 'em!"

In drunken droves, they come. Screaming, yelling, banging their fists on the cart, their mouths sticky and stained purple, orange and blue, they crowd around us, shouting their orders and demanding our attention. "Get your butts in line or you'll get no dogs," I screech, my voice tinged with panic.

For the next four hours Alice and I cram Lucky Dogs into buns and slap change in palms. But no matter how fast we work, they just keep coming. By two in the morning we're out of relish. And still they come. At three o'clock, we toss out the warming rack where the dogs usually rest and plunge a few more bags of meat directly into the steamer. As the line backs up, tempers grow short. When a smarmy kid reaches into the cart to grab a napkin, Alice bellows, "Keep your hands out of my cart or I'll kick your ass!" When a bull-necked drunk with a sneer on his face spills beer on my feet and questions whether the Lucky Dog I made for him is worth the price, I catch myself screaming, "It's $4.25 buddy; $4.25 or –" Profanity spews from my mouth like water from a fire hose. Fortunately, he takes the dog. I pocket the money. And the night rolls on.

By four the line is gone. By half past four, we are out of ketchup and down to three dogs in the steamer. Alice says she has had enough and I have to agree. Though some of the other vendors will stay on the street until past dawn, we pack up and begin the long push back to the shop.

Across Bourbon, down Royal and out of the French Quarter I push the top-heavy cart down a one-way street and into oncoming traffic, swerving to avoid open car doors and bottomless potholes. With Alice at my side, shouting directions, we cross six lanes of speeding taxicabs at Canal Street. Halfway through the intersection, the cart fishtails and I almost lose control. Two blocks later we take a hard left onto Gravier Street and gather speed to push up the ramp and into the shop.

My first attempt at pushing our cart up the slight incline fails when the seven-foot-long metal wienie careens to the left and gouges yet another hole in the narrow doorframe. By the time I stop its recoil, the cart has rolled into the middle of the street. Exhausted, agitated and close to quitting, I begin the second push just as Alice leans over and whispers in my ear.

"You were great out there. You didn't take any sh– from anybody. You're just like the rest of us. You can come back and work a cart with me any time."

And the cart clears the door.

DEAN FAULKNER WELLS

Letter from South Lamar

Miss Daisye Wade Hampton is a four star general in a predominately female Southern army that wages war against fathers, grandfathers, husbands, sons, and even against its own kind in defense of its cause: the absolute abstaining of everybody from alcohol.

The Miss Daisyes of this world are clean livers who have never sipped an alcoholic beverage and do not intend to. Yet something strange happens in kitchens all over the South as the holiday season approaches. These devout supporters of the Women's Christian Temperance Union haul out the Bacardi, the Jack Daniels, the George Dickel called for in their recipes, and pour them with a heavy a hand as a country club bartender on New Year's Eve.

Perhaps it is the uninhibiting, festive air of the season that so affects them. But there is also a refusal on their part to recognize, much less admit, that the same demon that lurked in Big Dad's rum bottle could possibly be released on a bright, sunny morning in *their* kitchens. Nothing could be wrong with a liquid that looks and smells that good, not if it's thoroughly beaten into a batter of flour, sugar, eggs, vanilla, and cream. Served their way, 90 proof Jack Daniels becomes little more than a kissing cousin to vanilla extract.

There ought to be a law against operating a motor vehicle after eating Miss Daisye's branded date nut bread. She has been bringing it to us, around New Year's Day, for the past 15 years and, before that, to my grandmother for just as many. First comes an early morning phone call. "Daisye Wade Hampton *Hello*. The bread is ready. I'll deliver yours around about four o'clock this evening." *Clunk* goes her receiver.

Later, we watch her coming up South Street toward our house, a small trim figure even in her heavy winter coat and wide, floppy brimmed hat. She walks with the quick, determined stride of someone much younger than her 80 years, handling a large wicker basket with ease. Up the front steps she marches, raps smartly on the door with a kid-gloved hand, then opens the door and calls from the front hallway:

"Daisye Wade Hampton's here. So's your bread. Come and get it."

We hurry to greet her, to extend a perennial, futile invitation for her to come sit by the fire. Even as we speak, she reaches into her basket and removes one of a dozen packages, a small tin-foil wrapped loaf. Our thank yous are made to her steadily retreating back.

"More to deliver," she says. "Don't forget to keep it wrapped up tight so it will stay moist."

Miss Daisye's delivery route has never varied. Once you have made her list, you stay on it, alive or dead. Many of her friends are indeed gone, but if a family member resides in the old house, he inherits her seasonal cheer.

The size and shape of her date nut loaves are a constant, as well. The ingredients vary only slightly. If her pecan trees have born well, she uses more nuts than dates. If the harvest has been skimpy, she might substitute walnuts. Sometimes she uses more cherries than dates.

One ingredient, however, never varies: the brandy. It is her one absolute—essential to the success of the bread—and yet the one that has begun to test her ingenuity. It has become, in fact, a test of Miss Daisye's fortitude.

When her father was alive, he bought the brandy for her. After his death, she relied on his bootlegger to supply her annual needs. "Red" operated his business out of a store located several miles out in the county. She could place her order by phone. She relied on Red's discretion, trusted him to view their relationship as confidential as that between lawyer and client, doctor and patient, sanctified not so much by law, perhaps, as by civility. Besides, he delivered.

In later years, with the demise of gentlemanly bootleggers and the advent of liquor stores up and down Main Street, the brandy purchase became more complicated.

Miss Daisye would circle on her kitchen calendar a date early in November. It would become for her as inevitable, as inescapable, as filled with dread as an appointment for a root canal might be for the rest of us. Once she chose the date for buying her brandy, it became irrevocable. On the given morning, she would leave her house at exactly five minutes until 10, knowing to the minute how long it took to walk to the nearest liquor store.

As the owner unlocked his door, Miss Daisye would arrive and quickly step inside. A man of sensitivity, he would make no sign of recognition, nor would he presume to anticipate what he knew her exact words would be:

"A bottle of Courvoisier, please."

"Yes ma'am."

By the time he found the bottle, she would have the money ready, snapping shut her silk coin purse. It is easy to imagine that as he wrapped the bottle tightly in a snug-fitting paper sack, their eyes might meet. The silhouette of the parcel was too revealing for a lady of her convictions to carry in public. Accordingly, he would shake open a large grocery bag, place the Courvoisier in it, and fold the top down securely.

As far as the town was concerned, Miss Daisye might be on her way home from the Jitney with a half-dozen apples.

Only once have I been privileged to see Miss Daisye actually at work on her bread. In her high-ceilinged, old fashioned kitchen with the porcelain sink and vintage gas stove, she made her batter with a hand-turned beater. I was only a girl then, but already a head taller. I watched over her shoulder as she splashed in the vanilla extract, which I felt sure was the last ingredient. I expected to see her spoon the batter into the tins. Instead she turned to me.

"Isn't it time for you to go home?"

"No'm. I can stay till they're done. I want to see them come out of the oven."

"Hmmph."

She walked past me and picked up her red kitchen stool and moved it to the farthest cabinet. She climbed on the stool and reached into the highest shelf. She handed down the heavy bottle. I felt honored to be admitted into her confidence. Stepping lightly to the floor, she took the bottle from me and wiped a coating of dust away with her long apron. She uncorked it with a sure twist and held the bottle up to the light to check the contents.

"Half full," she said. "That ought to do it." And into the batter it went.

She dropped the empty bottle into the garbage can, gave her batter another good beating, spooned it into the cake tins, then slid them carefully into the oven. She wiped her hands on her apron with satisfaction, then turned to me.

"That was the secret ingredient," she said.

"Yes'm," I replied, feeling much older than my years.

She let me wash up.

* * *

Years later, during a typically beautiful Oxford April, my husband Larry and I decided that we would, and could, become gardeners. This bold leap into troweling was due to my impatience with a measly, nonproductive, monotonous bed of irises.

We had lived for some 20 years in the house that my grandmother Maud Butler Faulkner built in the 1930s in Oxford, Mississippi, without too much interest in our half-acre yard. Over the years, Larry attempted various gardening experiments with little or no help from me.

After we were married in 1972, he remarked that it would be nice if we had grass in the front yard. I was puzzled. The yard was green, wasn't it? It was exactly the way my grandmother kept it. He tactfully convinced me that most yards were not solid moss. I pitched in, and we plugged sprigs of centipede grass we had from Mr. Wilson's yard across the street.

Nearly every summer, Larry planted tomatoes—Big Boys, Bigger Boys, Best Boys—in a neat row on the side of the house where nothing had grown before. He tied them up, fought bloom rot, and cajoled them into bearing fruit. He was devoted to his plants. I became just as devoted to fresh tomato and mayo sandwiches.

Gardeners are born, not made. Larry has green genes. His mother grew roses, azaleas, and hydrangeas in Alabama. She crossbred daylilies to produce new strains. His cousin in Virginia created a seven-acre park where flower-lined paths are open to the public.

My genes, on the other hand, are at war. My mother's people were successful farmers. My grandfather's tomatoes always came in, it seemed, "too fast and too many." I remember as a girl being handed a butcher knife and told to sit on the back porch and "help out with the womenfolk." It was a rite of passage. Years later, part of my dowry was quart size Mason jars of my grandmother's canned tomatoes. I cherished them.

The Faulkners contributed a few desultory genes to my gardening makeup. I distinctly remember the spring when Pappy—my uncle William Faulkner—first grew his victory garden, a patch behind his Oxford home, Rowan Oak, that supplied the table and provided a surplus for friends and family. Pappy plowed the garden himself behind a mule and was exceedingly proud of his vegetables. His wife, Estelle, planted peonies and roses in an intricate maze of privet and azaleas.

Then there was Maud, Pappy's mother and my grandmother. The original black-thumbed lady. She of moss in the front yard. At four feet eight inches tall and 89 pounds, Maud cast a shadow in which nothing grew. She could kill a blooming plant at 20 paces by looking at it. And yet she painted delicate florals of gardenias or magnolias so real they seemed to bruise if I breathed on them.

No seed catalog had more beautiful flowers. It was as if she believed that the only good flower was a painted one.

Until 1992, I—being a green thumb/black thumb schizophrenic—contented myself with growing houseplants, using the tried-and-true method of benign neglect (water them when you think about it).

That spring, a cedar tree had to be cut down on the south side of the house. It had been surrounded by irises my Faulkner ancestors planted years ago. I never had considered it a place for a garden, but after Larry planted zinnias around the trunk and produced a blaze of color, I was seduced by its sunny possibilities.

I called in Henry Jones, the yardman who worked for us and everyone else on the block. He has no telephone, by choice. One makes a Henry sighting and phones a neighbor to ask him to please come to the house next Saturday. He came expecting to mow the lawn as usual or perhaps rake leaves left from the fall. I pointed at the cedar stump and said, "Henry, let's make a flower bed."

There we stood, armed with shovels, hatchets, spades, and trowels. Four hours later, half the stump obstinately remained. Henry lay on the ground, panting. Larry and I were appalled at the unexpected number of iris bulbs we had destroyed. There were roots, bricks, and bits of metal toys or rusted tools lost during the Great Depression (Maud never threw anything away). We stared at the chaos we had wrought from what, in retrospect, seemed a respectable kind of order. The "flower bed" looked as though it had been hit by a small bomb.

Henry heaved himself up, sighed, and without mention of pay, walked out of our lives forever.

We had created our own postage stamp of raw earth. Nevertheless, we could not simply abandon it.

I have a friend, Joe Ann Allen—code name "Garden Center" — whose garden is the envy of all of Oxford and beyond. I borrowed my first garden catalogs from GC and was fascinated—obsessed—with the full-color pictures of flowers with names I could not begin to pronounce, much less spell. The text was as magical as the photographs, "Add enduring charm to your garden . . . attractive year-round . . . elegant and unusual . . . flowers *in abundance* from late spring to early fall . . . golden flowers *glow even on cloudy days*." One phrase leaped out, "EASY CARE!"

I was hooked. Visions of gorgeous blossoms danced in my head. It was going to be so easy.

Pouring over the catalogs, I noticed that each photograph was marked with a tiny symbol. The symbols indicated at least six hours of sun each day; partial sun or shade; or just shade. After I arbitrarily decided that our flower bed fell in the shady category, I called an 800-number and ordered my own "shade-loving garden." This catastrophic decision led to Garden Failure Number One.

When the perennials arrived, I was disconcerted by the small size of the carton. The Lilliputian plants had no "sprays of tiny yellow flowers . . . handsome ribbed leaves . . . masses of violet blue saucer-shaped flowers." Instead, they were a dirty, brownish gray and, to all appearances, dead.

My optimism soon returned. Within the hour, I was digging away, planting honeybells hosta, lady's mantle, hardy geraniums, and hardy gloxinia. When I finished, however, it looked as if my bundles of twigs had created a mini Stonehenge.

When the sprigs did turn green, exposure to 10 hours of daily sunshine throughout the summer burned them to crisps. I was relieved when the first frost came so that I did not have to hope any longer.

By January, though, I was raring to go, telling myself that this year the garden would be perfect. After careful catalog consideration, I selected a sun-loving "Magic Garden."

To my immense surprise, each plant lived. I had not bothered to learn their names: "funny looking blue flowers" (blue pincushions), "two tall pink things" (coneflowers), "scruffy looking whites" (omega wedding phlox), and "pink and yellow fuzzies" (coreopsis). Since they produced one single flower per plant, I could only identify them by holding the catalog next to their leaves. This, I fear, was Garden Failure Number Two.

The next year, I branched out, becoming a bit more creative and adding to my already established perennials—I planted zinnias and Texas wildflowers for height and color. I graduated to such executive decisions as "put the tall ones in the back and short ones in the front."

A friend gave me a statue of St. Francis of Assisi and, miraculously, *everything* bloomed. It would have been a glorious spring if the zinnias had not quit on me.

This year, as I look forward to my garden, I still have a few problems to work out. St. Francis cannot be seen over the five-foot purple coneflowers. There are gaping spots of barren ground. The bed looks better from behind than from the front—my dogs Lion and Murphy, have the best view from their fenced-in backyard, where it is pointless to plant anything.

I'm ready to start again, irrepressible optimist that I am. This version could turn out to be Garden Failure Number Four, but no matter.

Telling you all this, recounting my struggles, has inspired me. Confession is good for the soil.

Larry Wells

Farewell to the SEC

This was the Saturday of Saturdays, October 22, 1994. Alcorn State's Steve (Air II) McNair was poised to break the NCAA career yardage record against Southern University's Jaguars. My wife Dean and I were on our way to Lorman, driving the Natchez Trace. Accompanying us was author, and inveterate sports fan, Willie Morris, who asked me to stop at every historical marker so he could read them out loud. On the Trace, with Willie, the past was never passed.

In Lorman, state troopers directing traffic stopped our car about two miles from the campus. We had no parking sticker. Willie was prepared. He had stopped at a Kinko's and had a sign printed that read, "PRESS – The New York Times" (using Old English script). "Hold it up, Deanie," he whispered, "and look like a reporter!" The troopers, who thought they'd seen it all, laughed and waved us through.

We parked near the stadium, where a festive crowd was tailgating. The fragrance of barbeque rose from a hundred grills like a sonata. Mozart was playing on the stadium public address system. Willie had packed a picnic of vodka and fried chicken. Sustained by the provisions, we approached Jack Spinks Stadium.

Former Alcorn State Coach Mario (The Godfather) Casem famously observed that in the Deep South football is religion and Saturday is the holy day. In that spirit the minister who delivered the invocation asked the Lord to bless the contest and grant Alcorn State victory. The audience began to cheer before he could say Amen, because an invocation is only words whereas the game itself is prayer in motion—bands competing, drum majors athletically cavorting, bare-chested Alcorn "Brave" mascot in war bonnet hoisting an Alcorn banner, players in gold helmets and purple jerseys running onto the field.

Number Nine leads his teammates into the stadium. They circle the field at a lope, making right angles at the corners. Each player spins and leaps in a war dance. The Southern fans join in the applause. It is McNair's moment. He knows it. The players know it. The fans know it.

When were warm-ups anything other than players getting loose? At Alcorn, no activity is unworthy of ritual. The team captains assume their places in front of the players like drum majors. Their warm-up exercises are a study in precision. "We know who we are," this team seems to be saying. They end their warm-ups with a chant, "Alcorn, Alcorn, Alcorn." The Braves group closely together, heads bowed, helmets held in the air.

Southern kicks off. On the first series of downs, McNair uncharacteristically throws an interception. He's tight! He's going for too much, too soon. Southern scores first. Alcorn looks to answer.

In Coach Cardell Jones' high-powered, no-huddle, run-and-shoot offense, McNair takes the snap in a shotgun formation with a single blocking back and three wide receivers on one side of the line, sometimes a split end opposite. At home in the pocket, he checks his receivers. Primary receiver covered, McNair effortlessly scrambles to avoid the rush and wills his secondary receivers to go deep. One of his favorite targets is his brother, Tim, Number Seven. Go on, Steve, throw it to your brother. Make your mama happy!

McNair's calm, unhurried throwing motion is one with the choreography of talent on display all around us—bandleader pointing at his trumpet section, cheerleader doing a back flip, referee patting a player on the back after a dropped pass—grace absolute and sublime. McNair is mainlined into his receivers' moves, putting exactly enough lead on the pass, no chance for an interception, pro scouts in the skybox scribbling notes and shaking their heads. Hey, Number Nine, throw it in the air and run down the field and catch it your own self.

I've been recording McNair's yardage on a check stub. Willie announces to the fans sitting around us, "My computer analyst says McNair has sixty yards and needs two hundred and four to break the record. After every gain by McNair, people are asking, 'How many to go?' Willie says, "Let me check with my computer analyst . . . It's one hundred sixty-four."

Midway in the second quarter the magic number is 82, then 74, then 57, shrinking like a shroud being lifted, like the Lord fast-forwarding the clouds. A single sunbeam breaks through. We squint in anticipation of being dazzled. How many more plays will it take? Ten dollars says two.

McNair fades back for a pass. His receivers covered, he scrambles around right end. It is happening, as we all knew it would. Providence slows it down for our collective memory. McNair runs with deceptive speed, starting slow, waiting until the last moment for his receivers to get open, then committing to the run, exploding past defenders who hesitate too long. He gains ten yards, then cuts back against the grain. Needing six yards to break the record, he gets twenty-two.

We sit stunned by good fortune. In an indefinable way, an athlete has redefined existence and given us hope. The crowd's standing ovation swells into a roar of benediction. God is good! Thank you, God.

The team isn't aware the record has been broken. In both end zones students are loosening ties of plastic bags containing gold and purple balloons. The announcement is given over the public address system: 'Steve McNair has broken the career yardage record of 15,049 set by Brigham Young quarterback Ty Detmer.' Time is called. The band plays the fight song. Fans sustain an unending, thunderous applause. Balloons fill the air. Coach Jones and his staff and players rush onto the field to congratulate Number Nine. The Southern players line up to shake his hand.

McNair, who has made history by gaining nearly 300 yards in less than two quarters, and who will, in the fading moments of this game, prove that second down and forty-yards-to-go is no big deal, now demonstrates he has not forgotten the source. He trots over to the stands and hands the ball to his mother.

"He has three games left," Morris muses. "Who knows, he may leave behind a record that won't be broken. It'll be a crime if they don't give him the Heisman."

CURTIS WILKIE

A Magic Death

On Labor Day 2001, the holiday weekend started in Lafayette County with a promising victory by the Ole Miss Football team and ended with a young man dying under strange circumstances. No news story appeared in the local paper, not even an obituary, to mark the passing of 21-year old Chad Durley; nothing at all to hint that his case would be turned into an unprecedented criminal prosecution or that the incident would reveal a deadly nature to a rite of youth culture. Under a gravestone bearing a passage from Ephesians, Durley was buried near his home in Harmontown, a rural community on the far side of Sardis Lake from the college town of Oxford and a world removed from the hedonistic palaces of the beautiful people. There the case lay for more than a year.

A short article in the *Daily Mississippian*, the student newspaper at Ole Miss, appeared in October, 2002. It reported that two teenagers had been indicted for manslaughter after "their friend died in Harmontown from consuming mushrooms" they had given him. Few details were included; the victim's name was not even mentioned. Despite its routine appearance—just another entry on the Circuit Court docket—the story seemed to have the elements of a dark, Donna Tarrt novel in which young people poison an acquaintance while justice blinks.

I had been looking for a case to assign to twenty students in an advanced reporting course I was teaching that fall. Ideally, I wanted the class to cover a trial of some sort but figured that would be too time-consuming. After reading the story, I thought the class—composed, for the most part, of seniors and graduate students—might dig into the background of the manslaughter charges. To see if the mushroom case warranted our interests, I telephoned a local lawyer who agreed that it seemed intriguing. I also called Jere Hoar, an Oxford resident who taught journalism at Ole Miss before retiring to write fiction with a decidedly Southern Gothic tone. Jere said the story sounded "damned interesting." It reminded him of an old Clint Eastwood movie in which a man preys on a girl's school and is fed a fatal dose of mushrooms and toadstools in revenge.

My class was winding up their reports on a Congressional election in Mississippi, so before assigning them the mushroom case in early November, I did a bit of legwork myself. I climbed the creaking steps inside the old Lafayette County Courthouse—the whitewashed building in the center of the Oxford Square that provided so much color for Faulkner—to the second floor offices of the circuit clerk to inspect the court file. The document for Case No. LK 02-333 amounted to a few pages of bare facts: Adam Robertson, 19, and Randall Geeslin, 18, had been indicted in September, 2002, on charges that a year earlier they "did unlawfully, willfully, feloniously, and by their culpable negligence kill Byron Chadwick Durley." If convicted, they faced as much as twenty years imprisonment. After they were arrested following the indictment, Robertson and Geeslin pleaded not guilty. But I saw that Geeslin had since changed his plea to guilty. A clerk told me there had been a further development and additional papers would be put in the file later in the week.

Leaving the courthouse, I made a call to another Oxford lawyer I knew and learned that three days earlier, in a hearing attended by only a handful of people and no reporters, there had been an emotional exchange between Geeslin and the victim's parents before he was sentenced to spend a year in the county jail.

Our class had missed the opportunity to witness this drama, but I felt we still had a chance to track down other aspects of an interesting case. The assignment grew more fascinating with each fresh detail.

Had the victim and defendants been the sons of celebrities, their story would have been the stuff of tabloid headlines.

There were sensational elements: death, exotic evidence, criminal charges, mystery. And there was poignancy; a sad tragedy in which the life of one young man was lost and the future of two others—as well as members of all three families—were left irrevocably diminished and haunted. All the result of a weekend lark that went terribly wrong.

Since neither Durley nor his friends attended Ole Miss, they had not been preoccupied with the festivities surrounding a new season of football on that first Saturday of September. The young men from Harmontown were "country boys," and they looked elsewhere for entertainment. Geeslin and Robertson, whose previous brushes with the law were described by authorities as "run of the mill" juvenile charges, spent Saturday afternoon in neighboring Marshall County, picking mushrooms in the expectation that they would enjoy a high from consuming them. The next day, in the lassitude of late summer, the three young men ate the mushrooms at lunchtime. Durley became violently ill. Through hours of pain, Durley slowly expired on a pallet in the kitchen of the little house he shared with Robertson. He was pronounced dead shortly after arrival at Baptist Memorial Hospital in Oxford on Monday afternoon.

More than a year later, the state moved to prosecute his friends for manslaughter. At first, we found Rashomon-like discrepancies in the various accounts, stories that yielded more questions than answers. Had Durley been abandoned and left alone to die? Why the long delay in bringing charges? Why, indeed, make an effort to send two teenagers to prison? There were even questions regarding the fatal mushrooms. If they were not illegal, how could a criminal case be constructed around their consumption?

While I tried to instruct my class on the techniques of reporting a criminal case, they educated me on the popularity of mushrooms—or 'shrooms, as they are known colloquially. There was nothing unusual, they told me, about young people going into the Mississippi woods in search of "magic mushrooms" and using the plants to induce LSD-like visions. The practice was known to college kids as well as rural youths.

When I attended Ole Miss forty years ago, we were unfamiliar with recreational drugs. The only mention of marijuana came up in tales of Mose Allison growing weed in his dormitory window box before leaving campus for fame as a jazz musician. We would have more likely found cassoulet on the menu at the school cafeteria than marijuana at a fraternity party. My generation thought we were hip, but our extrasensory pleasures were obtained outside "dry" Lafayette County in the beer joints of Holly Springs and Quitman County. We were relatively innocent and hopelessly naive. By the time I was a senior, there were whispers about perception-altering cactus plant indigenous to the American Southwest. Peyote buttons, which supposedly produced visions when chewed, were ordered from New Mexico and distributed among a few of my friends. But when students thought of illicit drugs at Ole Miss back then, one thought of nothing more daring than Dexedrine during final examinations.

Even as an adult—and I did not exactly live under cloistered conditions—I was only vaguely aware of the psychedelic powers of mushrooms; the sort of "psilocybin mushrooms soaked in honey and used to sweeten tea" that Anthony Bourdain wrote about in *Kitchen Confidential.*

Members of my class laughed at my naiveté.

Magic mushrooms were readily available in Mississippi, Joy told me. They sprang up in "cow patties" after rains, and it was not unusual for young people to pick them to get a free high. Another student, Michele, said magic mushrooms were sold openly by youthful entrepreneurs in the audience of a Widespread Panic concert she attended in Alabama the week before: fifty dollars for an eighth of a pound.

Almost on cue, days after we began looking into the Lafayette County case, the (Memphis) *Commercial Appeal* reported that narcotics officers in Memphis busted more than a dozen spectators at another concert by Widespread Panic. The band is a popular "jam band" that has inspired a cult fashioned after the camp followers of the Grateful Dead. According to the article, one undercover officer was offered "mind-altering" mushrooms for sixty dollars each. Another suspect was arrested when the bottom of a cooler he was carrying collapsed and four bags of mushrooms fell out.

With one young man dead in Lafayette County, I wondered about the danger.

Lucille McCook, a biology professor at Ole Miss, gave a professional assessment of the magic mushrooms for Hays, one of my students.

"There are lots of urban legends out there when it comes to mushrooms," she told him. "It's really hard to identify the different kinds of mushrooms out in the wild. Some have deadly neurotoxins and there are no antidotes for them. They can cause painful damage to humans when consumed."

The mushrooms with hallucinogenic properties similar to lysergic acid diethylamide (LSD) "grow in cow patties and farmers' fields after it rains," she said.

"There are other kinds of mushrooms growing in cow patties that are poisonous. It's really Russian roulette."

As my class fanned out in search of the story, I assigned individual students to contact specific law enforcement officers, prosecutors and defense attorneys to avoid having all twenty students overwhelm the sources with calls. At class meetings on Tuesday and Thursday mornings, the information was shared. Each student would be expected to supplement these "pool reports" with their own independent reporting and be prepared to turn in a story by Thanksgiving.

The students found that most of the people they approached were helpful. But as budding reporters, they also learned that not every one was courteous. Jennifer told her classmates that she had been cut short by Tom Levidiotis, the lawyer who represented Geeslin. When she asked about the year's delay in bringing charges, Jennifer said Levidiotis snapped, "Talk to the assholes who charged them." He closed their phone conversation with another insult, "I feel quite confident you'll get the information wrong."

I told the class they should take that remark as a challenge.

Since Joanna was dating the son of Thomas R. Trout, the assistant district attorney in charge of the prosecution, she agreed to interview him. Joanna talked to Trout at his home while he watched a football game on TV. She turned in a transcript of their discussion, and it provided several laconic details:

Q: When and where did the death occur?

A: Well, Geeslin and Robertson picked the mushrooms and brought them back to where Chad Durley was and they ate the mushrooms. Durley died.

Q: Where did they get the mushrooms?

A: I don't know exactly . . . they picked them on the side of the road.

Q: Did Geeslin and Robertson eat the mushrooms too?

Q: Yes.

Q: Did the two defendants know that the mushrooms were poisonous?

A: No.

Q: Why was Durley the only one to die?

A: Well, you never know what the circumstances were, but it's a good chance that they picked more than one variety of mushrooms.

Q: Did they get sick?

A: Geeslin did. I don't know about Robertson.

Q: Why were charges delayed so long?

A: Well, there were many people who investigated to try to determine the particular mushrooms, and it was difficult to isolate the type of mushroom.

Lafayette County Sheriff Buddy East blamed the delay on extensive laboratory work.

"In any type of case involving investigation by the crime lab, you can almost guarantee that there will be a long period of delay," East told Chris, another member of our class.

"The lab is responsible for analyzing every single bit of evidence—blonde hair, fabric samples, etc.—and this type of investigation takes much time."

Jay Hill, an investigative officer for the sheriff, was more voluble about events leading up to Durley's death in his talk with Clara.

"Adam and Chad lived together in Harmontown," Hill said, "and Randall lived down the road. They were hanging out together all weekend in Harmontown."

For the first time, we learned that a fourth person was on hand when the young men ate the mushrooms—a young woman identified as "Chad's girlfriend" but not named. (Benita, another student in our class, would later find that her name was Candace White; she did not eat any of the mushrooms and no charges were filed against her.)

"Chad got sick," Hill said. "Apparently Chad had a cold, and when he got sick his friends left." His condition worsened.

"He called his mother, who was a nurse, to get him some medicine. Eventually she stopped by to check on him and realized he was in very bad condition." She called an ambulance and he was taken to the hospital, but it was too late.

Ron Rychlak, a professor of criminal law at the University of Mississippi Law School, told Lisa that the operative words in the indictment were "culpable negligences." He explained, "If you neglected to take someone to the hospital because you're afraid they'll turn you in for something wrong that you've done, then it's definitely an act of manslaughter."

Other attorneys and law professors we contacted said they had heard of manslaughter cases in which defendants provided drugs that accidentally killed the victims. But no one had ever heard of criminal charges related to a death caused by mushrooms.

Michael Hughes, director of the Mississippi Regional Poison Control Center, told Allen of our class that his staff handled anywhere from 150 to 200 cases of "mushroom exposure" a year in the state. Most of these cases involved young children beguiled by plants that sprouted overnight in their own backyards. Not teenagers seeking a cheap thrill. Fatalities were very rare, he said.

Two of the key figures in the prosecution of the case suggested that the fatal mushrooms were not actually illegal. Trout, the assistant district attorney, said, "There are no mushrooms in Mississippi that are illegal to eat. The ones that contain illegal substance are found mostly in the Southwest United States." Hill, the investigator, told Clare, "There are no laws against mushrooms in Mississippi."

After scratching through the state's criminal code with the help of the law school, we determined that substances containing psilocybin are illegal. This satisfied the team of amateur sleuths and their clueless instructor that the charges had some legal basis.

But we were left with another question after Lindsey obtained a copy of the transcript of the hearing for Geeslin. Reading the testimony, we saw that before Geeslin was sentenced, the victim's mother, Pam Durley, asked for permission to speak to the defendant.

"Mr. Geeslin," Mrs. Durley began.

"Yes ma'am." (We were told he was weeping).

"I am sorry for you. I really am," Mrs. Durley said. "The last time I saw you, I was looking through a window and you were getting high while my son was dying."

According to the investigator's account to Clare, Durley's friends left after he became ill. How, then, could Mrs. Durley have seen Geeslin at the house while her son lay dying?

It took more interviews to reconcile this apparent discrepancy.

Amanda, a graduate student who worked part-time in another office at the courthouse, arranged to talk with Hill. According to Hill's clarification, there was an interval of nearly thirty hours between the time Durley ate the mushrooms and became ill and the following afternoon when his mother tried vainly to rescue him. During this period, the defendants and Durley's girlfriend left the house. Sometime before the mother arrived, the two men returned.

The investigator was still mystified by the appeal of the magic mushrooms. "I don't see why people want to lift up a piece of shit and eat what's growing out of it," he told Amanda.

Hill was pressed for more information in a separate interview with Benita. He said he had gone to the Harmontown house after the ambulance was called. "Adam was there at the scene. We had to locate Randall on a county road. He left the scene."

Amanda uncovered more excruciating details in a talk with a county official who did not want to be named. He said that Chad Durley had become desperately dehydrated in the hours after he ate the mushrooms. Before he sought help, Durley tried to slake his thirst with tea, water, soda and fruit drinks. "By the time he got to the hospital," the source said, "his lips were stained with Kool Aid."

We were winding up our exercise in news gathering and had dealt with most of the questions. The deadline was approaching, but members of the class asked for an extension of a few more days. A couple of students who had developed a special interest in the story asked privately if it would be okay to approach the Durley family.

We had already read their heartbreaking comments in the court transcript. "I have asked God to forgive you," Mrs. Durley told Geeslin, "and I hope that you will turn your life over to God." She said he owed it to his family as well as his friend, Chad.

"My son is gone," she said. "You have been given a second chance . . . This is all about accountability, son, when you make judgments you stand to take responsibility for what you do."

After she finished, her husband, Don, also addressed Geeslin, "I lost the most dear thing I have in this world when I lost him, and if you are responsible, you know, I hope you realize what we lost, what you lost and what the community lost . . . because you know and I know there weren't any better than that boy. He never hurt anybody. He never said anything bad about anybody and he is gone forever. I can't talk to him. I can't touch him. I can't even see him anymore. All I got is memories. They are good ones, but they hurt. And they hurt like hell, sir."

I didn't want our project to add to the Durleys' grief. But I felt it would be appropriate to call the family to see if they were willing to talk. They had, after all, spoken with humble eloquence in court. And a year had passed since their son had died. These are the toughest calls to make, to call a bereaved family for comment. But a journalist knows to take a deep breath and dial the number. Be polite, I advised, and be sensitive. If they don't want to talk to you, be understanding. Thank them. Apologize for bothering them. And hang up without trying to finagle some sort of comment.

A few nights later, Mrs. Durley called me at home. She said she had been contacted by two of my students and wanted to know if the assignment was legitimate. She said she was inclined to talk to them, but wanted to be sure. We had a pleasant conversation. She said she wanted the public to know about her son's death, to learn about the dangers found in magic mushrooms. So far, no one had seemed interested.

In the end, Mrs. Durley decided against talking publicly about the case until the charges against the second defendant, Adam Robertson, were resolved.

But before we ended our conversation that night, she confirmed the answer to the remaining riddle in the case: Why had the authorities waited so long to bring charges?

I had been told earlier by someone familiar with the case that it was not because of problems getting a report from the crime lab. The delay was caused by the state's reluctance to prosecute the case. But the Durleys were not mollified by the adage about the wheels of justice turning slowly. They wanted action and they pressured Lafayette County officials for months. Finally, the authorities agreed to make arrests if a grand jury agreed to hand up an indictment.

No one had wanted to do anything, Mrs. Durley told me. Still, she persisted. After she was allowed to tell her story to a grand jury, the testimony resulted in the indictment and the arrests. It was all about accountability, she told me, echoing her message to Randall Geeslin. It took her a year, she said, but someone had to be accountable for her son's death.

JANE MULLEN

The Ghost of Christmas Future

My mother had told us Uncle Andrew was coming for a visit because he'd been very sick and needed a good rest, but he kept going out for longer and longer walks. She kept trying to make him take my sister and me with him and when he left without us she would send us running after him.

He explained, not that patiently, that our mother just couldn't seem to understand that he really needed to walk a lot faster than we were able to; but he knew we would understand.

He'd give us each a quarter—a fortune; babysitters were paid twenty-five cents an hour—to stay on the swings in the park until he came back for us. When it was raining, he'd give us each fifty cents and leave us in a store where we bought red wax lips and black wax mustaches and cardboard cartons of little wax milk-bottles filled with green and blue and pink syrup. One time—the best time of all—when my sister couldn't come, he took me with him into a place where he said he had to see a man about a dog, only there wasn't any dog, and I got to kneel on a high leather stool at a counter and drink ginger ale and eat peanuts and listen to the beery cheery sound of men

talking to men.

The next time my mother took me downtown with her when she went to pay the bills and do some shopping, making the rounds from the bank to the electric company to the gas company to Holland's Department Store and on to the much nicer D.M. Read's, and we ended up as we always did at the soda fountain counter annexed to the first floor of Read's, I had a new thing to ask for when the waitress wanted to know what I would like to drink.

"A shot and beer, here," I called out in the way I'd heard one of the men do in the place without the dog. The waitress smiled and two men sitting at the counter laughed out loud. My mother took me home without anything to drink and made me sit on The Chair for an hour.

But I noticed that she did not tell my father.

For Easter that year we went to visit my uncle at West Point. After church there was an egg hunt on a grassy slope above the Hudson, and after the eggs and the prizes and consolation prizes, there was lunch in the officers' mess, where my sister and I drank iced tea for the first time and helped ourselves to scoops of vanilla ice cream that was mounded into big serving bowls like mashed potatoes and passed around the table. Our uncle kept telling us how pretty we were and how we would marry officers and wear wedding gowns made of pure white parachute silk. He kept drumming his fingers on the table. He kept leaving. My mother kept sending my father to look for him and my father kept getting more and more irritated.

When it was time to go back to the hotel my uncle said he'd bet that

my sister and I would like a ride in a real army jeep, but my father said absolutely not, and my mother said no as well. My sister got into the back seat of our car and slammed the door. I ran over to the jeep and put up my arms. My uncle lifted me in and we were off, moving so fast right from the start, the buildings flying by in a gray blur and the trees stepping out of the way just in time, that I couldn't even look over my shoulder to see if my parents were coming after us. I just held on to the grip with both hands.

We drove straight to the edge of a cliff—so it seemed—and parked. I stood up on the seat and looked over the windshield while my uncle pointed. "Look there. See how the river's carved that narrow channel into the Appalachians? Over there's where George Washington stood when he was planning how to take the Hudson River valley from the

British. And right here's where Benedict Arnold stood plotting how to give it back to them."

We stayed there until the wide streaks of flame in the sky had turned to dark, and I was already asleep when I bounced out of the jeep on the way to the hotel, breaking one of my arms and the other wrist.

When I was back home again my uncle sent presents. A blue stuffed rabbit I would keep for more than twenty years, a gardenia in a box, a book of stories about the Hudson River valley. But I never saw him again. He was not at Aunt Gen's for Memorial Day when we went to the cemetery with flowers. He was not at the lake in Pennsylvania that summer. Aunt Gen and Uncle Martin now owned the cottage they had been renting for several years. My family always rented another one nearby. The other three uncles came out, each for a couple of days. But Uncle Andrew did not come.

Two days before Thanksgiving two telegrams came; one from the Red Cross, and one from the army. My father was just coming home from work and he backed the car right out again to drive my mother to the railroad station. She boarded the train so fast— just a flash of her legs and her high heels as the conductor reached down to pull her up the steep step— that she forgot to turn and wave good-bye.

On Thanksgiving my father took us to dinner in a restaurant where we had roast chicken instead of turkey because we hadn't made a reservation, then to the red-carpeted, gold-trimmed Majestic to see "Singing in the Rain" to cheer us up after the chicken. When we got home the phone was ringing as we opened the door. My sister and I raced to answer it, but my father, who never answered the telephone if he could help it, yelled no, let him get it. We stood by, all ears. He said, "Sweetheart," so we knew it was our mother. Then he said he was sorry, that he really was sorry, that it was a shame, so young. He left the phone to get a paper and pencil so he could make a list, but neither of us dared pick up the receiver to say hello. When he got off the phone he just looked at us. My sister started to cry and ran upstairs to her room, and suddenly

I didn't want to hear what he had to say. I went to the piano and played "Chopsticks" over and over until my father scooped me off the piano bench, held me on his lap and told me he had to wash my hair because the next day we were going to Pennsylvania.

We sang along with the radio driving over Bear Mountain—When the values go up, up, up. And the prices go down, down, down—though it was snowing hard and all along the way up and down there were cars pulled off to the side of the road. We stopped only once to eat at a diner because, my father said, you never knew when you might get stranded and you couldn't count on Aunt Gen to give you a decent meal anyway. He asked the waitress to fill our thermos with hot chocolate. In the trunk of the car was a big box of sand, the fireplace shovel and the snow shovel. There were three blankets stacked on the back seat next to me and six Hershey bars in the glove compartment, and a green prune-juice bottle full of water on the floor. My father was always prepared for emergencies, always on the lookout for dangers and for ways—and alternate ways—out of them. Which is probably why death decided it had better take him completely by surprise, sneaking up behind him one morning—just three weeks after my mother died — as he carried his cereal bowl from the table to the sink.

At the house that used to be my grandmother's and was now Aunt Gen's there was another soldier who had come on the same train as my mother but who'd had to ride in the baggage car with my uncle. His name was Will and he was much younger than any of the uncles. Every time he sat down Vivien would crawl onto his lap. Ronan and I would sit on each side of him and move in close. My sister would sit across from him so she could look at him. He was very nice to look at, and he was the first southerner any of us had ever met. We kept making him say certain words over and over again, like Po-lice, and we kept calling our mothers Ma'am, the way he did, until our fathers told us to stop or we would get the back of their hands.

Will read us the newspaper story Aunt Gen's husband—Uncle Martin worked for the Scranton Times—had written about Uncle Andrew. It said he had enlisted in the army in 1937 and was made a corporal, a sergeant, a lieutenant, then a captain before giving up his rank to join the new parachute battalion when it opened up after the fall of France, a phrase that translated in my mind to a picture of the Eiffel Tower collapsing in tears to its broken knees. Uncle Andrew himself was quoted from a much earlier newspaper article, from an interview with him during the war.

There's nothing like jumping out into space, all the fellows behind you singing 'Ain't you Comin' Out? ' And dropping like a rock at a hundred miles an hour, then coming to a dead stop when your chute opens. It's like being hit with a ten-ten truck. But after it opens its just wonderful floating way above the earth. Though sometimes you hit the ground pretty hard. Oh, and you've got to pull that ripcord within three seconds after jumping, or it'll be too late.

There were two pictures, one in his major's dress uniform and one in which he was wearing a jumpsuit, standing sideways to show the packed parachute on his back. "He was a hero," Will said. "He was the first to win the Air Medal, and then he won another one. Y'all should be real proud." Another phrase we tried out on our grieving mothers.

The funeral was late in the afternoon because the ground was frozen and had to be opened with jackhammers, Will said. He said anybody else would have to wait for a thaw, but not a hero. The coffin was covered with a flag and carried by six soldiers instead of the uncles and fathers who had carried my grandmother. When the priest finished reading the prayers, it was so quiet you could hear the branches of the trees creaking under the ice and the hum of tire-chains on the road outside the cemetery.

We were sitting on rows of cold metal chairs under a green canopy that snapped in the wind. In the front row was my mother, Aunt Gen, Uncle Michael, Uncle Kerry, and Uncle Paul. In the next row was me, Ronan, my sister, Uncle Martin, and my father. I was on the end of the row. The ground under the green carpet was so uneven that Ronan kept sliding into me and I had to hold on to the edge of my seat with both hands to keep from falling off. The silence went on so long it seemed no one knew what to do next. Then one of the soldiers stepped forward and raised a bright brass bugle to his lips. He blew out the slowest and saddest sounds I had ever heard; the saddest, I think now, that have ever been conceived. He stood so close to where I sat at the end of the row that I could see the apple in his throat move in and out, so close that each note blew straight through me, moving my heart a little each time. Then Will and another soldier stepped snappily forward and whipped the flag off the coffin. They folded it quickly into a neat triangle, fat as a pillow. Will turned to where my mother and Aunt Gen sat. He hesitated, as if he weren't sure which to give it to, then presented the bundle to my mother. Ronan dug his elbow into my side and I turned to him triumphantly. We were getting the flag.

But he wasn't thinking about the flag. He leaned across me and pointed, like the ghost of Christmas Future, to the headstone. I had seen it before, had played around it on Memorial Days and birthdays and anniversaries when we would all bring flowers, but had never really looked at it. Most likely Ronan, who was the same age, hadn't either. But now that we could read, now that it was gathered under this tent with us, it seemed immense, the most immense object life had thus far presented for our consideration. There, etched in stone, were the names not only of our grandparents and of Ronan's sister Amy, who had died of polio before we were born, but my mother's name, and my father's and Ronan's mother and father, and all our other uncles, each name followed by a date and a dash.

It would be years before I would ask about this and my Uncle Paul would tell me that my grandmother had bought this huge plot after Amy died and had my grandfather moved there to keep her company. She had bought it in much the same spirit that she had chosen that big house the uncles bought for her after the war. Room for all: her husband, herself, her four sons, her two daughters and their husbands, four more spaces for those unknown and dreaded creatures, the women my uncles might possibly marry over her dead body. And she had bought this huge headstone and at a special discounted price—it is much easier to chisel letters and numbers into stone when it is lying on its side on a workbench than it is when it is standing on end embedded in the ground—had all their names and birth dates engraved. All that would be needed later was to supply the second date. No one else from my generation was there, only Amy.

Amy Genevieve Mathias 1941- 1946.

I contemplated the list of names and dates and what it must mean for those listed there. Were they so sure, then? Was it all arranged? Just a matter of time? No way out for them?

I looked at Ronan. His eyes were huge and bright and alive with excitement and something of what they held late at night when we scared ourselves silly with ghost stories we had made up, now that our grandmother wasn't there to tell us any. But there was something else; it was the look not of triumph so much as of the acknowledgment of having had a lucky break, a lucky escape from danger by the skin of our teeth. It was the look we exchanged when we arrived all out of breath at the door of the tall green fence that shut his back yard off from the alley and we managed to get inside and slide the bolt just in time, just ahead of the rough boys from Capouse Avenue who had chased us all the way up Harrison. Our names were not there. That headstone had nothing to do with us.

Then, from among the soldiers a voice barked three sharp commands. Rifle barrels rolled and clicked, ear drums cracked once, twice, twenty-one times. My cousin and I, shot through with terror, grabbed each other's arms and held on.

MASARU INOUE

The Clock Above the Courthouse

On the fifth of August, 2000, my Oxford friends, Jim Dees and Ronzo Shapiro, took me down to Yazoo City to visit the grave of our mutual friend, Willie Morris. Willie died of a heart attack on the 2nd of August, 1999, and I had wanted to make the trip on that day, but it was impossible for me to do so for I do not have a car, or even a driver's license. And Yazoo City is too far from Oxford on foot. Jim Dees and Ronzo Shapiro, who knew me well, decided to take me there. I really did feel much obliged to them.

At the cemetery, we saw that a year after the burial, the mound had settled and was completely covered with grass, and yet it did not have a headstone; instead, there was a bucket of flowers. Jim Dees read for Willie in the ground several impressive passages from Willie's *Terrains of the Heart and Other Essays on Home.* Ronzo Shapiro pronounced an eloquent eulogy for Willie. We drank from a bottle of George Dickel, one of Willie's favorite bourbon whiskeys, which I had brought from Oxford. I poured the remaining contents on the head part of the mound and folded my hands in silence.

It was very hot on the fifth of August, as the Mississippi summer usually is. It was more than hot especially in the open cemetery in the sun. The perspiration rose continually on my brow and never ceased dripping from my face. According to Jim Dees, Willie's funeral was held in the same boiling Mississippi heat as we were then enduring one year later. However, we were at Willie's grave for more than an hour in that blazing sun, recalling Willie in each of our hearts. I believe that Willie, chatting with the witch of Yazoo whose grave was next to his, was looking at us. I also believe that he surely chuckled as he told the witch that his friends had come from Oxford to see him.

On our way down to the Yazoo City cemetery, we happened to pass the courthouse of Yazoo County. I moved my eyes unconsciously up to the clock above the courthouse in the city. It said 8:18. "8:18 is it?" I thought, for we had left Taylor, Mississippi, at 10:55 a.m. so that I could not believe the time I saw on the clock. I moved my eyes to my wristwatch. I kept my watch adjusted to the hour on the Weather Channel on TV, so that, of course, it had the right time to the second: 1:30 p.m.

On our way back home, after staying for more than one hour at Willie's grave, we passed the courthouse of Yazoo County again. I moved my eyes again up to the clock and it said the same 8:18. Now my watch said 3:15 p.m. I thought that even the clock was so tired in the blazing Mississippi sun that it had given up ticking time.

I had spent a whole year studying and reading in Oxford, from April, 1986, to March, 1987. Willie had been a Writer-in-Residence there at the University of Mississippi at the time. He had told me that he would have enjoyed "viewing the landmarks of his past through the eyes of the visitor who knew the Delta through Faulkner's work."

Thus, Willie and I—with him at the wheel of his journeyman Buick—visited many places, not only in the Delta but also in other parts of Mississippi. A few among many were: Charleston, one of the two county seats in Tallahatchie County; the cemetery at Holly Springs in Marshall County, where several Confederate generals have been buried; and Vicksburg in Warren County, where one of the severest battles of the Civil War took place in 1863. In each town he showed me the clock above the courthouse for he knew that I was much interested in it.

In Charleston, four clocks on the four facades of the clock tower said four different hours, contradicting one another. So did the clocks on the courthouse in Holly Springs. In Vicksburg, when Willie and I visited his son, David Rae,

David took us to the old courthouse and said to me, pointing at the clock, "Masarou, this clock never moves anymore."

I replied, "Probably it has stopped ticking ever since the 4th of July, 1863."

Hearing this, Willie became excited, "Masarou, you know more Mississippi history than I expected."

"Thank you," I said, "The 4th of July, 1863, was also the day when Vicksburg was captured by troops led by General Ulysses S. Grant that is, tactically, when the South surrendered to him." Willie got mad at this, though not much. Perhaps invoking the name of Grant and the words "Southern surrender," struck a nerve. I added, in haste, "I just said a fact that I happened to know of."

He recovered quickly and became his amiable self. Apparently he was not alone in his passion. He told me that until the First World War, the 4th of July was not even celebrated in Mississippi.

My interest in errant clocks on the courthouse squares dates to my second or third reading of *The Sound and the Fury* when I was a young American Literature major in Japan. I was astonished to find, in the fourth and final section of the book, that the cabinet clock on the wall above the cupboard in the Compsons' kitchen was "three hours behind."

On the first day I arrived in Oxford in the summer of 1984, it was my first trip abroad in my life, the courthouse clock there was also behind by three hours. At 1:35 p.m. Central Standard Time, August 15, 1984, the clock said 4:35. Even if it was by accident. The next day, it said the wrong hour again. During that summer, I adjusted my wristwatch to the time displayed on the TV when I left my room in then Holiday Inn, just like I did in 1986 and 1999.

I was in a quiet excitement, muttering to myself, "I am now in Jefferson, Yoknapatawpha County. I finally came to the South Faulkner depicted in his novels. I am now in the world of *The Sound and the Fury.* Surely, the strokes of the clock that Joe Christmas heard in *Light in August* were those of the "wrong hour . . ."

And then I thought of Isaac McCaslin in "The Bear" (*Go Down Moses*) who actually sees Old Ben, the bear, only after he has relinquished not only the "gun" but also finally the "watch" and the "compass." Old Ben, the bear, is "not even a mortal beast but an anachronism indomitable and invincible out of an old dead time, a phantom, epitome and apotheosis of the old wild life" (1, 185).

It means that it was only after Isaac purified himself from those three symbols of the growth of civilization, which he calls the "taints," that he could see the bear. The watch, Faulkner writes, is "the old, heavy, biscuit-thick silver watch which had been his father's" (1, 199). That watch, in turn, reminded me of the "invisible watch" that could be heard "ticking at the end of the gold chain descending to her (Emily's) waist and vanishing into her belt" (2, 121).

On September 23, 1999, I returned to Oxford. And again I found that the clock above the courthouse said the wrong hour. However, almost a year later, in time for the 4th of July, 2000, the clock was fixed! It displayed the right hour, both the dial and the chime. This in fact made me very nervous. By that time, I had already started writing "The Clock above the Courthouse" using references from *The Sound and the Fury*. Apprehensively, I asked Jamie Kornegay, a promising young writer in town, "What is wrong with the clock? The clock is right! At the beginning of August." My question confused him much more than I thought. He looked puzzled as if it was a profound riddle to him. He surely must have thought, "What is this mysterious Japanese thinking? Nobody usually asks why the clock is right." But I did. As the question hung in the air, he noted my confusion, and advised me to go to the office of the courthouse or to that of City Hall. But I did not go then.

At the end of August, 1999, when I found the clock was wrong again, or as usual, I finally went to the office of the courthouse and asked an officer there if he knew anything about the clock. Unfortunately, he was too busy to talk with me about the clock but he suggested that I go to City Hall. At City Hall they suggested that I go and visit Mr. Will Lewis if I wanted to know about the clock. I began to get excited, thinking that I might be getting close to a clue to solve my question. I knew of Mr. Lewis because he was one of Willie's close friends, and because of Willie he treated me as one of his friends. "Mr. Will Lewis, Jr.? Is he the owner of Neilson's Department Store?" I asked.

I went to Neilson's and to Mr. Lewis' office, where I found him engaged in a phone call. He saw me standing hesitantly at his door and waved me in to take a seat. Finishing his phone call, Mr. Will Lewis, Jr. told me that the original builder of the clock was A. C. Hodkins who also built the clocks at Bolivar, Tennessee, and Holly Springs, Mississippi. He then was kind enough to show me the old pendulum that belonged to the clock and the old external counter weight, too. He also had several newspaper clippings with stories about the clock.

He even showed me a copy of a letter from a professor at the University of Mississippi addressed to the Lafayette County chancery clerk. The letter recounted the professor's inspection of the clock on December 29, 1998, and in it he suggested that "all the hands on all the clocks be replaced with aluminum hands." The clock, by now, has become too old to say the right hour, Mr. Lewis pointed out in one of the clippings. In a story from Memphis, the *Commercial Appeal* stated that "The clock at Oxford, Miss., was built in 1870." "The present courthouse in Oxford was actually completed and occupied in 1872," he said. Even stories about the clock get the time wrong!

As a reader of Faulkner's works I knew that clocks and watches and the hour are very important in understanding his work, and this is especially true in *The Sound and the Fury.* In the fourth and final section of it, entitled "April Eighth, 1928," we can find these passages:

On the wall above a cupboard, invisible save at night, by lamp light and even then evincing an enigmatic profundity because it had but one hand, a cabinet clock ticked, then with a preliminary sound as if it had cleared its throat, struck five times. 'Eight o'clock,' Dilsey said (3, 274).

While she (Dilsey) stood there the clock above the cupboard struck ten times, "One o'clock," she said aloud. "Jason ain't comin home. Ise seed de first en de last," she said, looking at the cold stove. "I seed de first and de last."(3,274)

These are the passages that came to me vividly and put me in a quiet frenzy of delight when I first saw the clock above the courthouse on the square in Oxford in the summer of 1984. As these passages demonstrate, there is a difference of three hours between the hour the cabinet clock strikes and the hour Dilsey says. Which hour is right, Dilsey's or the cabinet clock's?

Considering the cabinet clock, we discover that it has but one hand, which means that the cabinet clock is defective. It is obvious and plain that a defective clock with but one hand cannot display the right hour. Then, which hand is it that the defective clock has, the hour hand or the minute hand?

The one hand it has is construed as the minute hand, for the dial of the clock is visible in the night when they light the lamp. It means that anyone who looks up at it at least in the lamp light can see the dial. If one can see the dial, he or she can tell which hand it lost, or which hand survived. Dilsey, who has been the maid of the family for years, knows well that the hand it has is the minute hand, so she only reacts to its striking. When it strikes five times, she says, "Eight o'clock."

All the Compsons, in other words, the proprietors of the cabinet clock, live in a disordered time. For them, time unfolds not with the hour hand and its progression of a larger time unit, but with the minute hand. The minute hand, and the unending sound of the second, the smallest unit of time of the clock, as if it was the chaotic rhythm of clicking continuously to eternity, could in fact bring on a restlessness of sound and fury.

Readers of the novel recall the ticking sounds of the second in the first section, the Benjy section, when Benjy, the idiot, when he "could hear the clock and the roof and Caddy," and when he "could still hear the clock between his voice" (3,57-59).

However, in the Benjy section we do not know what kind of clock it is that makes the ticking sound. It is only in the final section that we learn the clock is defective. When we read the first section of *The Sound and the Fury*, we are forced to be involved in a chaos of time. The reader is confused by it, because Benjy is not only an idiot but also seemingly unconscious of time. Thus the past and present are jumbled together in his monologue as well as in his mind.

But it does not mean that Benjy has nothing to do with time as it progresses. It is only that we are confused with and betrayed by the jumbling together of past and present that we believe that Benjy's universe has nothing to do with it.

And yet, even in Benjy's universe, there is always a clock, and the clock is continually ticking, albeit with the wrong time. It exemplifies the fact that even Benjy, who gives us the impression that he is free from every worldly affair, is not completely free from the "mechanical progress of time." While Benjy's universe would seem to be one of jumbled disorder, he has a profound sense of order, more so, perhaps than the so-called sane members of the family. The ending of the book illustrates this dramatically.

Benjy is heading for the graveyard in a horse and surrey driven by Luster, a black boy Dilsey has charged with looking after Benjy. They come to the square. Luster sees Jason, his master, and also "a group of negroes" around the square. Wanting to show off to them, he hits Queenie, the horse, and tries to swing the surrey around. He intends to go around the Confederate monument to the left to show the assembled "how the quality does" by violating the traffic regulations. As the carriage moves "against his grain," Benjy begins to bellow. Bellow upon bellow, his voice mounts, with scarce intervals for breath. There is more than astonishment in his voice. It is "horror;" "shock;" "agony eyeless, tongueless."

Jason rushes over to them. He hurls Luster aside with a backhanded blow and catches the reins and saws Queenie about and doubles the reins and slashes her across the hips. He cuts Queenie again and again, into a plunging gallop. As Benjy's hoarse agony roars around them, he swings Queenie about to the right of the monument. And he jerks Queenie back and jumps down from the surrey.

Benjy's voice roars and roars. And Queenie moves again to the right, her feet begin to clop-clop steadily again, and "at once" Benjy "hushes." Luster drives on. Benjy's eyes are "empty and blue and serene again" as cornice and facade flows smoothly once more "from left to right, post and tree, window and doorway and signboard each in its ordered place."

In my personal opinion, these last few pages of the book show us Benjy's relation to the time ticked by the clock. They also show us that Benjy is conscious of time, that is, the "time of eternity." This is different from the hour the artificial measuring device says. We know that Benjy always "cries," "moans," or "bellows" at his house or in his yard that is fenced in. We also know that his home is a place with a defective clock that has but one hand and which is continually ticking and striking the wrong hour.

This is a universe that is filled with mechanical and disordered time and full of furies exemplified by "cries," "moans," and "bellows," as well as a mother's self-pitying grief over her own family, and the frustrated, shouted complaints of his brother about his own situation. All of this is related to the changes Caddy undergoes. She is the one and only daughter of the family, and the only one who has grown with the "natural progress of time," and because of this, she is denied and rejected by her own family.

To understand this, let us further examine Benjy's sense of order. What are the conditions that allow him to be "untroubled and serene." One is when Caddy, with her unselfish and fecund love, she soothes him when he cries, bellows and moans. He is also comforted when Dilsey takes him to Easter Sunday services, at the black peoples' church, or when he is headed to the graveyard. It is when he is in these places that he feels everything is in "order."

So what is the order here? Is it just because "cornice and facade flows from left to right, post and tree, window and doorway and signboard each in its ordered place"? In a sense, so it is. But the most important matter that we should not forget here is that cornice and facade flow "from left to right, not "from right to left." Cornice and facade are where they have been set. To Benjy, however, turning at the monument from the reverse direction is the thing that he can not accept.

When this happens, or anything else that he perceives as disrupting his sense of order, he cannot help bellowing and then roaring. Is his extreme vocal reaction caused by the mere violation of traffic regulations, because Luster dared to turn the surrey only to show the "group of negroes" what the "quality" can do?

Luster is with Benjy in the surrey and he knows Jason is in sight and he very well knows that turning to left at the monument is against the traffic regulations. Considering the violation of the traffic regulations as the cause that makes Benjy bellow is meaningless. It has nothing to do with Benjy's universe and he does not, needless to say, pay any attention to anything of the kind; moreover, he does not even know what the traffic regulations are. We have already known, in the third section, that Benjy "tried to run a little girl down on the street with her own father looking at him." Which finally leads up to his being "gelded" (3, 263).

Again, consider the fact that Benjy "cries," "moans" and "bellows" in his own house. A house, as we also have seen, that is governed by a defective clock that ticks the wrong hour. Benjy, who is a man in the "civilized" world, does repudiate the actual progress of time ticked by the clock, expressing himself in his "bellows," "cries" and "moans." He lives in accord with the "natural progress of time" and denies or repudiates instinctively the movement of the hands of the clock that "wears away" the natural progress of time that turns the hands of it "from right to left." Turning "from right to left" is called "clockwise" and turning "from left to right" is "counter-clockwise." Turning "from left to right" at the monument on the Square which has in the center of it the courthouse above which the clock is placed exemplifies "counter-clockwise." It is against the movement of the hands of the clock.

In thinking of Benjy's "sense of order," it never occurred to me that the simple fact of turning to the left at the monument on the Square, or anywhere else, is "clockwise." Again, it was my friend Jamie Kornegay who saw me standing in front of Square Books looking up at the clock above the courthouse.

Kornegay knew well that I was interested in the clock. When he saw me staring at it, he said to me, "Masaru, it is just a simple fact that turning to the left here is clockwise." I said to him in an excitement, "Yes, it is! Please let me use your idea!" Probably, to him, I looked very silly because I was excited to know this simple fact. However, what he said nonchalantly was, to me, enlightening.

Sometimes a simple fact carries the most meaning. I want to emphasize again the simple fact that turning "to the right" at the monument is against the movement of the mechanical device, and it is in accord with the natural progress of time to be against the movement of the clock in the sense that Benjy, who can judge everything instinctively, denies or repudiates the movement of the cabinet clock in his house by his "bellow," "cry" and "moan." Any artificial and mechanical device that relates to time is repudiated in that it kills the natural progress of time. The clock above the courthouse also is, needless to say, one of the mechanical devices that seemingly measures the natural progress of time. But it only deforms "time." It is the clock that is defective in measuring "time." Time, or the natural progress of time, is the thing we should not cut into pieces by using any kind of mechanical device that just makes a restless sound of ticking. Conversely speaking, Benjy's bellows and roars at the monument on the square exemplifies the defect in the movement of the clock above the courthouse, whether the actual clock above the courthouse on the square shows us the correct time or not.

The approximately 56-year-old clock may have told the wrong hour even in 1928, because in the second section of the book, the Quentin section, we have already discovered that there are in this world no clocks that can tell the right natural time.

We have to go to the Quentin section entitled "June Second, 1910" that begins with this passage:

> When the shadow of the sash appeared on the curtains it was between seven and eight o'clock and then I was in time again, hearing the watch. It was Grandfather's and when Father gave it to me he said I give you the mausoleum of all hope and desire; it's rather excruciatingly apt that you will use it to gain the reducto absurdum of all human experience which can fit your individual needs no better than it fitted his or his father's. I give it to you not that you may remember time, but that you might forget it now and then for a moment and not spend all your breath trying to conquer it. Because no battle is ever won he said. They are not even fought. The field only reveals to man his own folly and despair, victory is an illusion of philosophers and fools (3,76).

The beginning sentence of the Quentin section, in a sense, governs the whole section, because in this sentence the "shadow" caused by sunlight and the "watch" are juxtaposed. The shadow here exemplifies the movement of the sun that shows us the natural progress of time, and it makes Quentin conscious of "time" and then of the watch, an artificial device that measures "time." In this section, we find the appearance of a shadow, a clock, a watch so many times that I have given up counting.

Of the sun and the shadow, I would like to remind you of Lena Grove in *Light in August* who came to Jefferson, Yoknapatawpha, from somewhere in Alabama—that is, from east to west like the movement of the sun, "The sun stands now high overhead; the shadow of the sunbonnet now falls across her lap. She looks up at the sun. 'I reckon it's time to eat,' she says" (4, 29).

She lives in accord with the natural progress of time, not with the movement of the hands of the clock, the artificial time. Like Caddy, she was denied and rejected by her own blood brother when she conceived a child with a man temporarily called Lucas Burch.

In the Quentin section of *The Sound and the Fury* we see the unfolding of the "metaphysical consideration of time" by Quentin. However, I can not afford to discuss it here, because I do not have the ability or knowledge to do so. I can only remind you that he is obsessed with time that continually progresses and its ceaseless progression, and that he is much conscious of, and too nervous about, the clock, the watch, and the time they say accordingly.

Who is Quentin Compson? He is the eldest and first son of the Compson family. He attends Harvard and lives in a dormitory, far away from his home in Jefferson, Mississippi. The second section, entitled "June Second, 1910," consists of a monologue delivered on the last day of his life, just before he commits suicide.

The Compson family was once prominent with a "governor" and "three generals" among their ranks. But in the year 1928, only about 100 years after Mississippi's admission to the United States, and at most 130 years after the establishment of the Mississippi Territory, the madness caused by "saneness" in "crass material world," on the one hand, and the "obsession with the natural progress of time," on the other, have now brought the clan to the point of decay.

The "governor" is the representative and figurehead of a state, and the "general" holds that same authority in the military. If so, it can be said that the old state of Mississippi was made up of people like the old Compsons. In this sense the history of the Compsons is not only the history of the family, but also of the region, in this case, the state of Mississippi.

The history is the sum of facts arranged in chronological order. In other words, the accumulation of time ticked with the mechanical device, the clock, in which notable things happened. It is the chronological sum of seconds, minutes, hours, days, and so on, "ticked by the clock." If the clock of the Compsons is defective, then the public clock of the state also has been ticking the wrong hour. Just like the old clock above the courthouse in the real Oxford.

Thus, Quentin is a member of a family that once was the representative of the state. He has the watch that has been inherited from his grandfather to his father and then to him who is the first son of the Compson family. This means that he has also inherited the history of his state. By being the heir of his family, his watch which he carries with him around Cambridge, Massachusetts, is thought to be linked and synchronized with the family clock that is on the wall in the kitchen in his Mississippi house.

The family clock, the cabinet clock, is continually ticking and is always striking the wrong hour. By carrying this watch with him up in New England, Quentin also carries the accumulated past of his family and of his state. As long as he keeps the watch that ticks the history of his family, Quentin, like his brothers, Jason and Benjy, can never be free of the wrong hour. When he does finally try to free himself from his agonies, the first act he thinks of is to break his watch. Unlike Benjy who can only bellow when the clock is wrong, Quentin takes a physical action to attempt to "free" the natural progress of time. He breaks his watch that has ticked the history of his family and of his state:

I went to the dresser and took up the watch, with the face still down. I tapped the crystal on the corner of the dresser and caught the fragments of glass in my hand and put them into the ashtray and twisted the hands off and put them in the tray. The watch ticked on. I turned the face up, the blank dial with little wheels clicking and clicking behind it, not knowing any better.... There was a red smear on the dial. When I saw it my thumb began to smart. I put the watch down and went into Shreve's room and got the iodine and painted the cut. I cleaned the rest of the glass out of the rim with a towel (3, 80).

It is symbolical that Quentin finds "a red smear on the dial" of his watch. He was wounded in action. It means that he lost in the hand-to-hand fight with the "time" ticked by the watch, an artificial device that measures time, because while his watch may have lost its function on the surface, in its depths it keeps ticking on. As his father said to him, "no battle is ever won," and "the field only reveals to man his own folly and despair, and victory is an illusion of philosophers and fools."

His attempt to stop the watch was in vain. He finds then that it is impossible to stop the ticking of the watch. Finally, the only way he can think of to retrieve the natural progress of time was to stop his own natural time—his own life.

After breaking his watch, Quentin wanders into a jeweler's. Here he finds that "there are about a dozen watches in the window, a dozen different hours and each with the same assertive and contradictory assurance that mine had, without any hands at all. Contradicting one another."

This is when and where he is assured, in despair, that there are no right artificial and mechanical watches in the world, because every watch has its own hour, each with the "same assertive and contradictory assurance." Thus, the final way that he attempts to retrieve the natural progress of time was to commit suicide.

He throws himself into the river, because the river to him is a metaphor for returning the natural sense of time. "I could see the smoke stack. That's where the waters would be, heading out to the sea and the peaceful grottoes. Tumbling peacefully . . ." Quentin thinks that the waters would flow to the sea and finally to the peaceful grottoes. The word "grotto" stands for "a small cave or cavern." Its original meaning is derived from "crypt," and "crypt" is an anatomical term for "a small pit, recess, or glandular cavity in the body." So the "peaceful grottoes" here might be considered as the birth canal or as the vagina. It is through this "crypt" that the fetus is expelled during parturition. When Quentin commits suicide by throwing himself into the river, he is trying to return to the womb, the place where life originates. It is where the natural progress of time begins ontologically.

Even so, he could not and can not return to the origin of his life by committing suicide. It is an illusion. He probably knows his committing suicide by throwing himself into the river is an illusion; and that there is no way anyone can return to the origin of his or her being except growing old and finally going back to the soil. In this sense, it is very symbolic that in the final section Benjy's eyes are "serene and ineffable" when he is heading to the graveyard where all the dead are in their eternal time. On the other hand, Quentin thinks, "If I could say Mother. Mother." Because he also feels and knows that he, Caddy and Benjy are deserted by their own blood mother—he once heard his mother say to her husband:

Jason you must let me go away I cannot stand it let me have Jason (their son) and you keep the others (Quentin, Caddy and Benjamin) they're not my flesh and blood like he is, strangers, nothing of mine and I am afraid of them I can take Jason and go where we are not known I'll go down on my knees and pray for the absolution of my sins that he may escape this curse try to forget that the others ever were (3, 104).

However, for Quentin, the society or the family he was born and raised in is so full of sound and fury that he cannot help but to commit suicide by throwing himself into the river. To Quentin, "Jesus was not crucified: he was worn away by a minute clicking of little wheels," even if it was his father's opinion. Or it can be said that he inherited not only the watch, the accumulation of the family history, from his father but also, in the same sense, the way of understanding life itself. "Jesus was worn away by a minute clicking of little wheels," and His initials are "JC." And "JC" are also the initials of Jason Compson.

This brings us to the world of Jason Compson, the third section, entitled "April Sixth, 1928." Jason, the only child their mother loves, is ironically said in "Appendix" to *The Sound and the Fury* to be "The first sane Compson since before Culloden (a childless bachelor) and hence the last."

He assigns a cash value to every thought and movement. This "sane man" always needs money, the currency of this "crass material world." He invests his money and the money he steals deceiving his mother, sister and anyone else he gets involved with. His interest is always on how much he earns or loses, and he is usually losing his money by misreading the stock market, because the market is changing every moment.

If he is the only "sane" member of the family, he also is the only one who is committed to the movement of his contemporary world, which is completely overwhelmed by the cash value that is symbolized in the stock he is investing. So that the problem of his is whether he has the money or not. He has no love of his family, no pity for his sister, no pride in his family, no compassion for anyone else, and no sacrifice of himself to anything except for earning money. Love, pity, pride, compassion and sacrifice: these are all abstract and the abstract does not make money or profit.

For Jason, he is always driven by the movement of a hand on a clock, the minute hand, and by the ticking sound of the second, because the price of the stock market is changing every moment by the minute or by the second.

And in his rejecting or repudiating the virtues of or values of the abstract is the biggest irony—while time is seemingly concrete because it is realized by the movement of hands on the dial of a clock, it also is one of the most abstract of concepts.

In this sense, the poorest victim of the mechanical progress of time ticked by the clock is him, Jason Compson.

He is always conscious of the mechanical progress of time exemplified by the clock in a different way from Benjy or Quentin. In Jason's universe, time is cut and divided into pieces by the movement of the hands on the clock. As we have already verified before, time, when measured by the artificial device and cut into pieces, loses its meaning. When it is thus reduced to meaninglessness, it just produces the sound and fury, signifying nothing. And in this sense, again, it is very symbolic that the cabinet clock in his house has but one hand, which is thought to be the minute hand and has the ticking sound of the second.

For Jason, the ticking of the one-handed cabinet clock is particularly devastating. He is always behind by three hours, which means that he is destined to lose his money in stock investments. He can not catch up with the movement of the stock market. The information and reports he gets from "one of the biggest manipulators in New York" are coming late to him.

The situation Jason Compson, is put in reminds us of what Quentin recalls as what his father said to him, "Father said that. That Christ was not crucified: he was worn away by a minute clicking of little wheels."

If Jesus Christ had not been crucified but worn away by the minute clicking of little wheels of the clock, Jason Compson also has been worn away by the ticking sounds of little wheels. In this sense, it is no accident that both have the same initials, J. C. And these initials remind us of another character in a work by Faulkner, *Light in August*. Joe (Joseph) Christmas, who has the same initials, and has also always been driven by the movements of the hands of the clock.

In his monologue, when he tells of what he says, Jason Compson says, "I says," using the present tense. In the colloquial expression "I says" is equivalent to "I said." But it is not just a colloquialism in that sense in *The Sound and the Fury*, because when we read the book carefully, we find that "I says" is applied only in the third section, the Jason section, not in any other sections.

It means that we can reason about the meaning of the use of "I says." That is, in the third section, there are two Jason Compsons or Jason Compson split into two. One Jason is talking of himself at the same time the other Jason is doing something. While he is doing something, he is looking at himself doing it and talking about what he is doing.

Or we may reason and say the writer of genius shows us the terrible situation of modern people in alienation. The terrible thing here is that Jason is both a "doer" and a "teller" of what he is doing at the same time. He is said to have fallen into an absolute loneliness caused by the modern alienation.

He is completely frustrated and he cannot find any clue to get out of the situation. This is where we have the difficulty in understanding or realizing the relation between time and existence, because in our existence we will know time, and our existence is limited in the progress of time. I am not a Martin Heidegger (1889-1976) or a Jean-Paul Sartre (1905-1980). When we read the Jason section from this point of view, we discover that the Jason section has a significant meaning. Jason Compson can be a theme which demands attention in the category of ontology, for "There is no such thing as was—only is. If was existed there would be no grief or sorrow."

By being alienated even from his own family, by being uprooted from the society to which he belongs, and by being frustrated with his situation, Jason Compson becomes a philosopher of existentialism without knowing it: He is confused and baffled in the middle of the present ticked by the mechanical device with which we measure time, and because he tries to see and read the future. Jason makes it possible for us to hear the thunderous roar of existence in the silence. He takes us to the canvas of *The Scream* (1898) painted by Edovard Munch (1863-1944), a Norwegian artist, that is, to a world of the scream with no sound in it.

Regarding Dilsey who is the main character in the fourth and final section, I have mentioned her several times earlier, so that now it is enough just to quote her words, " . . . Ise seed de first en de last." She sees and knows everything, and I know that she would never mind even if I did not make any more mention of her here. It is Dilsey whom the author of the book loves so much. And of her, the author wrote in "Appendix" "Dilsey. They endured."

Faulkner's *The Sound and the Fury* has also endured. And it is enlightening to remember the lines from *Macbeth* that gave Faulkner his title for what some say is his greatest work:

To-morrow, and to-morrow, and to-morrow, Creeps in this petty pace from day to day To the last syllable of recorded time, And all our yesterdays have lighted fools The way to dusty death. Out, out, brief candle! Life's but a walking shadow, a poor player That struts and frets his hour upon the stage And then is heard no more: it is a tale Told by an idiot, full of sound and fury, Signifying nothing (Act V, Scene V).

Works Cited

1. Faulkner, William. *Go Down, Moses.* Vintage International
2. ——. "A Rose for Emily." *Collected Short Stories of William Faulkner.* Edited by XX
3. ——. *The Sound and the Fury.* Modern Library Edition. 1992.
4. ——. *Light in August.*
5. Shakespeare, William. *Macbeth.* Act V, Scene V.

MARK RICHARD

A Letter of Deep Regret

Hoppin' Bob's Paralegal & Auto Recovery Services
2215 Via Anacapa Suite 1
Palos Verdes, CA 90274

Dear Mr. Dees,

Thank you for your kind invitation extended to my client Mark Richard to contribute to your collection of fictions, lively essays, and recipes peculiar to Oxford, Mississippi, tentatively entitled "They Who Must, Walk Among Us; the Other Ones Ride in Cars."

Beforehand, I would like to address certain matters regarding the incident (hereafter referred to as "The Incident") which transpired on my client's last visit to your humble burg. I would also like to stress to all parties (police, city fathers, citizens, attendant, litigants, et. al.) that in no regard is my client Mark Richard (AKA Marco Ricardo, Mark Rebar, Peter Lawford Action Figure, Tick Tock, Snort) responsible for the accident, the toxic spill, the conflagration, the alleged destruction of public and private property, the mental health of one Mz. Katie "Carl" Pointer, or any physical "health issues" attendant of but not limited to, Officer D.B.(AKA in local parlance "Dim Bulb (see private investigator report #12)) Frumway.

Is it not clear that no one, not even Jesus H. Christ Himself could have foreseen that Mz. Pointer's flailing leg at the time of my client's extraction of her from her minivan would misdirect her gear shift from "P" into "N" thereby setting off the chain of unfortunate events?

Wouldn't you think somebody with a seafood allergy would stay away from all forms of shellfish, including, but not limited to, alligator nuggets? Or at least consider alligator nuggets in the same allergy family of shellfish which precipitate iodine reductive seizures in those prone to such seizures? Or that those prone would at least wear one of those MedicAlert wrist things you can get in the old folks section at Wal-Mart that cost about $5?

And isn't the Good Samaritan Law in effect in Mississippi wherein a passerby or even backseat rider cannot be held for damage or injury in the course of administering in good faith, or rendering of aid even if said rendering of such aid may or may not have been a small precipitator in events that led to The Conflagration (hereafter referred to as The Big Ass Fire). And regarding Officer D.B. Frumway's alleged alligator bolus assault and resultant eye injury, I have personally witnessed the effect of a champagne cork driven by effervescence precipitated by beforehand agitation strike an unprotected eyeball and inflict less damage than is claimed sustained by the alleged alligator bolus. (By the way, are you yet in possession of the state forensic specialist's findings regarding Mz. Pointer's "choked bolus expectoratory trajectory"? In quaint local legal parlance, "That shit won't fly.") And supposing real eye injury suffered by Officer Frumway, some ladies even find eye patches attractive (see *Penthouse Forum Letters* Aug. 1979, the one starting out "I had just come home from work to find my neighbor dressing up for the Halloween Pirate's Ball").

Isn't the correct colloquialism Officer Frumway was so unable to articulate, regarding the physical ministration my client offered "gratis" to Officer Frumway, isn't the correct term "bitch slap"? My client would never have said Whomp. Whomp is not a word in my client's vocabulary. My client went to school where Robert E. Lee was president after The War. They don't teach you to say "whomp" there.

Though my client regrets in expressing regard for Officer Frumway in such a manner, he can not be found to be liable for slander when he uttered "inbred idiot with a single-firing brain cell," since we can find solid scientific evidence supporting his assertion in U.S. Government Printing Office pamphlet #440943 entitled "When Cousins Marry."

I would like to point out that my client has two artificial hips and exerted tremendous strength and resolve merely by determinedly removing Mz. Pointer from her vehicle, seeing that Mz. Pointer was convulsive and outweighs my client by more than 100 (one hundred) pounds. My client reports waiting behind Mz. Pointer's minivan while the traffic light accomplished two cycles before gently "tapping" his horn, then getting out of his car to investigate the reasons why the purplish minivan (Vermont license plate 2BUTCH4U) had not traversed the intersection. It was at that time my client noticed Mz. Pointer experiencing some form of distress. My client interpreted her bluing face, bulging eyes, protruding tongue, flailing limbs and open take-out carton of alligator nuggets half-eaten on the passenger seat as indicative of someone in the immediate need of the administration of the Heimlich maneuver and in dire need of a hair-to-shoes makeover.

The State of Mississippi Arson Report and Summation No. 13-874 reveals that Mz. Pointer's van, at the time of The Incident, contained approximately 600 (six hundred) "giveaway" vials of "scent" as a promotional accompaniment to the marketing of her book *Bird in the Hand; Hand in the Bush.* State laboratory reports concluded the base element used in the scent is in fact grain alcohol, a known highly flammable liquid. My client, who did not attend the prior reading from Mz. Pointer's book (as did not many others attend, apparently by the paucity of books signed and the huge number subsequently transferred to an alternative nearby venue for immediate markdown), could not have known the deadly contents of that van; no, in fact, my client's primary focus was on rescuing Mz. Pointer from her obvious distress. Furthermore, prosecutors and law enforcement officials should be alerted to the State's own assertion that the "sparking" of the fire may have indeed been caused by a smoldering marijuana cigarette in the ashtray, and not the impact of the unoccupied van rolling down the hill and slamming into the paint store at the bottom of said hill after my client valiantly extracted Mz. Pointer from her minivan while making every effort to expel the alligator nugget (or nuggets) lodged in her said throat.

Should not have Officer Frumway's primary attentions have been toward the health and safety of Mz. Pointer rather than his attempts to erroneously arrest my client for blocking traffic with his car which my client admits leaving unattended to assist Mz. Pointer? And surely, the window-shattering explosions that occurred after the van slammed into the paint store at the bottom of the hill coupled with the wind-driven fire that immediately consumed the adjacent Debutante Maternity Shop, Pizza Hut and Tommy's TermPaperMill in less than ten minutes, should not have these five alarm fires—punctuated by the subsequent propane tank detonations—have given Officer Frumway pause or at least reason to think that something more important than my client's car blocking traffic was occurring in real time?

It was only in this frustration that my client uttered the words he now regrets in addressing Officer Frumway causing the officer to remove his service pistol from his belt at about the same time that my client, by gripping Mz. Pointer from behind, in a Herculean effort, was able to expel, with his thumb and fist pressing firmly just below the ample sternum of Mz. Pointer, a large alligator bolus that apparently struck Officer Frumway in his left eye. Do I even have to begin to attack the allegation of Officer Frumway that my client in some way aimed the alligator bolus (or boli) as it was propelled from the mouth of Mz. Pointer in Officer Frumway's direction? I think not.

As you know, my client narrowly escaped an extensive manhunt through Faulkner's Woods and the girls' dorms at Ole Miss. It was only through an underground railway of C—- G—- bar patrons that he was able to flee, all the while fearing retribution at the hands of an overheated police posse led by the sputtering Officer Frumway. (We neither confirm nor deny his route, south/southwestward via Taylor where some anonymous good souls have been accused of harboring him. His 1979 Cadillac Sedan DeVille was impounded but later claimed by same good souls upon redemption of the towing charges.)

Mr. Dees, unless the above questions are answered, the arson, assault, conspiracy, reckless endangerment, and slander charges are dropped, I cannot in good faith allow my client to be liable in any way to the legal vulnerability I feel he would be exposed to by contributing to your book, not to mention the financial liens that would be placed against any monies you would pay for his contribution. Therefore, it is with deep regret that we must decline to participate in your project, and I, along with my client, wish you all the best.

Sincerely,

Hoppin' Bob Rodriquez
California Certified Paralegal Lic. #334ABVD6

P.S. My client wants to know if you were able to get his Bootsy Collins dance mix tapes and sunglasses out of the Caddy, and did he leave his Zuma Jay sweatshirt at your house? Could you send them to the "good" address? Thanks.

Notes on Contributors

Ace Atkins is the author of three critically acclaimed novels, *Crossroad Blues, Leavin' Trunk Blues, Dark End of the Street*, and the forthcoming *Dirty South.* Atkins lives on a century-old farm outside Oxford, Mississippi, with five faithful mutts and two indifferent cats.

Larry Brown is the author of nine books including *Dirty Work*, the memoirs *On Fire*, and *Billy Ray's Farm*, and the forthcoming novel, *The Rabbit Factory.* He lives near Oxford on family land.

Jim Dees is the host of *Thacker Mountain Radio*, a literature and music program on Mississippi Public Radio. He is a former editor of *Oxford Town* for which he still contributes a weekly humor column. He lives in a two-room bungalow in Taylor, Mississippi.

John T. Edge has covered southern culture for *Cooking Light*, *Food & Wine*, *Gourmet*, *The Oxford American*, *Saveur*, and *Southern Living.* He is the author of several travel and food books including the James Beard Award-nominated, *A Gracious Plenty: Recipes and Recollections from the American South* and *Southern Belly: The Ultimate Food Lover's Companion to the South.* He lives just off the square in Oxford.

Beth Ann Fennelly is the author of *Open House*, winner of the 2001 Kenyon Review Prize for a First Book, and *Tender Hooks*, forthcoming from W. W. Norton in April, 2004. Her work has won a Pushcart Prize and an NEA grant. She's an Assistant Professor of English at the University of Mississippi and lives in Oxford.

Tom Franklin is the author of the novel, *Hell at the Breech*, and the acclaimed story collection, *Poachers.* He is a former Guggenheim Fellow and John and Renee Grisham Writer-in-Residence at the University of Mississippi. Franklin lives in Oxford with his wife, poet Beth Ann Fennelly, and their young daughter, Claire.

William Gay is the author of the novels *The Long Home* and *Provinces of Light* and the recent story collection, *I Hate to See that Evening Sun Go Down.* Gay, a frequent and welcome visitor to Oxford, is a long-time resident of Hohenwald, Tennessee.

Carly Grace's poetry has appeared in *Snake Nation* and other journals. A former writing student of Larry Brown and Barry Hannah, Grace is a recent graduate of the University of Mississippi. She lives in Oxford with her dog, Moon Pie.

Barry Hannah, an Oxford resident for more than 20 years, is regarded by all local writers as the master of the craft. Hannah is the author of twelve books, including the critically acclaimed *Airships.* His selection in *They Write Among Us*, "All the Harkening Faces at the Rail," first appeared in *Airships* in 1978 and is reprinted courtesy of Grove/Atlantic.

Lisa Neumann Howorth has edited *The South: A Treasury of Art and Literature* and *Yellowdogs, Hushpuppies and Bluetick Hounds: The Official Encyclopedia of Southern Culture Quiz Book.* In Oxford, where she may have lived for way too long, she is known as the Nightmayor.

Masaru Ioune is a professor of American Literature at Ferris University in Yokohama, Japan. His numerous published works include a critical study of Willie Morris' essay collection, *Terrains of the Heart.* He is a frequent visitor to Oxford and has also written extensively on the works of William Faulkner.

Jamie Kornegay's fiction has appeared in the second *Blue Moon Café* anthology and elsewhere. He is a bookseller with Square Books in Oxford and lives in Water Valley, Mississippi, with his wife Kelly.

David Magee is the author of the non-fiction book, *Turnaround: How Carlos Goshn Rescued Nissan* and the upcoming book *Ford Tough*, to be released in October, 2004. He is an Oxford native who lived in the town for 36 years before recently moving to Lookout Mountain, Tennessee, with his wife and three children.

Jonathan Miles is a Contributing Editor at *Men's Journal* and *Field & Stream*. His essays, journalism, fiction and literary criticism have appeared in *GQ*, the *New York Times Book Review*, *Salon.com*, the *New York Observer*, *Food & Wine*, and many other national magazines, and his work has twice been selected for inclusion in the *Best American Sports Writing* series. A former longtime Oxford resident, he now lives with his wife and four dogs in New York, and is at work on a novel.

Willie Morris is the author of numerous works of non-fiction including *North Toward Home, My Dog Skip, Yazoo, My Mississippi,* and *The Ghost of Medgar Evers: A Tale of Race, Murder, Mississippi, and Hollywood.* His fiction includes The *Last of the Southern Girls*, and *Taps.* He lived in Oxford from 1984 until 1995 and changed the town forever. Morris died on August 3, 1999 in Jackson, Mississippi.

Jane Mullen is the author of a short story collection, *A Complicated Situation*. Her stories have appeared in a number of magazines and journals, including *Shenandoah*, the *North American Review*, *Mademoiselle*, *Sun* magazine, and the *Oxford American*. The *Ghost of Christmas Future* is part of a work in progress called *God's Country.*

Anne Rapp is a screenwriter whose credits include the teleplay, *All the President's Women*, and screenplays *Cookie's*

Fortune, and *Dr. T and the Women.* All were directed by Robert Altman. She has also worked on movies with Sydney Pollack, Tom Hanks, Steven Spielberg, Lawrence Kasdan, David Mamet, Robert Benton, Rob Reiner and many others. She currently resides in Austin, Texas, but has considered Oxford a second home for the last decade.

Mark Richard is the author of three books of fiction: *Charity, Fishboy*, and *The Ice at the Bottom of the World*, which won the 1990 PEN/Ernest Hemingway Foundation Award. His stories have appeared in *The New Yorker, Esquire, The Paris Review, Harper's, The Quarterly, Grand Street, Shenandoah, Antaeus*, and numerous anthologies.
Richard is working on his next novel and also writing for television. He lives in Los Angeles with his wife, Jennifer, and two sons, Roman and Deacon.

George Singleton is the author of the story collections, *These People are Us* and *The Half-Mammals of Dixie.* His stories have appeared in a variety of magazines and literary journals, including *The Atlantic Monthly, Harper's, Playboy, Book, Zoetrope, The Southern Review, The Georgia Review, The North American Review*, and *Shenandoah.*
He currently teaches fiction writing at the South Carolina Governor's School for the Arts and Humanities. He once got his head shaved during happy hour in Oxford.

Dick Waterman's involvement in the blues began when he promoted a series of concerts with Mississippi John Hurt in 1963. The following year, he came to Mississippi and eventually rediscovered the great Delta blues man Son House. His long career as a manager, agent, promoter, writer and photographer earned him induction into the Blues Hall of Fame, where he remains the only member who was not either a musician or a record company executive. Waterman's long-awaited first book, *Between Midnight and Day* will be published this fall, coinciding with his appearance in the seven-segment PBS series on the blues.

Dean Faulkner Wells is the co-publisher at Yoknapatawpha Press. Her books include *The Ghosts of Rowan Oak, The Great American Writer's Cookbook* (editor), *The Best of Bad Faulkner* (editor) and the forthcoming *The New Great American Writer's Cookbook* (editor).

Lawrence Wells is the author of the novels *Rommel and the Rebel* and *Let the Band Play Dixie.* He also wrote an Emmy-winning TV documentary, "Return to the River," and contributes to the *New York Times Syndicate.*

Curtis Wilkie is the author of the non-fiction books, *Dixie,* and *Arkansas Mischief,* the latter co-authored with the late Whitewater figure, Jim McDougal. Wilkie was a national and foreign correspondent for the *Boston Globe* from 1975 until 2000, covering eight presidential campaigns. He also established the Globe's Middle East bureau. Wilkie has written for numerous national magazines including *Newsweek, George, The Nation, The New Republic* and others.

Claude Wilkinson is the author of the poetry collection, *Reading the Earth.* His poems have appeared in the *Atlanta Review*, the *Oxford American*, and *The Southern Review.* Wilkinson was the first poet to serve as Writer-in-Residence at the University of Mississippi. He currently resides in Nesbit, Mississippi.

Shay Youngblood is the author of the novels *Black Girls in Paris, Soul Kiss,* and the plays, *Big Mama Stories* and *Shakin' the Mess Outta Misery, Talking Bone & Amazing Grace.* She was the 2002-2003 John and Renee Grisham Writer-in-Residence at the University of Mississippi where she lived across the street from William Faulkner's home.

Acknowledgments

Many people contributed to this project but none more so than the staff of Oxford's Square Books. Their contributions may not have been direct, but they work hard every day to serve the readers of Oxford to make it truly a unique place.

Special thanks also go to: Bruce Newman, the eyes of Oxford; Michael Wilson, a writer and editor who spent four years in Oxford and Kelly Tidwell Kornegay, a gifted designer who also loves books.